A
BRAND X
MURDER

Also by Don Flynn

MURDER ISN'T ENOUGH
MURDER ON THE HUDSON
ORDINARY MURDER
MURDER IN A-FLAT
A SUITCASE IN BERLIN

BRAND X MURDER

A "Fitz" Fitzgerald Mystery

Don Flynn

Thomas Dunne Books
St. Martin's Minotaur

THOMAS DUNNE BOOKS.
An imprint of St. Martin's Press.

Book design by Jane Adele Regina

ISBN: 0-312-24373-1

First Edition: December 1999

10 9 8 7 6 5 4 3 2 1

For Char . . .
And shipmates
Betty and Wayne, Elaine and Bob,
Claire and Doug, Trudy and Frank,
Stella and Norm

ACKNOWLEDGMENTS

The author wishes to thank the Ironhead Matthews of editors, Ruth Cavin, for her patience and fortitude, his agent, Don Gastwirth, for various miracles, and "Elaine."

A
BRAND X
MURDER

ONE

"LIFE IS MORE LIKE WRESTLING THAN DANCING, IN THAT it should stand ready and firm to meet onsets, however unexpected," advises Marcus Aurelius.

Alas, Bobo Watson was neither a wrestler nor a dancer but a guy who played the piano at Elaine's on the Upper East Side of Manhattan and who wasn't ready for the onset. The tardy warning from the wise ancient Roman emperor-philosopher jumped into my head that afternoon in the city room of the New York *Daily Press* when I saw the story. Bobo had played his last note.

It had come in from Dubbs Brewer at the police shack. Bobo had been set upon by a mugger early Sunday morning in Yorkville on the Upper East Side. His body was found crumpled between two parked cars on East Ninety-first Street, a knife wound in his chest. He apparently had been walking to his car at about 4:30 A.M. after finishing his regular Saturday night job at Elaine's.

Bobo had finally gotten his name in the paper, which was something he had always been after. But even in his final exit he was cast as a minor player; the story was mostly about the fact that he had played at Elaine's, the celebrity hangout, and some of the celebs were quoted as saying how sad it was and what a nice fellow he had been. And, too, he had picked the most prosaic way to go in New York: by some anonymous, shadowy mugger with a knife.

I knew Bobo from his piano playing because when summer rolled around and the staff took vacations, I'd get bumped around to cover other people's shifts. So I had filled in on the late trick, working for Bruce, the night news editor, finishing up at about two-thirty or three in the morning. Bruce and I would then drive up the East Side to P. J. Clarke's or Elaine's in time to make the last call, and we'd find Bobo at his sawed-off upright piano playing "Danny Boy" or some Cole Porter ditty for the last few drunks.

"Fitz!"

Ironhead Matthews, my city editor, stirred at his desk, crawling and growling back into action after the boredom of his civilian weekend. He was once more at the helm of the SS *Daily Press*, ready to set sail.

He was beginning his week by piping me to his side.

I walked up to the city desk and stood under the big four-sided clock on the ceiling awaiting Ironhead's pleasure. He was tossing paper into a trash can, scribbling eviscerating notes on copy, and punching angrily on the keys of his computer, which always stuck.

"Goddamn computers," he muttered. "Crash if you sneeze on them!"

Clamped in his mouth was an insult of an elongated, blimp-shaped cigar, which shook and scattered ashes over the computer keys. Ironhead swiped at them and blew them away.

"Shit!"

Nobody was supposed to smoke in the Daily Press Building in the antiseptic Prohibition Era new world being clamped down upon New York, but no one dared tell that to Ironhead. The irascible city editor did not tolerate such nonsense, and barely tolerated computers since the day he spilled coffee onto his keyboard and the damned thing crashed in an electronic sulk.

Ironhead, who, as a young reporter, survived being

conked on the head by a nightstick during a riot, came up in the business banging his fists on sturdy, cast-iron, indestructible Underwood typewriters that survived cigar ashes, coffee and beer spills, and even being tossed across the room in moments of stress. Ironhead barely tolerated reporters or, if you ask me, the world at large. But never mind that. He got even with the puny, arrogant computers by savaging his underlings, which at the moment happened to be me.

He suddenly noticed me standing over him and sputtered, "Why do the damn keys stick? What do you want?"

I was going to suggest that dousing delicate computer keys and their mysterious innards with cigar ashes might have something to do with it, but thought better of it. Finally, he got squared away enough—meaning he threw most of the releases, tips, memos, and crip-crap into the trash can—and held up a sheet of paper.

"Now, don't sneak away again, Fitz," he snapped, although I wasn't going anywhere. "They're here, Fitz," he declared, his face mellowing out pleasantly.

"Who are?" I managed, curious as to what could cause Mr. Hyde to turn into Dr. Jekyll just like that.

"The *Bounty*!" he exclaimed dreamily.

"The what?"

"They'll be sailing up the Hudson like ships of the line! The HMS *Bounty* among them. The tall ships, Fitz."

I had noticed earlier on the Associated Press news budget that the tall ships were returning to New York Harbor again for another sail-through, always a lighthearted summer gala, but was surprised that Ironhead would care, since he forever cursed soft feature news for eating up his hard news pages.

"Yeah, they're pretty," I allowed rather airily, which turned out to be a mistake.

"Pretty?" The press release slapped his desk. His face was at me. "Pretty! Ships of the line! Barkentines! Ninety-eights! Drake and Captain Bligh! Those were the days of real men, and real newspapers, too! Today . . . phewie!" he spat. "What have we got? Pisswillie reporters and plastic typewriters!"

Well, I could understand that his hero certainly could have been Captain Bligh.

"Now, Fitz, we want daily coverage on the tall ships while they're here. Admiral Nelson had wooden ships and iron men."

I frowned a little, unfortunately, considering it a dumb assignment suitable for one of the new ponytailed reporters who were invading newspaper offices. The tall ships were gorgeous, all right, but mostly as big, blowup photos.

"You figure on any follow on Bobo Watson?" I asked.

"Who?"

"That piano player at Elaine's."

"What?" Ironhead was still with Nelson at the Battle of Trafalgar. "What kind of a follow?"

"Well, our story was mostly about Elaine's."

"So?"

"Well, Bobo was practically buried in the story."

"He wasn't Bobby Short at the Carlyle. He was just another piano player," Ironhead tossed off.

"What do you mean?" I heard myself saying with more impudence than was wise. "Ironhead, you never heard him. Listen, Bruce and I used to catch the last call, and Bobo played those great old Gershwin and Jerome Kern numbers. . . ."

I ran down as I realized Ironhead was staring at me as though I were an escapee from Bellevue.

"It's just a shame for a guy like that to be dumped under a car and forgotten," I finished lamely.

Ironhead glared at me. "What are you talking about?"

"A murder story," I piped up. "That's what made the *Daily Press*."

Ironhead stood up and turned into Captain Bligh. His face was red-going-on-purple, and the vein in his forehead stood out and throbbed. Was I, a mere goddamn pisswillie excuse of an insignificant general-assignment reporter trying to tell Ironhead Matthews, city editor of the New York *Daily Press*, veteran of newspaper wars, blackouts, jet plane collisions, gang wars, and World Trade Center bombings, what a story was?

"Well, but . . ."

He had directed the coverage of the mob hit on Big Paulie Castellano in front of Sparks Steak House, as well as fires, kidnappings, assassinations, ship sinkings, and real murders at the Waldorf-Astoria and the Metropolitan Opera while I was still a goddamn legman in St. Joseph, Missouri, or wherever the hell I had come from. Nobody had to tell Ironhead what a story was.

"No, but I mean . . . the murder angle was just kissed off."

"We don't want it anymore!" he yelled. "Murders are a dime a dozen now, and they're all nobodies. Brand X! Now we want Madonna showing off her goodies, or rappers telling everybody to screw the Statue of Liberty!"

Suddenly I heard the pain in Ironhead's tirade. The kind of stories he had grown up on were slipping away, replaced by interviews with radio and TV freaks talking about their privates. Celebrities and sickos and sex harassment cases and, yes, nice, big, hollow stories about tall ships. But real news? Only if the murderer slaughtered twenty victims at McDonald's or a Hollywood star turned up dead at the hands of Madame Slapbottom the Dominatrix in a Times Square whipping emporium.

"I've got no space for nobodies!" he declared with what I thought was a tinge of strangled frustration. He shoved the sheet of paper at me. "Go get me stories about the goddamn tall ships!"

When Ironhead blasts off like that, it's time to drop it. I slid away, back to my desk, and pulled up some copy on my computer about the sail-through.

"What'd you get?" Bike O'Malley was just sliding into his chair at his VDT terminal across from me.

"Tall ships."

Bike beamed. "All right!"

I knew what he meant; he was glad it was me instead of him. Bike O'Malley is about six-four and looks something like the old Green Bay Packers lineman Ray Nitschke; in other words, he's formidable and rather intimidating. This sometimes causes city councilmen or the street commissioner to assume he is dim-witted, and they say more than they might otherwise. This is a mistake, however, because Bike is a shrewd giant, smart enough, for instance, to always be away from his desk early during his shift on Mondays when he knows Ironhead will be casting about looking for somebody to dump a slop bucket on.

"Mondays the Bike sleeps late," is his motto.

Of course, we all knew that weekends were perilous times for us, because they gave Ironhead time to mull things over and think of amazing new features or series. Ironhead's idle hours were the devil's workshop. He had no other life than the *Daily Press* and detested every wasted minute away from the city room. He didn't seem to enjoy his hours in the city room, either, but that's something else. There was another insidious aspect to his weekends off, too, because weekends were the time when our publisher, Mr. McFadden, or some other front-office geek, could call Ironhead at home and have his full attention. The vital importance of garden shows, Kennel Club French-poodle parades at Madison Square Garden, or one of Mrs. McFadden's pet projects, like Red Cross blood drives or the desperate importance of scrubbing the statues in Central Park, was explained to Ironhead then; it did not improve his already irascible personality.

"Goddamn front-office loonies," he often muttered on Mondays, even as he was dumping one of their brilliant stories on us. Being late on Mondays or digging busily through clips in the news library for the first hour was a good idea, and Bike had mastered it. Unfortunately, I usually forgot such good examples.

Once he had blasted off, Ironhead had a paper to run, and nobody could talk to him calmly, not even the McFaddens. I printed out enough stuff from the Associated Press wire on the sail-through to get started, and was on my way out when the phone rang.

"Yeah?"

"Ed Fitzgerald?" The voice was distant, as though coming out of a barrel.

"Speaking."

"Fitz? Is it you? It's me, Ellie." She was talking fast, like somebody who was afraid of being cut off. I searched my mind for a connection.

"Ellie . . . sure," I said.

"I didn't want to bother you. Is this a bad time? I wondered if I could talk to you a minute."

"It's all right," I said.

That's the way it is with people who call reporters; they have the idea you're desperately busy, on deadline, or on the line with the White House, and they don't want to interrupt. Actually, it's true a lot of times, and also you're wary of calls from strangers who want to tell you about the Biggest Story of the Century, which turns out to be that their neighbor is the secret daughter of Newt Gingrich, or that the woman across the street has buried four husbands under her rhododendrons. You start off defensive and answer the phone, "Yeah!"

"What's the matter?"

"It's about Bobo."

"Bobo Watson?" Then I had it. It was Ellie, Bobo's girl, who used to hang around Elaine's waiting for him to finish playing and who sometimes sang at the piano with him.

"I just saw the story," I said. "I'm sorry. Do you know what happened?"

"No, Fitz. We just found him there, and . . ."

"You found him?"

"The bartender and I. When Bobo didn't come back to

drive me home, we went to his car. We thought he'd been run down, the way he looked."

"The cops say it was a mugger."

"Yes, I know. He was all bloody. . . . I haven't been able to think about it."

"Yeah."

"Have you heard any more?" she asked hesitantly.

"No. I'm not on it."

"If you find out anything more, will you let me know?"

"Sure."

She went silent a moment then, and finally there came a barely audible whisper. "What can you say?"

I went silent, too. She was right; what could you say? But there was a purpose to her call, as it turned out, and she finally got it out.

"Fitz, I was just wondering, if there's another story, could you see if they could put in something about the funeral? I've arranged a mass at St. Catherine's, and I'd like his friends to know. Do you think you could use a picture?"

I sighed, hearing Ironhead's sneer about nobody Brand X piano players.

"Well, uh . . ."

Ellie's image leaped into my consciousness: a pretty face surrounded by sculpted black hair; tall and slim and very well mannered, like somebody from the Midwest. My heart went out to her.

"I'll see what I can do," I said, rather recklessly.

"He always thought a lot of you, Fitz. I can't stand him disappearing without a word, without a trace."

Well, there you were. What could I do? Sometimes your instincts about calls from strangers are right. Some of them are nuts, but some put you through the wringer.

TWO

I WROTE A LITTLE FOLLOW-UP ABOUT BOBO, BASICALLY AN obit, and mentioned the funeral service. It wasn't much but it was the best I could hope to sneak past Ironhead. The *Daily Press* was never big on obits, any more than on minor murders. I walked up to the city desk and asked if we could use a couple of graphs.

"All right, all right," Ironhead mumbled.

"I think we've got a headshot of him in the library," I offered, and got an overheated glare.

"Did you pick a ship to ride?" he grumped.

"On my way."

I pulled up some stuff on the computer about America Sail from the Convention and Visitors Bureau press release and printed it out. The tall ships would be sailing into New York harbor under the Verrazano Bridge: full-rigged windjammers, barks, barkentines; the *Libertad* from Argentina; the *Gorch Fock* from Germany; the 295-foot Coast Guard training ship *Eagle* festooned with young cadet sailors in mainsail white on the lofty yardarms ninety feet above the deck. It would be a two-week long gala, the ships arriving on no particular schedule during the first week, depending on the winds. Then during the second week, they would be docked at various piers all over Manhattan and Brooklyn and hold open houses for New Yorkers to clamber aboard them. It would all lead up to Sunday, the Fourth of July, two weeks off when there would come the Parade of Ships up the Hudson River to the George Washington Bridge.

It would be a glorious sight, all right, but there was another vision in my wavering mind, that of a grieving, gentle face surrounded by a helmet of black hair. Actually, there was a second vision, too, that of bouncy Bobo Watson behind his piano, rocking and playing and singing like Hoagy Carmichael.

"Get with it, Fitz," I told myself.

I walked out onto Forty-second Street and down to the New York Press parking zone on Fortieth Street to my car, a little white Toyota Tercel I had picked up from John the Chevron station guy on Second Avenue. Second Avenue John had told me it belonged to an elderly schoolteacher. She must have been a very small one, because the Toyota was a miniature space capsule. But it was all right for Manhattan, where you don't want a big or fancy car, which is just as well since I never had one.

I went down the FDR Drive along the East River toward Lower Manhattan and the South Street Seaport. That's where some of the ships would be moored during their stay, including the *Eagle*, the *Danmark* from Denmark, and the comely, 240-foot *Christian Radich* from Norway. I would scout around to see if I could find a slip where one would put in. It was a glorious summer day, June 21, the first day of summer, and the breeze off the water was tangy and salty fresh. I left the drive at the Civic Center near the Brooklyn Bridge, and I was about to turn down toward the waterfront to the seaport when I found myself pulling into the NYP parking zone behind police headquarters.

"What the hell, it won't hurt," I heard myself rationalizing, and was out of the Toyota and walking into the massive, mustard-colored police complex that huddles beside the sprawling courthouses of Foley Square.

I entered One Police Plaza and found my way to the pressroom and our debonair police reporter, Dubbs Brewer, who claimed to have covered five thousand murders in his long career. You know when you hear an expert on the radio talking about crime in New York with some pompous talk-show pseudo-expert? The expert is usually Walter "Dubbs" Brewer holding forth.

"Fitz!" he said, looking up, his ruddy face set in a big hello. As always, Dubbs wore a sharp, slate gray suit and a red power tie and looked like a police inspector, which is what he sometimes passed himself off as.

"Hey, Dubbs."

"So, what brings you down here?" he wanted to know, always on the alert that a good story might be breaking and had been assigned to some hotshot from the office. Dubbs was territorial that way; police stories were his, by God! Reporters sent down to the police bureau by Ironhead to check out a story on Dubbs's beat often discovered that the biggest obstacle to getting the story was Dubbs himself.

"Nothing," I assured him. I told him about the tall ships assignment, and he smiled knowingly.

"That's Brain Dead for you," he laughed, relieved. "Ironhead's got a boat, you know. A dinky thing in Sheepshead Bay. Thinks he's Donald Trump."

"Working anything good?" I asked offhandedly.

"Such as what?" He was still suspicious that I had come down there to steal one of his stories.

"I saw your piece about the Chinatown gangs," I told him.

He brightened at that. "Yeah! They're running their protection rackets again and shooting each other up. It might work into something if a merchant gets caught in a crossfire."

It wasn't really what I was interested in. Crime in Chinatown didn't get much news either, because Chinatown seemed like a foreign country, Hong Kong or somewhere. Chinatown is an exotic, blurry little enclave of its own, and we didn't pay much attention to it except when the Flying Dragons or Ghost Shadows or some other vicious street gang staged wild gun battles on Mott Street or left a Chinese bean-curd shop owner dead because he wouldn't pay up. It was all pretty much Brand X, too.

I finally got around to what had brought me there. "That bit about Bobo Watson," I said. "You sent in something on that, right?"

"Watson?" Dubbs cocked his head. "Yeah. Out of the Nineteenth Precinct. Wasn't much to it."

He pulled a printout slip from the spike on his desk, and I looked it over. No, it certainly wasn't much. A couple of sentences stating that Robert Watson, white, male, thirty-seven, had been found early Sunday morning between two parked cars on East Ninety-first Street.

"DOA at the scene," the slip noted laconically. "Victim had multiple knife wounds." Multiple wounds? Sounded like more than one mugger. Police reports don't waste words. There's never anything in them saying that Bobo Watson wore yellow suspenders over a red striped shirt and a bow tie, played Jerome Kern and Cole Porter tunes, and patterned himself after Hoagy Carmichael. "DOA at the scene." That's the signature of the NYPD.

"Ironhead putting you on this?" Dubbs wanted to know, looking over my shoulder suspiciously.

"Naw. I knew him. He played piano at Elaine's."

"That joint up on Second Avenue where you and Brucey go?"

"Yeah."

Dubbs nodded dismissively. It wasn't his kind of place. Elaine's is a place where a lot of writers and show-business types hang out. Woody Allen walks in wearing tennis shoes, and Clint Eastwood and Kirk Douglas stop in when they're in town. I even saw Norman Mailer there one time. Everybody at every table cautions you that they simply can't talk about the humongous movie deal they've just sewn up. Dubbs had his own table at P. J. Clarke's on Third Avenue at Fifty-fifth Street, where he held court every early morning after finishing at the police shack. He was a regular fixture, and politicians strolled by and called him "Inspector." Bruce had taken me there a few times, but he and Dubbs both had big egos, and they wouldn't always fit in the same saloon.

"The guy's girl called me, and I just thought I'd have a look at the slip," I told him, and started out. Dubbs pumped me for office gossip, as usual, wondering if "Brain Dead" was hiring any new geniuses from Yale—or somewhere—to replace him at police headquarters. Dubbs was territorial all right, and always suspicious that he wasn't appreciated.

I drove down to the East River and then back up past the South Street Seaport, noting the few old clipper ships docked there permanently. It was enough to get an idea of how to cover the story.

Driving back uptown, I found myself thinking about Hoagy Carmichael Watson, whose passing had caused such a small ripple. Of course, murders don't matter much anymore, not when there are so many of them. These days, only Brand Name killings get noticed. There's so much of everything in New York that only news about The Four Hundred gets covered. That's the way I thought of it, anyway.

Back in the gilded age of robber barons, Ward McAllister, a New York society toady, decided there were only four hundred people who mattered, because that was how many could fit into the ballroom of Mrs. Astor's brownstone on Fifth Avenue. Today the equivalent of the Four Hundred are the celebrities who appear on TV. They make news by chatting with each other, or by interviewing or insulting other Brand Names. If you're not a Brand Name, you can only make news by blowing up the World Trade Center. Outsiders can get the impression that only Donald Trumps, Kathie Lee Giffords and Madonnas live in New York.

I got off the FDR Drive at Forty-second Street to go back to the office, but kept thinking about Bobo's multiple wounds. I'd have to meet Ellie again sooner or later, and she'd ask if I had found out any more. It wasn't my story, and I probably should have steered clear of it, but when something happens to a friend, you sometimes stick your nose where you shouldn't. I decided on one more brief stop, and headed up to the Nineteenth Precinct on East Sixty-seventh Street. Walking in, I told myself I was just doing a once-over-lightly check on Bobo's murder.

The desk sergeant glanced down at me from his raised desk.

"Yeah?"

"Hi, Sarge. Ed Fitzgerald, *Daily Press.*"

"Um," he humphed and made a face, showing half-annoyance. Sergeants are a little like city editors: they, too, barely tolerate nosy reporters.

"You got anything on a DOA on East Ninety-first?" I asked. "Bobo Watson. He played piano at Elaine's over on Second Avenue."

"Watson," he mumbled, shuffling slips of paper. "Yeah. I saw an aided on that. What about it?"

"Well, I just wondered if your squad dug up anything on it."

The sarge leaned over to squint at me. "Squad? I don't think the squad even got it. He was DOA."

Wasn't that cute? Bobo's murder was so insignificant they hadn't even assigned detectives to the case. I saw his nameplate on the desk. Sergeant Dugan.

"Come on, Dugan, somebody must have signed off on it," I pressed him.

Sergeant Dugan frowned, realizing he wasn't going to get rid of me that easily. "What's the name, again?"

"Fitzgerald. *Daily Press.*"

"All right, all right," he muttered, wrinkling a slip. "Hanley and Jacobs caught it. Upstairs."

I went up the scarred, well-traveled stairs to the second floor and along a hall to a room with frosted glass and a fading "SQUAD" painted on it. At a rear desk in the squad room sat Detective Dennis Hanley, six-foot-four, bald above the ears, and as impassive as one of the stone lions in front of the New York Public Library. I knew him slightly from past stories. I sat down across from him, which caused a raising and lowering of his eyebrows.

"Fitzgerald, right?"

"Yeah. Hi. Listen, a friend asked if I could find out anything on the Bobo Watson murder."

"Watson," he nodded slowly. "The butcher job."

"What?"

"The piano player who was all cut up. Yeah, the box-cutter gang."

"Box cutters?"

Hanley sat back and stared over my head, which apparently helped him think. "Yeah. Kids use these box cutters, you know. Blades sharp as razors. They cut out his pants pockets."

"You think that's what this was? A local street gang of muggers?"

"We've got some cases working," he said.

"Other murders?"

Hanley stopped looking over my head and zeroed in on me. "No. If this one's theirs, it's their first homicide."

I sat back and lit a Tiparillo. A street gang of box cutters. What a travesty. A finely tuned, painstakingly created musical mind, nimble fingers trained through endless years of careful practice, a blithe bow-tie spirit of melody and rhythm, an always upbeat, optimistic Robert W. Watson, aka Bobo the piano player, casually eliminated as though by roving wild dogs on the Serengeti Plain.

"Street muggers," I muttered helplessly.

Detective Hanley's brow rose and fell, and his bald head tilted slightly to the side. A veteran cop's reaction.

"New York," he said fatalistically. "We'll get them."

"Sure," I said, and got up. What good would that do?

I walked out of the squad room, down the stairs, and back out onto East Sixty-seventh Street to the Toyota. I don't know what I had expected to learn, but I wanted to be able to tell

Ellie something that might help when I met her again. Hanley's squalid little tale wouldn't measure up.

The way it is with murders in New York—and, I guess, anywhere—is that you expect or at least hope for some kind of sensible explanation. People can never accept the assassination of a famous, glittering figure, like JFK, by an insignificant nerd like Lee Harvey Oswald. Predator and prey have to have something approaching equal weight, or at least the motive has to be big enough to balance the crime and the criminal. Of course, in reality, it doesn't work that way. People are murdered for careless reasons—or no reason at all—wasted almost casually, leaving a few anonymous mourners to stare at the wall and sob or scream, "Why? . . . For what?"

"It doesn't make sense!" is the quote you see crying out in news columns in a hundred New York murders. And if the dead person is a "nobody," the "Why?" and the "For what?" and the senselessness very often never get answered. No wonder the Fourth Estate doesn't dwell on the unimportant ends of unimportant people. It only matters when the murdered John Doe in that little short buried in the paper isn't a nobody to you, but is somebody with a chirpy face who wears yellow suspenders.

"Be ready for the time when your soul shall fall out of this envelope," says Marcus Aurelius. "How ridiculous and how strange to be surprised by anything that happens in life."

But we always are, Marcus.

THREE

I DROPPED INTO ELAINE'S THAT NIGHT. I WAS THE ONLY one at the bar at first, but it was early. Even though it was Monday night, there would be plenty doing before long. Every day, and every hour of every day or night, is the start of somebody's weekend in New York. For people who work weekends—and there are a lot of them, including the casts of Broadway shows—Monday is their Friday night.

I remember when I first started out as a newspaperman in New York, I worked the lobster trick, midnight to 8 A.M., and was off on Tuesdays and Wednesdays. For us in those days, the TGIF cocktail hour began at 8 A.M. Monday, when Mutchie opened his doors. We hung out in Mutchie's, a waterfront bar on South Street, starting in with beer or silver bullets shoulder-to-shoulder with longshoremen stumbling in for morning wake-up shots. They accepted us as comrades and fellow drunks, which in a way I suppose we were. Then, too, there were guys, including some at the *Daily Press,* who used Monday night as their bust-out night, because they'd been marooned over the weekend out in Brooklyn or Queens or Long Island with their wives and kids. Actually, there are three or four subcultures in New York who hang out around the clock depending on what kind of jobs they have. The nine-to-five office types who come in for the happy hour and go home early. The guys like me who start about one in the afternoon, finish at eight or nine or ten, and stay out till the wee hours. People like Bruce the night news editor, Bobo himself, bartenders, and cops who finish up at three or four in the morning. Cab drivers who work 5 P.M. till 5 A.M. Then there's a crowd who don't seem to work at all, who flock to these Greenwich Village clubs where nothing starts till midnight, and they go on till dawn. They don't call it "the city that never sleeps" for nothing.

Anyway, I stopped by the place on Second Avenue at Eighty-eighth Street. I was trying to feel a good-bye to Bobo, I guess.

"Harp," I told big Kevin Duffy the bartender, and he put a bottle of Irish lager on the bar.

"Can you believe that about Bobo?" he said, looking away out over Second Avenue and blinking a little.

"Yeah." I took a slug, lit a Tiparillo, and did a little blinking myself. "Ellie called me."

Big Duffy nodded silently. The subject of Bobo's demise had a way of stopping all our mouths with mud.

"You and Ellie found him?" I asked.

Big Duffy's open Irish face clouded. He's a tall, youngish guy with big teeth who goes to Fordham by day and bartends by night and has some cops in his family.

"Jesus!" he said. "I wouldn't let her look at him."

"The cops say it was a gang of muggers."

"I thought he'd been hit by a sanitation truck. He was all bloody. He goes out to go to his car, and was coming back for Ellie. When he didn't come back, we went looking for him where he always parks."

That was right, of course. Bobo used to finish up after the last call, around four in the morning on Friday and Saturday nights. And sometimes he and the last few hangers-on, including Bruce and me on occasion, would lounge at the bar over a final drink after the doors were closed till almost five. There were always a few diehards who ordered drinks just before closing time and never wanted to leave.

Duffy's story of Bobo's final night was quickly told. Bobo

had banged his little sawed-off piano across from the bar till about 4 A.M.

"Ellie sat at the little table by the front window or stood at the end of his piano, the way she always did," he recalled.

"So, he just finishes up and goes for his car?"

Duffy shrugged. "He never came back."

I could fill in a little of what must have happened after that. There went Bobo out into the night some time after 4 A.M. to walk to his car on East Ninety-first Street, and then come back and pick up Ellie to drive her home. He must have walked up Second Avenue, then east across Ninety-first Street to his car parked over beyond First Avenue. He could park on the street there after seven.

"The cops said there were multiple wounds," I told him.

Another silence between us.

I ordered another Harp, lit another Tiparillo, and sat there. Some good-bye.

And then Ellie walked in.

There she was, pale as a ghost, walking like a zombie on wooden legs. She looked at Duffy and me and then sat at the bar beside me.

"Fitz."

"Hi."

She was in a semi-sleepwalking state, her eyes flat and dull, like a person who has been going for hours on adrenaline and routine, plodding ahead one step at a time on automatic pilot, with no time to think.

"You want anything?" Duffy asked, and she shook her head.

"I just wanted to get some of Bobo's music," she said in a flat voice. "I want Larry to play some of his songs at the funeral service."

An even longer silence.

I knew I'd run into Ellie sooner or later, and maybe that's why I had stopped by. Ellie—Eleanor Cunningham—was a very nice kid. Actually, she was no kid. She was in her late twenties, maybe even early thirties, and was from the Midwest somewhere. A tall, slim, good-looker with black hair, who wore navy blue sheaths with gold cinch belts and walked with her back straight, smiling quietly beside the ebullient Bobo.

She didn't want anything, but big Duffy served her a pot of tea at the bar anyway. He had to do something. It was like an Irish wake in a way. You had to go through some sort of mourning ritual.

"Sorry I bothered you at the office, Fitz," she managed to say.

"Hey. No problem." People in trouble are always humble, it seems.

"Did the cops tell you anything more?" Duffy wanted to know, leaning over the bar.

"Not really," she sighed. "I told them what I knew. I went down there. . . . He was in the basement at Bellevue . . . on a table."

So she had gone down to see Bobo's body at the county medical examiner's office at the Bellevue Hospital morgue. I had looked over a few bodies there myself, all of them lying still and pale as wax, stretched out on metal tables. It was always chilling and maddeningly institutional. No wonder Ellie looked like a zombie.

"You had to identify him?" Duffy asked.

"I did, but it wasn't official. His ex-wife did it."

"You met Claire?" Duffy asked.

"I saw her. She was with some man. I didn't talk to her. I didn't know what to say."

"So Claire claimed the body?" Duffy asked.

"All she wanted was the death certificate," Ellie said softly. "Something about insurance. After they left, I asked the morgue people what they were going to do, and they said she told them cremation. I wanted them to send him to Campbell's Funeral Home, but I wasn't a relative, and . . ."

So it would be a memorial service without a body. Bobo

was being completely obliterated. I wanted to ask what Claire was going to do with his ashes, but she probably had no idea.

"You've had a couple of days," I managed inadequately.

"I can't sleep. I'm all cried out. I just walk."

She slumped over the bar, her back no longer straight, and stared listlessly at the cup of tea. She was hardly there.

"A man's character shows itself in his voice and eyes," observes Marcus Aurelius. At the moment, Eleanor Cunningham's voice and eyes showed a character dissolving before us. I had to look away. I puffed on the Tiparillo and allowed my mind to conjure up a different image, that of Ellie on other occasions when she stood at the piano watching Bobo with lively eyes, her face full of the future.

You understand, Bobo was a piano player and an entertainer, and so he showed his game face to everyone. Nobody likes a grim piano player. So, he called himself Bobo instead of Bob, dressed like Hoagy Carmichael, and sang like him, too. Oh, there were times, early in the morning after Bobo had finished, when Bruce and I would sit at the bar with him and he'd talk about the years when he knocked around the country playing in bands. Bobo was no angel—none of us are—and he had his darker moments. But piano players, like newspapermen, seldom pull long faces.

The gig at Elaine's finally rescued him from the road, and he became a fixture there, warbling away in his hoarse Hoagy voice. And then he met Ellie. She came in one night on the arm of what Duffy called a "suit," a tall, blond, straight-arrow-looking young man in a conservative blue suit, with every hair in place, who apparently brought her there to hear Bobo. This turned out to be a mistake on the part of the suit.

They sat at the bar in the corner at Elaine's, and she waved Duffy over after a while.

"Who's the piano player?" she wanted to know. "He's terrific."

"Bobo Watson. But you can call him Hoagy."

After that, Ellie started showing up by herself. For a few

nights she sat at the corner of the bar, and then she began standing at the end of the piano. Finally, she hung around till closing, and she and Bobo became an item. She changed his life.

Bobo didn't mind having a drink, he bought for others freely, and he didn't seem to contemplate the future beyond the end of his nose, or his piano keys.

"Everything's cool," he'd say, "cool as a fool in a pool."

I understood Bobo. There are lots of guys like him in the city, and I used to be one of them. There are times when you're first starting out, as a reporter or a piano player, when you're making a dollar-three-eighty, as we used to say—meaning not enough—times when you're behind in the rent and signing bar tabs till payday. The thing is, since you can't make sense of your financial situation, you don't try to. You just slog along and don't worry about it because there's no solution.

That's the way it had been with Bobo; he'd just been hanging on, badgered by his ex about maintenance—and by his ex's live-in boyfriend, too. So Bobo immersed himself in his piano, sang away, and grinned fatalistically at the world. He had a ratty basement room somewhere up in Inwood at the upper tip of Manhattan. His life was music and Elaine's, and if the future concerned him, he didn't show it. Then he hooked up with Ellie, and she started putting him back together, which is usually the way it happens if a guy ever does find his way out from behind the piano keys or his newsroom computer.

I remember the night Ellie stood at the end of the piano blushing, her hands over her laughing face, and Bobo announced they were going to get married.

"Here," he yelled, shoving his tip bowl—a brandy snifter—across the piano top to her. "The bank account!"

Bobo may have been teasing her, but Ellie took it seriously. After that, she religiously emptied the glass bowl and socked the money away toward a wedding.

"Why the hell did I do that?" he joked, but it was a real step, and Ellie slowly accumulated a nest egg. Now I guess the money would go for the memorial service.

Ellie sipped the tea with no interest. "I wanted to get him a new jacket," she said. "He still had his bow tie and suspenders. I wanted him to look like he looked. But . . ."

I couldn't stand it. Nobodies might not make news, but they leave real people behind.

"I couldn't find his keys," she went on, looking at Duffy. "Do you have a spare key to the piano bench?"

"Sure," said Duffy, and left the bar to go to the office.

"Oh, Fitz," she murmured.

I didn't know what to say, and so said nothing. She was suddenly alone in New York and lost. I knew the feeling. My place on East Eighty-second Street was empty, too, since things hadn't worked out with Audrey. It had looked for a while that my seminomadic existence in New York was going to resolve itself into something permanent. Until The Day.

"Fitz!" she had called me after an interview at CBS, full of triumph. "They want me!"

I remember the elation and pride I had felt. Of course they wanted Audrey McMillan! Why wouldn't they? She had paid her dues as a CBS reporter for six years on the tough streets of New York, just about obscuring the *Daily Press* reporter who had helped her get started.

"Good-o!" I had yelled. "You deserve it!"

Rather fanciful images fled through my head at the time. Finally tying the knot and maybe even buying a house in New Jersey. A real life, a family, something more than a knock-around life as a reporter. Let's face it, my place was pretty ratty, too, and my life wasn't much more than the streets of the city and the *Daily Press*.

Then the reality.

"Fitz—it's L.A.!"

My God! Los Angeles? But of course when the chance comes in the news business to move up, it often means a new address, sometimes a faraway one. I had made my own moves in the past. A few years back, a chance at New York had meant good-bye Chicago, and I'd left a girl behind.

I couldn't blame Audie. And we'd work it out, we were sure. Hey, the West Coast isn't so far away now, what with jet planes. But a TV reporter's life is not her own, once she has the spot. A red-eye trip to the coast, and another, and then. . . . Time and distance and reality and ambition had their way.

No, I couldn't blame Audie. But I could understand Ellie's lack of interest in a pot of tea at Elaine's. For a few wistful moments, I even thought fleetingly of Ellie and me. But Marcus put in his two cents' worth: "Look on the attractive loveliness of young persons with chaste eyes." Yes, Marcus.

Duffy came back with a key to Bobo's piano bench, and Ellie went over to the piano to dig out his folder of music sheets. She sat on the bench and shuffled the sheet music, all those pages with his notes of sharps and flats scrawled on them that he used when playing things like, "When I Fall in Love."

Then she was crying.

"Listen," I said to Duffy, "What the hell is this? My Harp is empty here."

FOUR

THE FIRST OF THE TALL SHIPS CAME SAILING IN THE NEXT day, Norway's *Christian Radich,* tacking up the lower bay under the Verrazano Bridge, gleaming in the sunlight of a lovely New York morning. I caught a glimpse of her on TV over coffee at home.

A long shot of the sailors on the stately tall ship floated before me: the agile young men, in mainsail white blouses on footropes in the yardarms, waving at the Statue of Liberty.

I found my little snippet on Bobo tucked away on the obit page, and felt inadequate all over again. I took a sip of coffee and then realized what was happening. Something was bothering me about Bobo's murder; it was that damned missing jacket.

"They cut his pants pockets out," Half-Dome Hanley had said. That was bad enough, but then there was the insult of stripping his corpse, like Achilles humiliating the fallen Hector at Troy. Why would they take his jacket? They could have gone through it and tossed it.

I put it out of my mind, since there wasn't much else I could do, and headed downtown to the *Daily Press* in the Toyota. When I got into the office just after 1 P.M. to begin my shift, Ironhead was watching for me. He came right over to my desk.

"Did you see her on TV?" he asked eagerly. "The *Christian Radich*? Gorgeous! Where's she going to dock?"

"Let's see . . . the South Street Seaport in Lower Manhattan."

"Did you get a place on any of them?"

"Not yet. Which one do you want me on, the *Bounty*?"

Ironhead rolled his eyes, as though surveying the vast flotilla of thirty-five tall ships that were due in, among 266 vessels, including the replicas of the *Bounty* and the *Nina*, the *Pinta*, and the *Santa Maria*.

"You want me on one of Columbus's caravels?"

Ironhead swayed back and forth, considering. "I'll ask Pippy," he finally decided.

That caught my ear. Pippy McFadden, the publisher's son? The lightfoot lad and aspiring commodore of the New York Yacht Club. A light began to dawn; the importance of this story.

"Not that it's up to him," Ironhead finished with a half-scowl.

So that was it. I could see this was Pippy McFadden's show, all right. Pippy's smiling, windblown figure always popped up in the paper in regatta stories, strolling around in a navy blue jacket with a gold monogrammed seal on the pocket, white duck trousers, and a captain's hat decorated with scrambled eggs. He kept a seventy- or eighty-footer in Long Island Sound at City Island—named *The Fourth Estate,* naturally—and was always sailing off to Majorca or some-place.

Ironhead detected that I understood the situation. That grumped him up because he couldn't stand front-office interference in his city room. But what could he do? He could do what city editors always do in such situations—rip into a hapless reporter—me.

"So, if you haven't got a berth on one of these wooden buckets, what the hell did you do yesterday?"

"I scouted out the South Street Seaport."

"That took you all day?"

"I've got to pick the right one. The *Radich* is a grand sight, okay. Nice blouses on those sailors. Did you know those muggers swiped his jacket?"

"What?" Ironhead asked, crooking his neck.

"They cut out his pockets, but they took the blazer. I mean, insulting him that way."

"Cut out his pockets?" Ironhead leaned toward me, trying to get it.

"Were they looking for something? Maybe there's more to this than a mugging."

"A mugging? One of the sailors got mugged already? Goddamnit! You'd better get on that right away. There could be some news in this after all."

"I'm talking about Bobo. That cop at the Nineteenth said they really butchered him."

Ironhead chewed the stump of his slimy stogie, and his eyes narrowed, zeroing in on me.

"The Nineteenth Precinct?" He was having trouble with the location. "Do you mean to tell me the *Christian Radich* is docking at a goddamn police station?"

"I just stopped by on the way."

"On the way where?"

"A friend asked me to check it out. I'm only saying it might be a better story than we thought."

Ironhead's face seized, like the battleship *Missouri*'s engines grinding in a chaotic, clashing tangle of colliding gears and pistons. His mouth worked, as though the Mighty Mo's sixteen-inch guns were trying to spit out shells.

"If I thought there were really a . . ." blurted out of him, and then the funnel of Hurricane Matthews swirled over me.

"Tall ships, not dinky murders, is your assignment!"

"Well, yeah, but . . ." I started, but got no further. Ironhead did not tolerate the word *but* from any of the lowly reporter-seamen who sailed before the mast on the Good Ship *Daily Press*. What I got was an explanation of just who the hell I was and who Ironhead was and a general suggestion of what happens to hopeless idiots who don't listen.

"Bleaghhh!" came first, and then . . . did I understand that Pippy McFadden, the publisher's son, was a weekend tar with a gleaming, white yacht moored at City Island? Did it penetrate my thick Irish skull that Pippy was the pride and joy of his parents, Mr. and Mrs. McFadden, our publishers? Was it vaguely possible for me to realize that Pippy was hosting a gala luncheon at the New York Yacht Club and had promised all his ritzy yacht-owning pals a regular armada of stories about the tall ships? Did I understand two and two? Was I possibly insane?

"I'm right on top of it," I insisted anxiously. "I just thought the mugging might develop into a real story, and while the ships are coming in and getting moored, I could use my spare time to . . ."

A plume of smoke spewed upward as though a genie were about to burst forth from the exploding stovepipe.

"Spare time!"

An unfortunate choice of words.

"You will find goddamn ships! You will explore their bowels and write colorful, seafaring yarns! You are off that goddamn piddling piece of crap! Have I made myself clear?" he spluttered.

"Yeah, sure!"

"Shut up!"

My exact thought.

Ironhead set sail across the city room, trailing indignation, a sure sign of displeasure that has been known to dump reporters who couldn't follow simple directions into the Brooklyn night police shack.

Ironhead had made his point. I hurried past the city desk, conspicuously waving the tall ships handout in front of Ironhead's nose, which drew a grumpy glance, and beat it down to the Toyota.

I drove across Forty-second Street to the West Side, parking in the NYP zone on Forty-fourth Street. It was a short stroll over to the Hudson River where the aircraft carrier USS *Intrepid* is docked as a permanent museum and floating forget-me-not monument to World War II.

And there, sailing majestically up the Hudson River, all canvas set, her top gallant bellying from the breeze, came another tall ship, a British man-of-war ship of the line that might have done Sir Francis Drake proud. She was the *Pandora* out of Liverpool, and I watched her being nudged into a slip across from the *Intrepid,* her nimble crew of tars scrambling like monkeys up and down her masts and across her spars, reefing her sails. A tall ship she might be, but she was dwarfed by the huge steel hull of the *Intrepid.*

Once her lines were set, I hung my press card around my neck in approved fashion and walked up the gangplank with other reporters. Ironhead was right about tall ships. They are majestic, though surprisingly small on board, and walking their decks swirls all sorts of seagoing history up your spine. The captain greeted us, a bluff, portly sea dog in a scrambled-egg decorated cap and a blue jacket with brass buttons. He was, he declared, "Royal Navy, retired, sir!" He had once been a skipper for the Monarch cruise line on the New York to Bermuda run, he said.

"Great to be ashore here, Yanks!" he smiled, "docked beside the gallant warship *Intrepid.* Those were the days, lads, the Big Two, British sailors and American ships. An unbeatable combination."

Captain Plummer, retired from Her Majesty's navy and from the New York–Bermuda run, was now handing on his experience to British tars on the training ship. Well, the Brits do know how to host guests on their ships. A nice buffet lunch was soon set up on the deck, with bangers, fish and chips, and rations of Guinness stout to wash it down. A pleasant assignment, all in all.

"Is there room aboard for a refugee from the *Daily Press*?" I asked Captain Plummer, and he said he would sign me on for the sail-through up the Hudson to the George Washington Bridge and back on the Sunday after next. I left HMS *Pandora* and noticed the crew of sailors were all scampering away on shore leave, eager for the feast of New York. It looked like about a third of them were women.

As the *Pandora*'s crew scattered into Manhattan, I spotted the reborn *Nina, Pinta*, and *Santa Maria,* looking wobbly and pitifully small, maneuvering into the dock across from the *Intrepid.* Maybe one of them would be more suitable for the sail-through, I thought. The grand gathering armada was an embarrassment of riches.

Back in the city room, I turned out the kind of colorful story expected, all about the new British invasion of America, this time as solid allies. I ran around Manhattan the rest of that day and the next interviewing gobs and captains, even journeying all the way to hell and gone out to Pier 6 in Brooklyn where HMS *Bounty* was moored, and wrote more stories about how wonderful it is to be in New York in the summer when the fleet's in.

Of course, there are always loose ends when somebody is murdered, and late that afternoon one of them dangled through my phone when Glenn the Switchboard called over to me.

"Hey, Fitz, you did that Watson obit, didn't you?"

"Yeah."

"Here's some guy asking about him."

I didn't recognize the voice, but the guy said he was Douglas Shippen, a friend of Claire Watson's. I gathered he was the man Bobo's ex-wife lived with out in Queens, the one who had been with her at the Bellevue morgue.

"You wrote that about Watson's funeral?" he asked, and I said I had.

"Who told you to put that in the paper?"

"Pardon me?"

"This Watson was a freakin' deadbeat," Doug the boyfriend informed me indignantly. "Claire, that's his wife . . . she's with me now . . . she didn't order any funeral service. Did that come from Ellie Cunningham?"

"Well, yes."

"What right's she got to hold a service?" he grumbled. "She's not his wife; she's nobody! Can you tell me how to reach her?"

"I have no idea," I lied.

"You got her address or phone number? We want to talk to her!"

"I can't give that out."

"Well, do you know if she's got any of his papers or anything?"

I remembered Ellie mentioning something about his insurance.

"I just did a little piece about the service."

"Some nerve she's got. We need his papers, his insurance policy. We got the death certificate. See, there's double indemnity if it's accidental death before he's forty."

"It wasn't exactly accidental," I suggested.

"Well, whatever you call it. Not natural. I handle insurance stuff at my auto body shop and can take it from there. So . . . you can't tell me where to find her?"

"Sorry."

He and Claire the ex had their eye on the prize, all right.

I did manage to order some flowers for Bobo's funeral and realized I'd see Ellie again that evening. I made one last call to Detective Dennis Hanley at the East Sixty-seventh Street squad to ask if he had any late details on the Bobo Watson case.

"We brought some kids in," he offered.

"Yeah? Any good?"

Well, he told me, there were some kids in a street gang who called themselves the Randall Raiders because they played soccer on Randall's Island and did a little purse-snatching and head-breaking on the side.

"Any admissions or statements?" I asked him.

"Not yet. We're sweating them. Couple of them had switchblades."

"Switchblades?" I felt a shiver. Just the item for a sharp jab between the ribs.

"We're running them for blood," he said.

"Is that what the M.E.'s office said did it? A switchblade?"

"We haven't got the medical examiner's report back yet. Looks like it, though."

"Did you find his jacket?" I wanted to know.

"Jacket?" That didn't register. "No. Why?"

"Well, if they ran off with it, it could tie them to the murder."

"Hey, Fitzgerald, you know we've got other cases up here. This one isn't high-priority."

"You mean you're dumping it?"

Half-Dome Hanley made a disgusted noise. "No. Of course not. It's active. We'll let you know if anything turns up."

"That's all right. I'm not on the story. I'm just checking for a friend."

"What?"

"I knew the guy and his girlfriend."

"Oh. Well, maybe you can help us. You know anything we don't?"

I told him about Doug Shippen calling me, and about Claire the widow.

"Okay," he said.

I hadn't talked with Ellie since seeing her at Elaine's and didn't want to, since I had nothing to offer her. I had the idea she would expect me to do something, being a New York reporter and a friend of Bobo's. People are like that with reporters. They think you can bully the cops or shake up city hall or run big stories to spook the killer. They think a reporter is a free agent who can chase any story he wants to. They don't realize you're a rather insignificant cog connected to and driven by a big wheel and that you're more likely to be assigned to inconsequential feature cream puffs than to the story of the year.

As far as I knew then, the Bobo Watson story was finished, another unsolved case lost in the files of the Nineteenth Precinct detective squad. But when I got to St. Catherine's Church Wednesday evening for Bobo Watson's funeral, everything changed.

Larry Swanson was there to play some of Bobo's favorite numbers using Bobo's own arrangements. Big Kevin Duffy, the bartender from Elaine's, was there. Even Bruce the night news editor showed up, and a lot of Ellie and Bobo's friends. But there was something not to be imagined or understood about that funeral service.

Father McMahan came out onto the altar, looked around, and finally came down the aisle to Duffy and me.

"Shall we get started?" he asked efficiently.

"Not yet," Duffy told him. "Ellie isn't here yet."

"Ellie . . . the wife?" Father McMahan asked. He looked at his watch.

"We can't start without her," Duffy said, and glanced at me.

"No," I answered, just as puzzled at her absence.

The main character, other than Bobo Watson himself, hadn't shown up. Eleanor Cunningham was among the missing.

FIVE

LARRY PLAYED SOME OF BOBO'S FAVORITE SELECTIONS softly on the church organ, and some of the plaster saints in their niches might have been bemused to hear Hoagy Carmichael tunes like "Old Buttermilk Sky" and "Stardust." But Ellie had wanted to fill the service with lively touches, because Bobo was never one to pull a long face.

"Funeral hymns wouldn't be Bobo," she had said.

A few more people arrived at St. Catherine's, but still no Ellie. Mourners were huddled together in the first few pews, talking softly. Friends and relatives; people I didn't know. They started turning around to look toward the rear of the church, getting restless. Duffy and I were just inside the doors, watching the street, and Bruce was outside, pacing the sidewalk, smoking away as usual.

"Where is she?" Duffy asked.

"Last-minute things," I suggested. "Flowers maybe . . . people calling her. Maybe she stopped at her own church to light a candle."

"I'm going to call her," Duffy decided.

He walked up a side aisle and into the church office. In a few minutes, he was back.

"No answer," he said, staring out at the street. "Just the answering machine. Must be on the way."

"Well, you know, Duffy. New York."

"Yeah."

It's easy to be late in New York, where there are always

traffic, subway breakdowns, and generally jammed-up streets. In New York, you very often can't get there on time. So, we waited, and Duffy was silent. He'd been chewing on things, all right.

"You know, Fitz," he said finally. "I've been thinking about that suit who brought Ellie to Elaine's that first time. He and Bobo knocked heads one night."

"Yeah?" That got my attention.

"Outside in front," he said, staring ahead and remembering. "When Bobo got there, this guy was waiting for him."

"What happened?"

"I was inside, and couldn't hear them. But the guy was in a sweat, you know? Grabbed Bobo by the shirt and yanked him around."

"A fight?"

"Not so much a fight as a couple of wild punches and a lot of yelling. The guy was, like, warning him. Sticking his finger in Bobo's face."

"It was the same guy who brought Ellie there? Who is he?"

Duffy shook his head. "Don't know. I never caught his name. When Bobo came in, he had a bloody nose and some blood on his shirt. He laughed it off."

"He would."

"He says, 'The guy's all bent out of shape. Thinks I'm not good enough for her.' "

Duffy said that when he looked out again, the guy was gone.

"Bobo asked me not to mention it to Ellie," Duffy went on. "He didn't want her to worry. Now I wish I had, or had gotten the guy's name. I should have thought of this before, but the cops were already after those muggers."

A jealous former boyfriend? I wondered. I'd have to ask Ellie about that. Duffy paced around again, and looked toward the front door.

"Maybe she had an accident," he finally said.

I went into the office and called her again.

"Hi. This is Ellie. I can't come to the phone right now, but . . ." I hung up impatiently.

Half an hour passed, and Larry Swanson was into his second rendition of "When I Fall in Love." Bruce stopped pacing and smoking outside and stepped in to me.

"Listen, Fitz, I have to move." He was due at the paper, where his shift as night news editor started at 8 P.M.

"Yeah, I know," I told him. "Go on."

"Tell Ellie, uh . . . you know." He left, and then I saw Father McMahan walking back to us.

"Say," he said with some annoyance, "she's been here all the time. I really have to get started."

"Who's been here all the time?" I asked.

"His wife, Ellie," he said, and led us back to the front to the first pew, where a wraithlike washed-out blond sat with a man.

"Here," he said, "Mrs. Watson is right here."

I looked at her, slim and rather faded. Beside her sat a gangly, scowling, uncomfortable-looking man with carelessly combed hair and a jacket that hung on him the way jackets hang on men not accustomed to wearing them. I had to figure this was Bobo's ex-wife, Claire, and the auto body mechanic, Doug Shippen, who had called me at the paper.

"Eleanor, can we get started?" Father McMahan asked impatiently.

"I'm not Eleanor," she said faintly, her eyes straying timidly to Doug for help.

"This is Mrs. Claire Watson, the lawful widow!" Doug Shippen snapped. "We want to talk to that woman! Who is she to order a service? She wasn't married to him, the slut!"

"Well!" Father McMahan looked abashed. "I don't know. Somebody called to arrange it."

Doug stood up and gave a sneering look around. "Is she here? I want to talk to her! She better not have taken any of his things or his papers! It's bad enough his wife had to put up with a deadbeat who forgot to send the check without this bitch meddling in things!"

I glanced at Duffy. Here was Bobo's ex-wife's boyfriend, who hassled him for maintenance. Could it have been he—and not the suit—who grabbed Bobo's shirt in front of Elaine's? Duffy understood my look and shook his head no. This was a different guy, and pretty burned up.

"Listen," I told Doug, "Ellie arranged this because nobody else did."

"Who are you?" he wanted to know.

"A friend of Ellie and Bobo's. Ed Fitzgerald." The guy annoyed me.

He glared at me. "Fitzgerald? The reporter? So you're on their side, huh? He better not have left anything to that woman!" He was annoyed with me, too.

Father McMahan was perplexed. "I don't know anything about this," he said rather stiffly. "My concern is with the soul of the departed. I'm going to begin."

Neither Duffy nor I could think of anything to say. We walked back to the rear of the church.

"I'm going to run over to her place," I told him. "She ought to know what she's walking in on."

"Some beauty that guy is," Duffy simmered.

"He wants Bobo's insurance," I told him.

Duffy gave me Ellie's address over on the Upper West Side, and I went out. I drove across town wondering what could have happened to her but not wanting to guess. There was no way Ellie would miss the funeral service.

She had an apartment in one of those big, sprawling old buildings on Riverside Drive above 113th Street, which used to be a pretty fancy address some years ago. Now the once opulent buildings are cut up into apartments and single rooms. Her name was on a plastic slip in the lobby: "E. Cunningham—6-B." I rang her bell, but there was no return buzz. I checked the listing for the building superintendent, but of course there was no indication. Supers don't like anyone to be able to find them easily. So I resorted to what all New Yorkers do under such circumstances: I pushed other buzzers until somebody buzzed back and let me into the lobby.

"Hello! Hello!" a woman was yelling into her intercom as I went in.

I rode the jerky elevator up to six, and went along the narrow, gloomy corridor to 6-B. Either the bell didn't work or there was no answer. I pounded on the door.

"Ellie! Are you there? It's Fitz!"

Frustrated, I tried the doorknob, and the door swung open.

I stepped inside. "Ellie?"

It was a nicely kept apartment, with a large sofa covered with green-and-yellow flowered upholstery, and with drapes at the front windows gathered partway down and held with tiebacks. I could see a bulletin board on the wall leading to a little kitchen. A smiling, blowup photo of Bobo Watson grinned out at me. I noticed that a window facing the drive was open. Something slid through me, a feeling of uncertain dread. The place was so silent, as though deserted. Then I heard soft music playing.

"Ellie?" I tried again, and walked cautiously toward the sound of the music, past the kitchen area to a door that stood partly open. Music floated out. It was a radio playing "oldies but goodies." When I pushed the door further open, there she was, sprawled facedown crossways on the bed, her face turned away from me, toward the headboard. It only took a second, a frozen pinpoint, to take it in. There is nothing stiller than death.

"Damn!" popped out of me.

I knew she was dead, all right, but to make sure I went over and put my fingers on her throat. Nothing. No pulse, no pneumatic trembling sensation of life. I was glad her face was turned away from me. I felt blood and adrenaline rushing through me, a warning aura of semipanic, and backed out of the bedroom and out of the apartment without touching anything.

You move automatically in situations like that. In a moment, I was down the corridor banging on the next apartment door.

"Hello? Hank, is that you?"

"Open up," I yelled. "Hey!"

The voice went silent, and then came again, cautiously, "Yes? Who is it?"

"Emergency," I shouted. "I need a phone!"

I tried to peer in through the glass peephole, but couldn't see anything—probably because the woman inside was trying to peer out at me.

"Who is it?" she called out again. "Were you ringing before?"

I banged the door. "Madam, this is the New York *Daily Press!* Please open the door!"

Well, that did it. The door swung halfway open, and a blowsy middle-aged woman stood looking out, her head propped around the door at me.

"The *Daily Press*?" she gawped. I didn't give her a chance for second thoughts, but brushed past her into her apartment, pulling my press card from my jacket pocket and shoving it at her.

"I need your phone!"

I spotted it on a table next to a sofa, and snatched it up.

"What's the matter?" she asked, alarmed and backing away. "Who are you?"

"I'm sorry, ma'am. Fitzgerald, *Daily Press*!" I was punching in numbers. "There's been a murder next door."

I thought she was going to run out of the apartment. Her eyes popped open like saucers, and she came out from behind the door.

"What! My God! What do you mean?"

"Daily Press," came the voice of Glenn the Switchboard.

"It's Fitz. Give me the desk," I told him, and in a bleep Del the nightside city editor was on the line.

"Fitz?" he said pleasantly. "What's up? Sailing on the *Bounty* yet?"

So word of my sensational assignment was around the office.

"Naw, Del. I've stumbled on a murder."

The blowsy woman had edged toward me a little, but now she leaped back again, her face flushed. She gasped and covered her mouth.

"Oh, my God!" she gawped again.

"Any good?" Del asked calmly. Naturally, that would be a city deskman's reaction. Murder was an everyday event at the *Daily Press*, and the first question always was whether it was a Brand Name.

"Well," I hedged, "I don't know. You might want to send a photog up. I'll call the precinct and get back to you when I've got enough to file something."

"Okay, Fitz," he said. "It isn't on one of the tall ships, is it?"

"No such luck." I gave him the address for the photographer and hung up.

The woman was staring at me as though I might be the killer. She tried to say something, gulped, and blurted, "Who is it?"

The name came out of me with a shock. I was off the phone now, not on automatic pilot anymore, and the murder victim wasn't just a name on a police slip.

"Eleanor Cunningham," I managed, and my mouth went dry.

"Ellie?" The poor woman let out a shriek, and then she bolted out the door, yammering hysterically.

I rubbed my eyes, held on, and called 911. The police dispatcher, like Del, was all business as he took down my name and the information. Were an EMS squad and ambulance needed?

"I'm no doctor," I said, "but I don't think so."

"Okay, stand by there, will you?"

I hung up, sat down, and lit a Tiparillo.

Everything drained out of me, and I willed my mind to function. I'd covered murders before, and I tried to make myself think of this as just another one.

But it wasn't just another one.

SIX

I WALKED BACK DOWN THE HALL TO ELLIE'S APARTMENT, where the door was still open, and went in to have a look around before the cops got there. There was a collection of photos on a bookcase, a couple of them showing Ellie with different hairdos. Well, women change their hairdos from time to time. I glommed on one of Ellie and another of Ellie and Bobo. They were sitting smiling into the camera, in front of Grant's Tomb of all places. Another glance into the back bedroom, and this time I noticed some dark, red stains on the bedspread beside her. I went around the bed to get a better look at her face. More blood from her mouth. There had to be a wound in front somewhere under her that I couldn't see. That was enough for me. I backed out. The medical examiners would figure out what killed her. Outside I heard sirens.

An absurd rush of fright gripped me as I thought, "What will I tell Bobo?"

What, indeed? I was hallucinating.

Figures floated before me, vague shapes, specters without substance. People standing at the apartment door, edging in, peering in; others looking over their shoulders; all of them silent and wide-eyed, squeezed together at the narrow door, watching me as though I, too, were dead or a ghost or maybe the killer.

"Nothing to do," I said dully. "The police will be here."

Finally, a short, swarthy man in a blue-and-white Yankee T-shirt stepped in hesitantly.

"What happened?" he asked blankly in an accent that sounded faintly Arabic. "I'm the super."

"Nothing." The word came out of me idiotically. "She's dead."

His lips moved to ask, "Dead?" but no sound came out. He stared at me, and then he looked back at the people at the door and nodded knowingly, as though to say that it was all right because he was there now. Reality walked through the door a few minutes later, when two uniformed cops from the Twenty-sixth Precinct pushed their way through the crush of stunned gawkers.

"In there," I gestured.

Right behind them came the EMS paramedics, who hurried into the back bedroom. I heard *oup-oup* sounds as they tried to revive her.

"You called it in?" one of the uniformed cops asked me.

"Yeah. Ed Fitzgerald, *Daily Press.*"

The cop's face opened up. "The press already?"

"I found her."

"*You* did?" he came back. "How come?"

"She was a friend of mine."

"Yeah?" His face got a little harder. My presence wasn't just in the way of business. "Is that so?"

The cop's hard, suspicious eyes and the EMS squad moving around gradually shocked me back into a semblance of control. Being on the scene of a murder before cops arrive—in the apartment of an attractive, murdered young woman who was a "friend"—was a very poor idea, I realized.

The cops shooed everybody out of the apartment except the super and me, and closed the door.

"Sit down," the hard-eyed cop told me. "The squad will be here."

"I have to call in," I said.

"No, you don't."

"What?"

"Later."

So, there I sat, marooned, more or less in custody, impatient to call Duffy, although I wanted to make that call about as much as Marcus Aurelius wanted to lead his Roman legions against the Sarmatians on the Danube. I needed to call the city desk back, too. My head was coming together, and this wasn't just the murder of a friend anymore. My other hat was on; I was a reporter, and this was turning into something a little better than a mugging murder. It wasn't my story, but I couldn't just walk away. But I knew better than to argue with a uniformed cop. I had to wait for the squad.

They showed up after a while—two detectives from the West 126th Street squad—and they were less than pleased when they found out I was a *Daily Press* reporter. The taller one, Detective Sergeant Thomas, looked me over in confusion, crossed his arms, and said, "What the hell were you doing here?"

I tried to explain as best I could, but Sergeant Thomas held up his hands and cut me off.

"This is part of another murder in the Nineteenth?" he asked. That interested him.

"That's what it looks like. Detective Hanley's got the case over there. Bobo Watson."

"What makes you think so?"

"Well, she's Bobo's girlfriend."

He leaned down at me. "I thought she was yours."

Wasn't that wonderful!

"Look, I just came over here as a friend because she didn't show up at his funeral."

"His funeral?"

"Yeah. I told you, he was murdered, too. That's why I think they might be hooked up somehow."

Sergeant Thomas gave me a look, and then walked into the kitchen area and talked softly with his partner, a pudgy guy wearing a straw hat with a feather in it.

"Let them have it!" I heard the straw-hat dick say.

You might say that that was the beginning of my troubles,

because after that, things got pretty confused and heated up, and I was in the middle of the stew.

The pudgy straw hat sauntered over, sat down beside me, smiled, and introduced himself.

"Renaldo Musso." He leaned back as though we were a couple of strollers passing the time of day on a bench in Central Park.

"*Daily Press*, huh?" he said genially. "I read the sports. You write sports?"

Here was a smooth detective trying to butter me up.

"No."

"So you and this Bobo had a thing for the same broad, huh?"

Terrific. About as subtle as a kick in the crotch.

"Look, if you're through with me, I've got to call the city desk."

But they weren't through with me. Not by a couple of miles. They had hardly even begun, as it turned out. Pretty soon, in walked tall, half-bald Detective Dennis Hanley from the Nineteenth Precinct on the East Side with his partner, Dan Jacobs, whom I had not met before.

"What are you doing here?" Hanley asked.

That's all they seemed to want to know. Listen, I wanted to know the answer to that, too. What the hell was I doing there? I should be out on the town with Brit sailors from the *Pandora*.

"He says this is your case," Detective Thomas explained, apparently ready to dump the whole thing.

"What?" Hanley's partner, Jacobs, a stubby guy with a fat rump, shoved into the group. "What the hell is he talking about?"

"He says it's part of your Watson case."

"Well . . . goddamnit!" Hanley muttered.

It certainly was lovely. Detective Hanley had been stuck with Bobo Watson's murder, and now here were three more ratcheted-up detectives from both sides of Manhattan arguing over who had jurisdiction. Each team seemed to want to dump the mess on the other. Sticking their fingers in each other's faces and getting loud and red-faced, the four of them forgot I was even there.

"What do you expect from one of these smart-ass reporters?" Hanley demanded, not so impassive now.

"He's hitting on his pal's girl," Sergeant Thomas got in.

"Evasive, won't talk. Better check him out!" insisted smoothie sports fan Renaldo Musso.

And then who joined their little circle but Syrian Jack, the super, leaning in to say, "He was snooping around, ringing all the bells."

"Who are you?"

"Jack. I'm the super. Missus Hooper, she's waiting for Hank to come by, and here's this bozo."

"Just hold on a minute."

I wish I could tell you that this muddle turned into an investigation of poor Ellie Cunningham's murder, but all the four dicks seemed to want was to get rid of it—and for me to explain why all my friends were being knocked off.

"Can I call my desk?" I asked Sergeant Thomas.

"Ask Hanley here. It's his case."

"The hell it is!"

"Listen, Hanley," I said, "there's a former boyfriend of Ellie's you ought to check out."

"Yeah? Who?"

"I don't know. I was going to ask Ellie, but . . ."

"Well, what about him?"

"He was after Bobo, and he may have been stalking Ellie. It was a triangle, I guess. He could have been after both of them."

Hanley didn't seem to know what to make of that, and I didn't either, since I didn't know who the guy was or anything about him.

"Thanks," he said, pretty sarcastically.

"There's another guy, too. Bobo's ex-wife's boyfriend,

Doug Shippen. He wanted to know where she lived."

"Is that who he is? The widow's boyfriend?"

"You've talked to him?"

No, he said, he hadn't, not yet. But a Doug Shippen had called and left messages, and had been down at the medical examiner's office to get a death certificate for Bobo. "He said he was calling for the wife, about insurance or his estate," Hanley said.

"Good luck with that. He lives with the ex out in Queens, and I guess he's looking for anything that was left."

I thought that over a minute. "You know, Hanley, he called me looking for any insurance policies. He said there's double indemnity if Bobo went before he was forty."

"How old was Watson?" Hanley wanted to know.

"Thirty-seven. Maybe somebody was trying to beat a deadline."

Hanley rolled his head around. "We'll see."

Nothing got resolved in that crowded apartment on Riverside Drive, except that I would be brought to the West 126th Street station to give a statement before there would be any phone calls to the snooping *Daily Press*.

On the way out, through a phalanx of apartment residents who had come out of the woodwork to watch the suspicious bell-ringing hoople escorted out by four detectives, Johnny Roche, the *Daily Press* photog, snapped a picture of Ellie in a body bag being wheeled out on a gurney to an ambulance.

"Hey, Fitz," the Roach said, coming over. "Where you going?"

I shrugged. "To the pokey. Tell the desk. Take my notes." I slipped him the photos of Ellie and the one with Bobo, and he beat it up the street to his *Daily Press* radio car. I was allowed to drive my Toyota to the station, in a caravan between the two squad cars, and up the stairs we went into another squad room. I noticed the clock on the wall over the desk sergeant as I came in; it was after nine. I was missing deadlines on the story. This would not please Del or Ironhead.

But that wasn't the worst of it. In the squad room, Sgt. Thomas sat me down and advised me to make a clean breast of it all.

"It'll be better for everybody if you give a full statement here, Fitzgerald."

"Well, hell, yes," I told him. "I've got nothing to hide. I told you, I was just checking in on her."

"Good. You want to call a *Daily Press* lawyer?"

That outraged me and brought me up short. A lawyer? What the hell did I need with nervous, Oh-My-God Charles W. Corcoran, the jittery newspaper lawyer who lived in terror that one of the reporters might be out there stepping on his cock?

"Why?"

"Never mind. Just put it all down."

I wish I could tell you that I realized this was a touchy situation, but the fact is reporters never think of themselves as news stories. I always wondered at suspects shooting off their mouths when they should have dummied up, but I was an innocent bystander. Well, I wrote out a statement, and Thomas and then Hanley kept cross-examining me on details, and it took about two hours before I could finally get out of there.

"I want you in my office in the morning," Detective Hanley snapped grumpily, and Sgt. Thomas looked smug. I gathered that the case had landed back in the file of Hanley and Jacobs. Good, I thought, pleased that maybe they accepted the idea of some connection.

"Good" wasn't on Half-Dome's puss, though. "Sour" was.

I finally got on a pay phone downstairs in the precinct and reached Del at the city desk.

"Del? Fitz."

"Jesus, where the hell have you been?"

I told him the frustrating tale of my semidetention.

"Christ, Fitz, you've blown three deadlines! Roche the photog filled us in a bit, but the damned story's full of holes."

"Okay, give me Tommy Toolen on rewrite, and I'll unload now."

"It better sing, Fitz. Ironhead's been calling in."

My head imploded. Ironhead? Why would he be calling in so late?

"What did he want?"

"He wanted to know how come the story's already all over the *Post*."

Jupiter Optimus Maximus! The *New York Post!?* While I was being held incommunicado, grilled by four squabbling dicks, the damned story had been leaked out to the opposition?

"Who wrote it?"

"Pat Whitestone."

Shit! That sneaky little weasel! He must have picked up the scent at the *Post's* police shack and worked the story by phone. I shuddered. Missing a story is a mortal sin in the journalistic profession, but getting beat on your own story is a path straight into Ironhead Matthews's doghouse.

I unloaded my notes to Tommy and finally headed for my place, going across town toward the East Side on Cathedral Parkway, which is 110th Street, the top of Central Park. It was late by then, after midnight anyway, and I was debating whether to stop by Elaine's on the way downtown to fill in Duffy. I didn't really feel like talking to Duffy just then, or to Ironhead either, or to anyone, if you really want to know. I drove on, wondering how the hell I get myself into these things, and I guess I wasn't concentrating on my driving because all of a sudden this large, dark car was swerving beside me. I thought I had strayed into his lane, but when I slid over into the inside lane, the damned thing slid over with me, crowding me toward the curb.

I tried to glance over at the car; it was an arrogant shape driven by somebody I couldn't make out in the darkness. Then I realized his lights were off. And the big car, a green or metallic blue Lincoln or Mercedes, swooped over toward me. Some damned idiot choked with road rage, apparently because I had cut him off. You never know what kind of crazies are on the streets of Manhattan.

I slowed, giving him time to pass me, letting him win the chicken game he was playing. Go on, screwball, the road's yours! But the dark hulk slowed too, and edged even closer toward me.

"Hey!" I yelled, trying to look at him.

And then, *scrunch!* The irritated driver scraped the enormous bulk of his heavy monster against the side of the Toyota, sending my little space capsule wobbling onto the curb, over it, and between parking meters across the sidewalk.

Terrific! A fender bender. All I needed to cap off the night. Fortunately, I hadn't hit anyone on the sidewalk, but strollers and street characters immediately materialized around the car, coming out of the park, along the sidewalk, and from across the street.

"Hey, mon, what you doing?" Somebody was glaring through the driver's-side window at me.

I looked past the angry gathering at the dark car, which had halted a little past me, expecting to see the demolition derby wacko come out of it and start screaming at me. Or worse. The driver's-side door opened, and the top of his head rose partway over the roof, glaring back toward me and the school of street fish surrounding me.

"He cut me off," I muttered, opening the door to get out. I glanced at the side of my Toyota; barely a scratch, nothing much.

"He *the Man!*" one of the street fish standing in front of the car and glancing at my license plates muttered. "*Mr. Charley*!"

I realized the gawker had seen my NYP plates and thought they meant New York Police, which is what a lot of people think. I usually don't correct them, especially not in situations like this. Others were moving toward the dark car stopped in the street a little way beyond me, and I guess Mr.

Road Rage didn't think much of that, because the car started moving away.

"Hey, Mon! You run Mr. *Police* off the street!" All of a sudden, I had a street posse on my side.

The dark car slid away, moving ahead of the posse, and disappeared across town. That surprised me, because I expected at least an exchange of insurance information. Even a tiny scrape on the side of an expensive set of wheels like that could run into some bucks. But he apparently didn't want to deal with the street fish. Actually, I didn't, either.

I backed across the sidewalk, between the parking meters, and out onto the street again. The posse pushed on the car as I slid out.

"You get him, Mr. Charley!" one of them yelled as I drove off, apparently assuming that since I was *the Man*, I would chase him. No way! Let him go. Anybody crazy enough to bump me off the street over a little thing like that was not somebody I wanted to tangle with.

I was so relieved, in fact, that at first I didn't think much about it; just an ordinary New York fender bender. But as I drove on, I realized this was a queer sort of accident, and maybe not an accident at all. Even after I had given him the street, that dark car had kept crowding me, kept trying to cut me off, to stop me. Driving with lights off, too. That swarm of street fish had perhaps saved me from a worse confrontation. I tried to figure out the make of that car, but all I had been able to see in the gloom was that it was big, dark, and looked like a Mercedes or a Lincoln Town Car.

I was getting skittery. By the time I reached my place late that night, I wasn't sure if it had been just another crazy driver or somebody who had tailed me for a reason.

SEVEN

"HE WHO FOLLOWS REASON IN ALL THINGS IS BOTH TRANquil and active at the same time, and also cheerful and collected," Marcus Aurelius remarks. The musings of my ancient mentor in his *Meditations,* which I relied upon in moments of uncertainty, were not always pertinent, it occurred to me. I had followed reason and tried to assist a friend in trouble and explain things to the blockhead cops, but Marcus was an idiot to suggest that this resulted in tranquility.

What I was, when I woke up the next morning, was in a five-way mess involving two murders, one on each side of Manhattan, four detectives, and a body they wanted to connect me with. If that wasn't enough, when I opened the apartment door to grab up the *Daily Press* from the hallway, any hope of being either cheerful or collected sank like a tall ship trying to negotiate Cape Horn in a typhoon.

There it was on page five with the pictures that I had snatched, along with Johnny the Roach's photo of Ellie's body being wheeled out.

SHE'S MURDERED ON WAY
TO SLAIN FIANCE'S FUNERAL

Finally, the *Daily Press* had run a decent story about Bobo's murder, since it now involved a second one, the killing of his girlfriend Eleanor Cunningham. The murder of a nobody might die on the obit page, but two nobodies hooked romantically couldn't be ignored. And it now had a decent angle: a grieving young woman killed on the way to her murdered fiancé's funeral. Attractive, deserving young lovers, planning a wedding and now poignantly going to their graves together. A *Daily Press* story now, all right.

Tommy Toolen had banged it out nicely from my notes. It was dripping with pathos, but it knocked me for a loop. There was no *By Edward Fitzgerald* on it, as was standard when a story came in from a reporter on the scene; there was not even a double byline. Instead, the byline read *By Tom Toolen.* I cringed, figuring I was definitely on Ironhead's shit list. But then, as I read the copy, it got even scarier, and I understood what had happened.

". . . The body was discovered by *Daily Press* reporter Edward Fitzgerald, a close friend of Cunningham and of her murdered fiance, Robert 'Bobo' Watson . . ."

No wonder I didn't get a byline. I was part of the story. A witness, for crissake! I've already said reporters never think of themselves as news. We all sort of float around a story, gather it, and put it down, but we are basically invisible, except for our bylines. I had tumbled from the more or less detached, disinterested observer in a byline into the body of the damned story.

You might think that a newspaper would be pleased to have one of its derring-do reporters as a major player in a story. You might think the *Daily Press* would crow about his dashing initiative. You might think he would even get a bonus. But the fact is, it's a pain in the grumper. Because it means you can get dragged into court, and stiff-necked newspaper counsel Charles W. Corcoran has to spend time and effort representing you and fending off the cops and the district attorney's office, and it might gag you from using your inside stuff, as Half-Dome Dennis Hanley had already suggested. Reporters who call attention to themselves by winding up in stories or winning the Pulitzer Prize are often soon out the door for the mistake of being noticed or getting too much credit. A low profile is definitely more healthy.

But it was too late. This was brought to my attention in the form of Ironhead blasting through the phone like Wolf Larson on Jack London's whaler *The Ghost* looming out of the fog firing its cannon. The ship's bell bonged across the water, and I grabbed it up.

"Yeah?"

"Fitz! What the goddamn hell is going on?"

Ironhead wasn't tranquil, either. He was, in fact, in a combustible state, his cannon lobbing shells from Forty-second Street across the bow of my place on East Eighty-second Street. They exploded into hot shrapnel about what I had been up to and, more to the point, why?

"What the hell happened? What were you doing over there?"

"I was at Bobo's funeral, and his girl didn't show up, so I went to check on her."

"Is that so? A funeral service, huh?"

"For Bobo Watson."

"You mean that piano player I told you to drop?"

I had been on my own time, I explained, minding my own business in a church and went to check up on Ellie and somehow had stumbled upon a second murder.

Ironhead didn't like that. There was no such thing as "my own time," for one thing, and no business for me to mind but that of the goddamn newspaper I worked for.

"We've finally gotten a story out of it, Ironhead," I launched in hopefully, a mouse cozying up to a snarling, feral cat.

"You know who's been on my phone forty times?" he demanded, veering off dangerously toward the ammunition locker.

"Those dumb cops?" I ventured, conjuring up the Four Stooges I had dueled with.

"Cops? No! Yes! Cops, too! What the hell are you doing

with four detectives after you? Never mind! Goddamnit, Pippy wants to know what ship you're riding!"

Oh, boy! The tall ships gala.

"I don't know if I can handle that now, Ironhead. Those cops have dragged me into this thing, and . . ."

"What!"

Whomp! Splat! Noises over the phone. Ironhead had dropped his cigar or spilled coffee on his computer keys, or maybe he was just incinerating. He didn't seem to be able to sort out what outraged him the most.

"Dragged into the story?" he finally spouted. He at last got to the one that caused the vein in his forehead to throb.

"I send you to find a ship," he raged. "But where do you go?"

"I wasn't working the story, Ironhead. The damned thing found me. I couldn't ignore a story dropped into my lap like that."

He sort of gargled, was momentarily speechless. But not for long. "All right, of course you couldn't. But now you're practically a suspect, goddamnit, and you let the *Post* steal it from under your nose!"

"Yeah," I complained, "they keep me incommunicado and leak the damn thing on me!"

Alas, this, as every other word I uttered on that unfortunate morning, was a blunder. It jogged Ironhead's already inflamed brain about what had happened the night before when the damned thing came in. Not only had I gotten mixed up in a story I had been warned not to touch with a barge pole, it was explained to me heatedly, but I had let the *Post* make a sap out of me and, more desperately, had embarrassed Ironhead and the New York *Daily Press.*

I hadn't seen the *Post* yet, and innocently I asked, what was in it? Another lamentable question, which had a fuse attached to it.

What was in it? Oh, nothing. Nothing at all. Merely that a bumbling *Daily Press* reporter had been found in a Riverside

Drive love nest with the fiancée of his best friend, Bobo Watson, the famous piano player from Elaine's, the hottest celebrity café in New York.

Wonderful! Bobo Watson, a nobody piano player one day, suddenly finding the fame that had eluded him while alive. And me with him.

"Aw, that's a lot of bullshit, Ironhead; you know that."

Oh, he was perfectly aware what bullshit was, he informed me. Bullshit was snide *New York Post* reporter Pat Whitestone gleefully calling the *Daily Press* city desk for a "comment" about one of its reporters being a goddamned murder suspect! Bullshit was Del Weisskopf, the night city editor, calling Ironhead at home for guidance.

Bullshit and various other scatological effluvia was Ironhead being forced to call the *Post* back and tell them that the *Daily Press* was pleased, as always, to let them pick up the scraps from one of our exclusives and that we would expect to be credited with our scoop.

Bullshit was the opposition hanging us out to dry on a story that could absolutely not be by me because it was at least in part *about* me. Bullshit was the damned *Post*'s story forcing the *Daily Press* to put me in our own story at the goddamned murder scene!

The only decent result was that, since I was part of the murder scenario, I could not possibly pursue it any longer and could get back to the tall ships armada and Pippy McFadden.

Yes, I immediately agreed, I was definitely working the tall ships gala. "I was on the *Pandora*, and I'm sailing with the Brits a week from Sunday," I got in hopefully.

"Yes, you damn well are! Now, you listen to me," he shouted. "I'm putting Dubbs on that murder. He can wrap it up! Dubbs knows how to get a story without getting arrested. Now, get your ass in here!"

"Detective Hanley wants me up at the Nineteenth."

"You stay away from any detectives! Now, get in here!

Corcoran's been in and out of here. We've got to figure out where we stand in this before you talk to those damned dicks."

"Oh," was all I could get out.

I shuddered. Wait till he and Corcoran learn that I had already unburdened myself at the 126th Street squad.

"Listen," I started, "the thing is . . ."

"I don't want to hear it! I don't want one of your goofy goddamn Irish explanations! Get your ass in here!"

He finally hung up, and I went in to shower and shave and try to come back to life. The water poured over me soothingly, but all it did was clear up my head enough to ponder how I could stay away from detectives when they considered me a damned material witness.

Well, the hell with it. It was Dubbs Brewer's headache now. Sometimes I wondered wistfully why I had not stayed back in St. Louis, working on the dock with my father, loading trucks. But no, I had to be a newspaperman.

After some coffee at the kitchen-nook table, I finally put in a phone call to Duffy, waking him up.

"Fitz!" he said groggily. "I saw the paper! My God! What happened to you?"

I filled him in on the lugubrious doings of the long, painful night.

"It's crazy," he said. "Both of them!"

I told him I had the same thought. There had to be some connection here.

"Did you get anything from the cops?" he asked.

Yeah, I thought, a hard time.

"Not really," I said. "They're still dragging their feet."

"Well, you can goose them in the paper, right?" he said, looking for some action. "They can't ignore it if you keep the heat on."

I was going to tell him that I wasn't on the story. But I didn't bother. Here was another one who thought a reporter could go after any story he wished.

"Did you ever notice anything funny at Elaine's when they were there together?" I asked.

"I don't know. Like what?"

I didn't know either. Anything unusual, out of the ordinary.

"No," he said, pausing, trying to think. "There was that boyfriend outside one night. And then some woman called Elaine's one time looking for Ellie."

"Who was she?"

"I don't know. I didn't take the call."

"When was that?"

"Let's see . . . uh, Monday or Tuesday. She wanted to send her a condolence card and asked for her address."

My blood froze. Some stranger calling to get Ellie's address?

"Did you give it to her?"

"No. The day bartender didn't have it."

"Did she say who she was?"

"No. Tommy just said it was a friend. She said she knew Bobo and Ellie. I didn't think anything of it, you know. The story about Bobo was in the paper by then."

"Did you ever see Claire's boyfriend, Doug the auto body shop guy, in there?" I asked.

Duffy pondered that a moment. "Well, she was in a few times talking to Bobo. I don't remember seeing him, but he might have been with her, because Bobo used to say this Doug hassled him sometimes."

I told him about the dark car that had cut me off.

"You think it was Doug?"

"I don't know. It was somebody."

So somebody had called looking for Ellie. It didn't necessarily mean anything. Friends could have called to send her a card, or to send flowers to St. Catherine's. But somebody had been looking for her address, and somebody had found it.

Big Duffy's stunned remark hung in my head. "Both of

them." He had voiced my own thoughts. This had to be about something linking them together. But what? That jealous former suitor of Ellie's? Bobo's divorced wife? That mechanic in the ill-fitting jacket who maybe owned a big, dark car or worked on them in his shop?

I realized then that I really didn't know Bobo or Ellie very well; they were casual friends, bar friends. I should have left it that way. I got myself together and headed out of the apartment. Outside, I skipped down the front stoop, and there, double-parked, sat Detective Dan Jacobs of the protruding rump, watching for me.

"Hey, reporter."

He was out of the car and had my arm.

"Let's go."

"No, listen, I'm due at the office."

"Yeah. My office."

"I'm not supposed to talk to you guys," I said, trying to pull away. "You'll have to call the *Daily Press* lawyer."

"Okay," he said. "We'll do that. Get in."

He walked me around the squad car, opened the door, and shoved me in.

"When?" I asked.

"Whenever." And we drove off.

The squad car went over to Second Avenue and then downtown, heading, I had no doubt, for the Nineteenth Precinct and Detective Dennis Hanley, the one place and the one person I was supposed to avoid.

"I already gave you a statement," I complained.

"Somebody wants to talk to you."

"Who? Look, this isn't really my story."

"Yeah? Well, you're part of our case."

"So you guys caught the case after all?"

"Under the circumstances."

I didn't quite know what that meant. What circumstances?

Jacobs kept driving. He was a stubby guy, as I've said, with a pinched prune face, wearing a cream-colored summer suit. He wasn't impassive like Hanley the stone lion; he was more like Grumpy of the Seven Dwarfs.

"Something new developed?"

"We checked out your suspect."

"You checked out *my* suspect?"

"Yeah! What do you think we do all day, ride sailboats in Central Park?"

Even they knew about my assignment.

"I don't exactly have any suspects," I muttered defensively.

"Oh, you don't? So you admit you don't know what the hell you're talking about, but still you guys come up with this bullshit, and we've got to check it out. We've got no time to find the real killer; we've got to check out your tips!"

"Who?"

"The ex's boyfriend, Doug the fender-banger in Queens. He and Watson's ex are looking to scoop up anything left."

"So he's a real suspect, then," I suggested. "They can collect insurance if Bobo's dead. This Doug didn't like Bobo spending money on some other woman."

Jacob's didn't say anything.

"So, did he check out? Has he got an alibi for the time Bobo was killed?"

"That's good, Fitz! Watson's knocked off at four in the morning, and you want to know does the guy have an alibi? Everybody's got an alibi at four in the morning! They're all home in bed, except piano players and reporters who never go home!"

"Where was he Wednesday afternoon when Ellie got it?"

"He says he was in his shop on Myrtle Avenue banging out a quarter panel on a Ford Galaxie. Alone."

That jogged my mind. "A Ford Galaxie? You sure it wasn't a dark green Mercedes?"

"What?"

"Listen, somebody ran me off the road last night."

"What's this? You think it was this Doug?"

"Well, I couldn't see who it was. But he's hot after Bobo's insurance. He can't account for his whereabouts for either murder!"

"Cute! We can't place him at either one. He and the ex had a motive: Watson's insurance. But they're each other's alibis. We've got nothing on them. Why would he run you off the road?"

"I don't know! He knows I'm Ellie's friend. He's a hot-head."

Jacobs let out an annoyed breath and drove on. It's always a surprise to find out that something you do gooses the cops into action, but sometimes it happens. And the cops don't like it, especially if they think your story's bullshit, which is almost always.

"What about Ellie's boyfriend?"

"Will you stay the hell out of our detail?"

We got to the precinct and went in.

"Look," I told him, "if you're going to question me again, I have to notify the company lawyer. They've gagged me on this."

"It's a little late," he tossed off, and herded me upstairs to the squad room.

"I'm not saying any more," I declared as officiously as I could. "I've got lockjaw."

He opened the detective squad room door and ushered me in, and only then did I realize the truth of what I had said.

Half-Dome Hanley was at his desk at the back of the room, and all of a sudden my jaw was locked for real, my head in a whirl. I couldn't have spoken if I had wanted to. For a second, I thought I was going to faint.

There at Hanley's desk, back straight, black hair sculpted, staring intently at me, was Eleanor Cunningham.

EIGHT

DETECTIVE HANLEY STOOD AND NODDED HIS HEAD TOward me.

"Ed Fitzgerald."

"Hello, Mr. Fitzgerald," she said softly, mutilating a handkerchief in her nervous, trembling hands.

"Eleanor's sister, Kathleen Cunningham, from Grand Rapids, Michigan," Hanley explained. He sat down again.

"Hello."

I stared at her for a long moment. Her sister? She wasn't just Ellie's sister but an absolute double, her twin. The same straight back, the same sculpted black hair. It was like something out of the *Twilight Zone*. Here was Ellie back from the dead in a blue traveling suit, a reconstituted ghost or doppelgänger in the flesh.

"I didn't know she had a sister," I said.

Jacobs drew me back toward the squad room door and turned his back on her, speaking softly so she couldn't hear him. I wish I hadn't had to hear him, either.

"We took her by the morgue this morning to identify her sister," he half-whispered.

I looked around at her, sitting rigidly at Hanley's desk, her hands in her lap. She glanced around at me, and I walked over.

"She wanted to get a fill-in from you about what happened," Detective Hanley said gently.

"You found her?" Kathleen asked softly.

I nodded. I really didn't know what to say.

"I gave them a statement," I told her.

"I just wondered if you knew any more. You knew Ellie and . . . Mr. Watson?"

"Well, yeah," I said, wondering a little at her calling her sister's fiancé Mr. Watson. "I don't know what else I can tell you."

Her shoulders slumped. "Oh. Well, I wanted to thank you, anyway. Ellie called me about the funeral and said you were such a help. I just thought . . . since you knew them both, and officer Hanley said you're the only real witness . . ."

I didn't like that much, and glanced at Hanley. He and Jacobs might consider me a witness, but I thought of myself only as somebody who had shown up at the wrong place at the wrong time. Hanley sort of half-smiled, as though enjoying watching an ambushed reporter. Newspaper guys like me were always riding the cops on cases, writing snide stories insinuating they're all either a bunch of bumbling Inspector Clouseaus or on the take. How did I like being on the receiving end? That's what I got from his satisfied, tit-for-tat expression.

"Maybe the stories you're writing will get somebody to come forward with something," she said hopefully.

I looked away, then back. "I'm not really on it, Kathleen," I told her. "I only happened to be there."

"Oh." She looked away and stood up, turning to Hanley. "I'll get out of your way," she said. "I don't know what I'm going to do. I came here straight from the airport. I guess I'll stay at Ellie's."

Her little "oh" made me feel like an insect. I wish I could tell you I didn't offer to run her over to Ellie's place, but she looked so lost and forlorn.

"All right, good. I've got a key to her apartment," Hanley offered, handing it to her. "We'll know where to reach you."

She picked up an overnight bag I hadn't noticed before. Outside, I remembered my Toyota was back uptown since I had been dragooned off my front stoop into Detective Jacobs's squad car. I got us a cab and gave the cabby Eleanor's address on Riverside Drive.

Kathleen sat back, her traveling bag on her lap, arms on top of it, staring listlessly out the cab window, looking at nothing, I thought.

"The police called me, and I was in shock," she said distractedly. She trailed off into silence.

"I didn't really know Ellie very well," I said, breaking the silence. "I knew Bobo a little."

She focused on me then. "Was he all right?" she asked.

"All right?" I wasn't sure what she meant.

"We hardly knew him, you know, and the last thing Ellie told me was they were going to be married."

"Oh, yeah. I was there when they announced it."

"You were? Where?"

"Elaine's. That's where Bobo played piano."

Kathleen wagged her head impatiently. "It's hard to take anyone seriously who calls himself Bobo."

"Well, a piano player, you know. They use stage names."

"A dope's name," she muttered. "Piano player! Ellie was a pianist!"

That surprised me. "Your sister was a piano player, too?"

"Not a piano player. A pianist, a musician. She played Mozart. She was a graduate of the Indiana University School of Music. I don't understand what she saw in him. Was he mixed up in anything?"

"No," I said. "He just played the piano. Everybody liked him."

"He had an ex-wife somewhere."

"Yeah, in Queens. She was at Bobo's funeral. What makes you think he was mixed up in something?"

"Oh, I don't know," she said warily. "But something happened. I had to go with those policemen to the morgue and . . . oh, God, Mr. Fitzgerald . . . it's so hard to believe. I don't know what to do."

She looked away, trembling with frustration and anxiety. I could understand her need to blame someone, and at the moment the only person she could think of was Bobo.

"Somebody got him, too," I reminded her.

"Yes, that's why I wonder what he was mixed up in. How did she meet him, anyway?"

"Some guy brought her to Elaine's. He might be the one they're looking for."

"Who was he?"

"Nobody seems to know. An old boyfriend of Ellie's? A jealous one?"

"What do you mean?" Her head jerked around.

I told her about the suit who had brought Ellie to Elaine's and about the confrontation with Bobo outside.

"This character could have reason to get both of them," I concluded.

"A boyfriend?" she asked, looking excited and troubled.

"Yeah." I examined her face. She was showing signs of deep interest. "You know who she might have been seeing out here?"

"Well, yes—Erik Coleman!"

"You know him?"

Well, of course she knew him, she said. She, Ellie, and Erik had all gone to school together back in Grand Rapids. Everybody had always assumed Erik and Ellie would marry, until Bobo Watson came out of the woodwork.

"What's this Erik look like?"

Erik Coleman, she told me, was tall, handsome, cultured, a gentleman, an old friend, a wonderful young man who was assistant manager of the New Jersey Symphony. He had moved out here about the same time Ellie had.

"I've known him all my life!" she said, her face flushed.

"You know where he lives?"

"Yes . . . in New Jersey. I've been trying to reach him."

"You can't reach him?"

"I've been calling, but there's no answer. Do the police think he had anything to do with this?"

"Well, it's usually somebody who knows the victim."

She stared at me, shaken, uncertain. "Well . . . he was so crazy about Ellie!"

I had the distinct impression she had mixed emotions about Erik.

"What kind of car does he drive?" I asked. I was still wondering about that road-rage character on Cathedral Parkway.

"What?" she replied, befuddled. "I don't know."

"Where can they find this Erik? I think the cops want to talk to him."

"Oh, no," she murmured. "He lives in Leonia, New Jersey. I've got his number."

Then Kathleen looked out the window again, clutching her traveling bag as though to hold onto something, and I could sense the inner turmoil in her, the percolating, bubbling rage that drives a murder victim's loved one to despair. Such an unfortunate is left behind, confronted with an impossibility, and no one seems to care. And now she suspected one of her closest friends of murdering her sister.

The cab rolled across Cathedral Parkway, passing St. John the Divine. An open-top double-decker sight-seeing bus ahead of us on 110th Street turned off and climbed toward the immense cathedral.

"Look at them," she said softly, "going on with their lives as though nothing has happened."

At the apartment building on Riverside Drive, I got out and told the cabby to wait. Kathleen climbed out, lugging her bag, and paused to dig the key to Ellie's apartment out of her purse.

"Well, listen," I said, "good luck. If there's anything I can do . . ."

I edged toward the cab door. I had to get across town and down to the *Daily Press*. In the back of my mind, I recalled Ironhead Matthews's gentle suggestion about what I was supposed to do that morning. "Get your ass in here!"

Kathleen was at the front door fiddling with the key, and then she leaned against it, motionless.

"You okay?"

"Yes, I guess so."

She didn't look very okay, though, and who could blame her?

"You go? You stay?" The cabby, who looked like he was from Bangladesh, leaned over and harassed me out the cab window. Goddamn pushy immigrant!

I sighed and paid the cabby. "Let's get you settled," I said.

We went into the gloomy, nondescript lobby with its typical New York iron-framed elevator door and rode up to the sixth floor in the jerking, claustrophobic car, Kathleen too close beside me, looking apprehensive.

"Have you been in her apartment before?" I asked.

She shook her head. "I was going to come for the wedding. . . . Thanks for coming in with me. I didn't want to walk in by myself."

Well, she had company: "Get-Your-Ass-in-Here" Fitzgerald, prize doofus of the *Daily Press*.

She put the key into the door of 6-B and opened it. Right away, I could sense it. You know that feeling when instinct takes over and your blood rushes into your head? I stepped in, Kathleen behind me, and the place was a shambles.

"Oh, my God!" she gasped.

Yeah.

The flowered sofa's pillows were thrown aside; a desk was opened and its papers scattered as if by a pipe bomb; the rug was ripped up. A scene of devastation.

"Did the police leave it like this?" Kathleen wondered aloud.

"No," I assured her.

NINE

I WANTED TO KICK MYSELF FOR HAVING COME UP TO THE apartment with Kathleen, but shuddered to think of the state she would have been in if she had walked in alone.

I noticed a window facing the drive was open, and outside it, there was a fire escape. Easy in and easy out.

"He came back," Kathleen said quietly.

"Yeah."

"What did he want?" she asked. I considered that a good question, too, whoever he was or they were.

And then who appeared in the apartment doorway, peeking in suspiciously, but Syrian Jack, the super.

"You're back?" he asked.

No, I wanted to say. Absolutely not!

Pretty soon, blowsy Missus Hooper from the next apartment was behind him, gawking in too. And then several other nosy residents.

"It's that reporter again!" announced Missus Hooper.

"I spotted him this time," Syrian Jack declared, the damned snoop. "What happened here?"

"We've been burglarized!" Kathleen told them excitedly.

Missus Hooper blinked and swayed. "My God! It's Ellie!"

Syrian Jack suddenly realized his dead tenant had returned. He jerked backward, gestured, and muttered, "In the name of Allah the compassionate, the merciful!"

"It's her sister," I explained.

"But she's dead!"

"Her twin sister."

He stared at her uncomprehendingly for a few more moments, and then turned to me.

"Every time you come, something happens!" he complained, eyeing me warily.

What was I supposed to say to that?

"We have to tell Detective Hanley," Kathleen blurted, coming back to life.

"I'll call 911!" Missus Hooper howled. "The neighborhood's gone!" She scooted away toward her apartment.

Wonderful. And I was supposed to be on my way to the paper.

First Detective Sergeant Thomas from the West 126th station showed up again, along with Renaldo Musso of the feathered hat and unctuous manner.

"What the hell is this, anyway?" was what Sgt. Thomas wanted to know, and he wanted to know it from me. This was my personal crime scene, wasn't it?

"The sportswriter?" Musso recalled.

Go to hell, fool!

And before long, Detectives Dennis Hanley and Dan Jacobs from across town showed up, too. They took a quick look around.

"You found it like this?" Hanley asked me.

"As you see."

"Every time he shows up, there are bodies and burglars," Syrian Jack told the cops. "Who is he?"

"A *Daily Press* reporter."

"He broke down my door and barged right in the other time," Missus Hooper declared.

"I didn't break down anything," I said in frustration.

"There," she said huffily, "you see?"

You may not believe this, but four detectives were not enough to handle the case. After a while, two more walked in from the Thirty-fourth Precinct and huddled with Hanley and

Jacobs, casting glances at me. Hanley strolled over to me with them.

"Detectives Dienst and Schaefer from the three-four," Hanley said. "They want to ask you a few questions."

"No way!"

Hanley tilted his head in resignation and turned the screws, telling the two new arrivals, "He's a pain in the ass. You may have to contact his lawyer at the *Daily Press*."

"Wait a minute!" I muttered, the image of Corcoran's pained face swimming up before me. More cops calling in about me might confuse him.

Detective Dienst studied me calmly, smiling faintly.

"No big deal, Fitzgerald. We just thought you could steer us a little since you're on the story."

I realized I had developed a ferocious headache.

Then Schaefer pushed in. "That story about Bobo Watson the piano player—that was yours, right?"

"Sort of."

Well, Dienst and Schaefer told me, Bobo Watson lived in their precinct up in Inwood, on the upper tip of Manhattan, and his basement room also had been broken into and ransacked.

It was a nothing burglary, and they didn't know if anything had even been taken, and they hadn't been able to locate the tenant, Bobo Watson. But when they filed a report, information eventually came back that the tenant had been murdered. That had led them to Hanley and Jacobs down in the one-nine, who had the homicide case, and now it had brought them to Riverside Drive, where the whole thing seemed to have a connection.

"Jesus, all I did was drop in for the last call!" I mumbled.

"Last call?"

"Forget it."

Would I be willing to give them a statement to clear this up?

Clear it up? Jupiter Optimus Maximus!

"Couldn't I just fill you in, and never mind any statement? See, the *Daily Press* doesn't want me to talk to you until I clear it with the office."

Detective Hanley, listening in, smiled at that, and I realized he understood. He surmised that I had stepped on my cock by blabbing already and that the office didn't know.

But I was fascinated at Dienst and Schaefer's report that Bobo Watson's apartment had also been ransacked.

"They were looking for something up there and here, too?" I mused.

"Who are 'they'?" Hanley asked.

"You got me."

"Any idea of what they're looking for?" Hanley added.

Of course, I had no idea. And when they all huddled around Kathleen to ask if she knew, she was equally in the dark. Whatever it was, somebody apparently wanted it enough to kill two people.

"I can't stay here!" Kathleen cried.

"No," Hanley agreed.

"Listen, Hanley," I said, "did you and Jacobs check out whether Doug Shippen was working on a Mercedes instead of a Ford Galaxie in his body shop?"

"Goddamnit," he shot back, "will you stay out of our hair!"

"All right, but listen, that boyfriend of Ellie's I told you about? Kathleen knows him—Erik Coleman. He lives in New Jersey."

Hanley turned to Kathleen and asked her about Coleman. She gave him Erik's address and his phone number.

"Was he pretty put out about Watson and your sister?" Hanley asked.

Kathleen's face was pale, and she looked away. She nodded. "Yes. I talked to him once about it."

"Have you talked to him since you got here?"

She shook her head no. "I just got here today."

Jacobs took notes in his logbook as Kathleen filled them in about Erik Coleman. Stumbling over her words, she was a reluctant informer, crushed by the terrible murder and the frightful suspicion.

They were through with me for the moment, although I was invited not to leave just yet, and so I sat on the windowsill and lit a Tiparillo. It was a wonderful situation, so full of submerged, floating mines that I didn't want to think about it, and so I just stared idly out the window.

Down below, there were a few more gawkers, ogling up at the window and now at me. There was something titillating going on up there in 6-B, the scene of a recent bloody murder. Some of the idlers looked like pals of Syrian Jack—vaguely foreign, maybe Arabs or maybe Bangladeshi like the cab-driver, or Indian, or from Hong Kong or who knew where. New York is an international feast these days, with Koreans running fruit-and-vegetable stands, and Indian Moslems and Hindus driving cabs, operating newsstands, and working in emergency rooms. There are people in other parts of the U.S. who call New York the capital of a foreign country.

I averted my gaze from the rubberneckers and glanced over them across Riverside Drive. There, out on the Hudson River, what did I see but a tall ship, sliding serenely up the river on what I supposed must be a practice run for the sail-through to the George Washington Bridge a week from Sunday.

From a hurried scan of the flotilla I had made earlier, I made her out to be the 399-footer *Sedov* out of Latvia. She was glorious, she was a vision, she was a cattle prod in my neck. I turned away from the sidewalk gawkers and the *Sedov*, and lurched to Detective Hanley. I told him I had to get out of there. I was already frightfully late. I had to get to the office before I was keelhauled.

"Sure," he said smugly, "go ahead. But you'll be available, right?"

"Yeah," I said sourly, and I could see that if I cooperated with him unofficially, he would not call the *Daily Press* and tell Ironhead that I had already shot my mouth off in a statement.

At the door, there was Kathleen Cunningham, grabbing me.

"Mr. Fitzgerald . . . are you leaving?"

"I'm overdue at the office!"

"Oh! Of course. I don't know what I'm going to do!"

I didn't either, but I was finally out the door, down the cramped elevator, out onto the street and moving between some of the window gawkers. I hurried to 113th Street and then over toward Broadway, where I might hope to hail a cab. I'd have to call Dubbs Brewer and alert him to the burglary, since it was his story now, but I didn't want him to mention that I had been back at the scene. Fat chance! Dubbs wasn't a police reporter for nothing.

I was in such a discombobulated rush that I wasn't paying any attention to anyone walking along behind me, and in New York you always instinctively watch your ass. But as I got away from Riverside Drive and headed toward Broadway, I realized that some of those rubberneckers were following me. Apparently they knew I was a reporter and wanted some of the gory details. Then one of them was holding my arm, and I yanked away, pretty annoyed at the nerve of them. Goddamn ghouls!

"Fitzgerra?" one of them said with some kind of an accent.

"Read the *Daily Press,*" I flung back, and hurried on. But then my arm was snagged again, and I realized it was rather importunate. The pushy character was trying to stop me.

I yanked my arm again, but didn't get loose this time. Then another hand was on my other arm. I glared around at whoever it was, and stared into the faces of two of those foreign-looking gawkers.

"You will come with us!" one commanded, and I was bewildered.

"What?"

Now I looked closer. They weren't Indians but East

Asians. One was short, and the other looked like he could play center on the Chinese Olympic basketball team. They wore rough, blue jackets—denim, maybe.

"Get outa here," I snapped. "I can't talk to you now."

An invisible fist landed on my ear, and I felt heat and saw stars. One of the maniacs had punched me! If they wanted my attention, they had it now. I was manhandled into an about-face, and was being marched along between an Asian Mutt and Jeff who appeared to be Chinese or Korean. I caught a glimpse of dark eyes and silky black hair. I was mesmerized momentarily by the size sixteen—at least—yellow lumberjack shoes of the giant one moving me along beside him in long strides.

"What are you doing? Let go of me! Hey!"

"Silence, wagging tongue!"

"What?"

That fist crashing on my ear had alerted me that something bizarre was happening, and instinct took over. It was like being mugged; you don't know what's happening. Two crazies are dragging me along the street. I knew that the best and probably only moment to do something in such a situation was immediately. I twisted my head down and back between and through them, jerked loose, and took off, running in the opposite direction.

They were after me.

"Stop, wagging tongue!"

A hoarse, singsongy curse.

I ran dementedly east along West 113th Street, away from Riverside Drive, going I didn't know where, but toward the next intersection. They panted behind me, yelling. I have no idea what I thought except that killers had staked out Ellie's apartment, and these characters had been waiting outside. Trying to sprint on a New York street has its problems, such as women with baby carriages and a Department of Sanitation truck picking up trash cans in front of apartment stoops.

I slanted away from the baby carriages onto the sidewalk

and plowed through Sanitation Department workers hefting large, metal trash cans. A thumping crash and some choice New York street language—mixed with clanging, exotic shouts in my wake—gave me hope.

Then I was at Broadway, and a desperate plan gripped me. I ran out into the traffic in the middle of Broadway and halted, throwing up my arms, jumping up and down like an exercise leader at Jack La Lanne's, causing a frantic squealing of brakes and an instant outburst of road rage as cars, cabs, and an Entenmann's Bakery truck screeched to a halt.

"Get out of the street, you hoople!"

But I stood fast, blocking traffic, jumping in front of anything that tried to move.

"Hey! What are ya, crazy!"

The intersection erupted with a blare of horns and some virulent tongue-lashings.

At the sidewalk, I spotted the two crazies shrinking back, gesturing at each other, temporarily frozen.

And then, deliverance! A blue-and-white police car slid through the madly congested, honking, cursing, traffic jam and up to me. Fresh blood or a traffic jam is the only guarantee of getting a cop in a hurry in New York.

A uniformed cop got out and strolled up to me.

"Okay, pal, what are you supposed to be? A Knicks cheerleader?"

TEN

AS THE COP SHOOED ME OUT OF THE INTERSECTION, I searched the corner for the two wackos who had tried to mug me, but I didn't see them. I had to hope the cops showing up had discouraged them.

A cabby leaned out his window. "Run that screwball in; he's a mile high on crack!"

"Go on, get moving," the cop's partner yelled disgustedly, waving the traffic back into motion.

"Hey! I hurt my back when you stopped!" the cabby's fare squealed.

"No, no," the cabby protested. "You fine!" He looked at me and the cop again. "It's his fault! You get his name!"

"Get outa here!"

"Juiced up are ya, pal?" the cop now asked me.

"No! Two guys tried to grab me. I had to do something."

"Yeah? Can you describe them?"

"They looked Chinese."

The cop frowned. "Chinese up here?" He examined me a little closer. "You been drinking?"

I sighed. "Look, I'm Ed Fitzgerald, *Daily Press*. Are there any Chinese gangs working this neighborhood?"

His partner walked over. "Guy says two Chinese grabbed him, Clancy."

The one called Clancy cocked his head. "Huh! New one on me. Did you see where they went?"

I looked back toward Riverside Drive. "Back that way, I guess. I don't see them now."

"Come on," Clancy said. "We'll have a look."

I got into the backseat, and the sector car went back across West 113th Street to Riverside Drive. They looped around the streets looking for them, but we didn't spot them.

"We'll put in a slip," Clancy said. "Maybe the Chinese squad can look at it."

After circling several blocks, the cops let me out on Broadway again. I'd told them I didn't want to go to the precinct and file a report. What was the use?

I stood on the corner looking to flag down a cab. What a day it was shaping up to be. Ambushed by a dead twin from Grand Rapids, manipulated into an apartment that had just been burgled, and chased into traffic by Ching and Chang.

Just another day in the life of a reporter in New York.

You know how it is when you have thirty-seven pressing things that you absolutely have to do at once, but you're in such a funk that you can't decide what to do first?

I decided I needed a drink.

I walked along Broadway and into a bar and ordered a Harp.

"We don't got no Harp."

I realized I was not in an Irish bar. The bartender was Hispanic.

"What've you got?"

He shrugged. "Everything."

"Such as what?"

"You like something gringo . . . Rheingold?"

"Why not?"

Rheingold? It was a famous old New York beer that I thought had disappeared. But here it was again. I didn't care; I would have drunk Japanese beer. Maybe not Chinese beer, though, if there is such a thing.

I sat there in a stupor and took a swig. It was time to try to think, to get myself organized, to knock my head back into working order. I lit a Tiparillo and tried to make sense of it.

Who the hell were they, and what did they want with me?

were the obvious questions. Dubbs Brewer was working stories about the Chinatown gangs, but I couldn't imagine them being this far uptown. More to the point, why would they want to talk to me? The short, wiry one with the invisible fist had called me "Fitzgerra," and seemed to know I was a *Daily Press* reporter. A little intimidation against the paper, maybe? Why me? Maybe they couldn't get at Dubbs inside the police shack. Could they have seen me leaving police headquarters and tailed me from Chinatown up to Riverside Drive? I couldn't make sense of it.

Marcus Aurelius had warned me to "stand firm and be ready to meet onsets, however unexpected." I had been no more ready than Bobo.

Then I remembered that Tommy Toolen had put my name in that story, identifying me as a close friend of Bobo and Ellie's. Was that it? They saw me coming out and knew I was that same "Fitzgerra"?

I took a gulp and looked at the clock over the bar. My God! It was late afternoon. But I knew that. Where had the day gone? A phrase and a vision flitted through my distracted head. "Get your ass in here!" was the phrase. Gorgeous tall ships pridefully bellying out their plumage was the vision. Fu Manchu and Invisible Fist then blotted out both.

I wish I could tell you that this feverish little review cleared my mind and jolted me into action, but unfortunately I was completely at sea, although sadly enough not on a tall ship.

A dark, ominous cloud identifiable as Hurricane Ironhead scudded across my horizon, but I willed it away for the moment. Even he would understand that I had something more important to deal with. A couple of Chinatown maniacs were stalking me, and I didn't know why. What had the one called me? "Wagging tongue?" What the hell was that?

I got on the pay phone in the bar and called Dubbs at the police bureau.

"Hey, Dubbs, have any of those Chinatown gangs hassled you?"

"What?" he asked, his voice sliding into annoyance. "So Brain Dead did put you on my story!"

"No, no! But two Chinese goons tried to grab me. Do you know any of them? One tall and one short?"

"What the hell are you talking about? Goddamnit, Ironhead's got me chasing your piano player story! Do your ship story!"

"Listen, Dubbs, I'm not poaching on your damn beat! I think these guys want to scare us off! They know my name!"

"Well, ain't this sweet!" he muttered. "You dump your crappy murder on me, and then come down here and go slinking around Chinatown behind my back . . ."

"It wasn't in Chinatown! It was up on Riverside Drive!"

"Where?" That confused him.

"Look, I'm just warning you! Watch your ass! I don't think they like your stories, and they're out to put the fear of God in somebody."

"Yeah, well, just stay out of their way, and keep the hell off my turf! Scare me off, huh? I'll wipe up Mott Street with them! Is that what they said—they're trying to scare me off?"

"Well, no."

"Are you working this story or not?"

"No, no. Absolutely not! I don't want any part of it."

"You uptown office hotshots better stick to dog shows! I'll handle this!"

"Okay, okay! By the way, there was a burgle on the piano player murder story up here."

"Is that so?" There was a note of smugness in his voice. "Well, that's some hot scoop! You're off that. I've got it, and it's all wrapped up."

"What?" I didn't think I had heard him correctly. "What's all wrapped up?"

"That Bobo-Watson-and-the-twin murder you've screwed up."

I still didn't understand him. "What do you mean? What happened?"

"They got him."

"They've got who?"

"The boyfriend."

"Erik Coleman?"

"He turned himself in."

ELEVEN

I HUNG UP THE PAY PHONE AND STARED AT IT BLANKLY. Erik Coleman had turned himself in? I dropped in another quarter and dialed rapidly, hoping I had heard Dubbs correctly and that he wasn't pulling my leg.

"Hanley, one-nine squad."

"It's Fitz. I just heard Erik came in on his own."

I heard a long, satisfied breath. "Yeah. Your police reporter, Dubbs Brewer, already got it."

"I'll be damned!"

"We went over to New Jersey to that address Miss Cunningham gave us, but he wasn't home. When we got back to the station house, there he was, waiting for us."

"What did he have to say?"

"We're talking to him now."

"Did he make a statement?"

"Interrogation is continuing."

I caught a whiff of official NYPD language there, and realized it was Dubbs's baby.

"By the way, how did he get there?"

"Get here?"

"Did he drive? What kind of car does he have?"

Hanley sputtered a little. "What kind of car? What the hell are you talking about?"

"A Mercedes by any chance?"

"Are you still imagining things? No! One of these pickup truck things. An Isuzu Trooper, I think it is. Why?"

"Well, you know—I'm just interested."

"Get interested in something else. This one's finished. Do us a favor, and disappear. Go back to covering sports."

He hung up.

I walked back to the bar and took another swig of Rheingold. Erik Coleman walking into the police station to cop a plea. It was deliverance! The whole damned thing wrapped up. I heard most of those thirty-seven grating problems that had been blocking my head winging away into the wind.

I paid up, went outside, and hailed a cab, and rode back down to my place, where I had left the Toyota a million years ago in another life. Just like that, the damned mess was out of my head. I ran upstairs for a moment to stop in the john to deal with that Rheingold.

Then the phone rang. Of course.

I wouldn't answer it, I decided. It was Ironhead in a state of agitation. I knew I had to talk to him face-to-face, because I had to explain why I had been back at Ellie's apartment on a burglary.

"*Wraaaannnng!*" the damn thing insisted.

With a phone in his hand, Ironhead uses only one end of it. Maybe it was the cops. Which one? I had six of them rattling my cage.

"*Wraaaannng!*"

I let the answering machine take it, and heard a trembly voice. "Mr. Fitzgerald?"

I picked it up. "Hello?"

"Mr. Fitzgerald? It's me, Kit."

"Kit?"

"Kathleen Cunningham. I've been trying to reach you."

"What happened?"

"They've arrested Erik!"

"Oh. Yeah. I just heard. I was going to tell you about it. I'm on my way to the office."

She was silent a moment. "How could he do it?"

I didn't know what to say. Losing a loved one can demolish your equilibrium, but finding out who did it doesn't help much, especially if it's somebody you know.

"Did you see him?" she asked hesitantly.

"Erik? No. He's at the police station. Where are you?"

"At the Edison Hotel in Times Square. They put me up here, and then they called and told me."

"What are you going to do?"

"I could come over to the paper," she said wearily. "If you need to know anything more for your story. It's the least I could do, I guess."

"No, no, Kit. It's not my story."

"It isn't?"

"No. Dubbs Brewer, the police reporter, picked it up. I'm still on the tall ships story."

"The what?"

"It's a top-priority assignment from Ironhead," I explained hopefully.

"Who?"

"My city editor."

"Ironhead?"

"Arnold Matthews, actually, but . . ."

"Well, I just want to help. I feel I owe the paper for helping me."

"Listen, I've got to get to the office. I'll tell you what. Meet me at the Greek's across from the paper."

"The Greek's?"

"It used to be the Greek's, but now it's Angelo's Café. Some Egyptians run it. And after I check in, I'll come over."

"All right." She sounded listless, defeated, strung out.

The second I hung up the phone it started jumping around like it had been invaded by a nest of bumblebees. This time I didn't answer it, but beat it out of there, chased by the wraanging swarm.

Driving down Second Avenue to the *Daily Press,* I felt relief and resignation that the Bobo-Ellie murders had slid into an understandable, even traditional, conclusion. Poor, disappointed, jilted Erik Coleman, scalded with embarrassment at being dumped for a nobody and boiling for revenge against both of them, lost it and went on a rampage. It was a sad tale and an old one, but almost a blueprint for what the cops call a crime of passion.

I parked on Fortieth Street in the NYP zone and walked up to the *Daily Press*, past the huge world globe in the lobby. Then I fell in step with Bike O'Malley, our NFL linebacker–sized, motorcycle-riding, demon reporter, who had once gone off a pier.

"Fitz!" he smiled as we stepped onto the elevator. "How're you doing on that swashbuckler story I helped you land?"

"Yeah, by dodging it yourself."

"I see Toolen gave you a plug in a story, too," he chuckled. "Talked to Corcoran yet?"

I swayed a little at that. "Was he looking for me?"

"Oh, no. Only every ten minutes. What's that all about? I thought you were playing midshipman."

I could see that my wonderful assignment and a hint that I had made a dog's dinner of it were topics of keen interest.

It was, more particularly, a topic situated in Ironhead's office. In fact, in his craw. This became apparent when I got to my desk and perky Betty Applegarth glanced at me, eyed the ceiling, fluffed her hair, and murmured, "Oh, oh!"

I risked a glance toward Ironhead's office, and he was on his feet, glaring out through the glass at me. He lit the damp stump in his mouth and then crooked his finger at me. Being summoned into Ironhead's office was never pleasant, because he was almost never in there except when he was chewing somebody out. Bike called it Ironhead's "attitude adjustment center."

Passing the city desk, Sam Graff, the assistant city editor, raised his eyebrows and smoothed the brush on his upper lip, but didn't want to look up.

"Hey, Sam," I asked quietly, "did Dubbs phone in anything on an arrest in the Watson murder?"

Sam glanced up and then back at his VDT. "Yeah, he sent in some notes. That's the thing you've been working instead of the ships?"

"I haven't been working it," I insisted.

From the end of the room, beyond the managing editor's office, I noticed a slumping hulk in a vest and with rumpled gray hair tacking toward Ironhead's office.

Ironhead sank down in the chair behind his desk as I entered, leaning forward, his eyes transfixing me like a butterfly in an entomologist's collection.

Charles W. Corcoran reached port, slouching at the door, a clipboard in his hand.

"Well?" said Ironhead.

An innocent sounding word, but not when it issues from the turned-down mouth of a city editor mangling a cigar stump and drumming a pen on the desktop. He started in again.

"What the hell were you doing back over on Riverside Drive?" His mouth rolled the slimy cigar around. "Dubbs says there was a burglary, and you were back up there this morning."

It was time to try to explain how I got hooked up in this thing.

"Ironhead, look, Ellie's twin sister from Grand Rapids showed up, and the cops brought me in to talk to her. So I took her to Ellie's apartment, which I guess wasn't too smart. But she was, you know, pretty upset. And finding the body . . . I was checking on Ellie. It's all sort of a mix-up."

"A mix-up!" he snorted.

Behind me, Corcoran shifted his bulk and cleared his throat. The clipboard smacked his knee. The mention of the Ellie Cunningham murder story had sparked him into action, and he stalked around behind Ironhead and waved his clipboard.

"The question here is how you got yourself involved in this thing as a witness!" he declared. "Now, we've got to work up a statement for the police before they talk to you."

I sank into a chair.

"It is our policy for reporters not to get involved in actual crimes!" he declared indignantly.

"I wasn't exactly involved," I protested.

Corcoran's mass of gray hair shook. He leaned toward me over Ironhead's shoulder.

"Not involved?" he snapped, as though grilling a lying witness in criminal court. "You found the body!"

"I was just trying to find out what had happened to her."

"Why didn't you simply absent yourself?" he wanted to know.

"Walk off a story?"

"Story?" He was considerably annoyed by that. "It was a homicide!"

"Aw, shut up!" Ironhead had found his tongue. "Goddamnit, no decent reporter would do that."

"But, Arnold . . ." Corcoran protested, sinking back to sit on the windowsill behind him.

A precedent, a miracle! Ironhead was sticking up for me. I nestled in my chair feeling vindicated. It was a trifle premature.

"But, goddamnit," he raged at me, "you weren't supposed to be anywhere near there!"

"Absolutely not!" Corcoran chimed in righteously. "This newspaper does not condone insubordination or improper, illegal activities that compromise the integrity and reflect upon the reputation of the *Daily Press!* Furthermore . . ."

"Hey!" Ironhead turned on the blustering lawyer. "He wasn't supposed to be there, but goddamnit, any man on my staff who walked away from a story would find himself on unemployment or working for some goddamn gossip sheet!"

"What am I supposed to tell Mr. McFadden?" Corcoran complained.

Well, you never know in this business—Ironhead exploded! Corcoran could go and tell our publisher, Mr. Mc-

Fadden, and his goofy sailor-suit son Pippy, and their goddamn dog, too, that their city editor was sick and tired of being given crappy features that waste the time of his reporters, and this city editor would absolutely no longer stand for a lot of stupid front-office interference!

Corcoran leaned back, and I thought he was going to topple backward out through the window.

"Excuse me?" he blurted out.

"You tell him that, and tell him I said so!"

It's an established practice for a city editor to tell off the publisher. Mr. McFadden, the damn-fool businessman who only cared about the bottom line, was not to ask for coverage of goddamn tea parties or tulip festivals or idiotic dog shows, but to stay the hell out of the way and let somebody who knows how run the *Daily Press!*

Ironhead's wastebasket made the mistake of being too close and was kicked across the room.

This show of bravado was directed at an intermediary, of course—Corcoran, a safe target. It would never reach the ears of Mr. McFadden, but it made Ironhead feel better. Having rescued his integrity, Ironhead now turned upon me. No, I could not have walked off that story, he grumbled, not that I was supposed to be covering it. And we had gotten a decent story out of it, Ironhead said.

"And now you can get back on the ship story. Pippy is on my butt! Have you had time to even look at a ship?"

"Oh, sure!"

"Which one?"

"The big Latvian ship *Sedov* went up the Hudson partway on a practice run," I tried.

"Latvian?"

"And the *Nina*, the *Pinta*, and the *Santa Maria* are in beside the *Intrepid*."

"All right. Get yourself signed on to sail on the *Nina,* the *Pinta*, or the *Santa Maria*, or some other damned sailboat!"

"Ironhead, there's another angle to this thing that I can't

figure out, and it may have nothing to do with it, but a couple of Chinese tried to grab me."

"Chinese?"

That stopped Ironhead.

"They were hanging around Ellie's apartment and grabbed me when I came out. They knew my name, and wanted me to go with them."

"What the hell is it about?"

"I don't know. Dubbs is doing some Chinese gang stories, but that doesn't seem to figure. Maybe just a couple of muggers. But they knew me and were up there."

Ironhead didn't know either, and he had other things on his mind. "Pippy's hosting a chichi luncheon at the yacht club next week. You will be there! You will regale him with everything anybody ever heard about ships!"

I escaped.

TWELVE

THAT SHOULD HAVE BEEN THE END OF MY INVOLVEMENT with the Bobo and Ellie murders. Dubbs had the story, and the cops had Erik Coleman. It had been a hell of a week, but it was Friday and I was looking at two days off. On Monday, I could get back to the ships. Most of them were in by now, and I would have a week to write them up. Then I'd have to catch that yacht club luncheon on Wednesday. And then the Parade of Ships up the Hudson a week from Sunday.

I was walking back to my desk when Glenn the Switchboard waved me over and told me Paul had called.

"Paul who?"

"I don't know. He said call him back."

That didn't compute for me. "Did he have a Chinese accent?" I asked, wondering about my pursuers.

"Huh? Naw . . . a what accent?"

"Never mind. Did he leave a number?"

Glenn shrugged. "No—he sounded like you knew him."

You get these calls at a paper, people certain you remember them when you might have chatted with them over a beer at the bar at Elaine's or Giambone's a month ago. The only Pauls I knew were Paul O'Neill of the Yankees, Paul Newman, or Pope Paul, and I didn't exactly *know* them.

There was one last loose end for me. Kit Cunningham wanted to meet me at the Greek's in case we needed anything more from her on the story. I wasn't looking forward to talking with her again.

I beat it across Forty-second Street to the Greek's and found Kit at a table. Right away, she looked at me anxiously.

"Did you hear any more about Erik, Mr. Fitzgerald?"

"Fitz," I said. "No. They've put the lid on for now."

She looked lost. "It's just so unbelievable. We all went to Mackinack High together. He was always so crazy about Ellie. I had a crush on him, too." She blushed a little and looked up in wonder at the recollection. "But, he was Ellie's. . . . Did he admit it?"

"I really don't have a lot of details, Kit. What we've got will be in Dubbs's story."

"Oh, if I could get my hands on him!" she simmered. "He always was so intense, so . . . oh, the dirty, rotten, son of a bitch!"

She looked away, and her eyelids trembled. She couldn't go on. She was wilting, trying to accept the unacceptable.

I explained the all-too-familiar pattern of the stalking, controlling male unable to let go, and that the killer in too many murder cases is not a stranger but somebody the victim knows well. In fact, too well.

"How sad," she said wearily, emotion draining out of her. She stared out over the street, and her eyes fluttered, teary. She blinked and rubbed the tears away.

"Oh, Fitz. She's really gone, isn't she?"

I don't think the enormity of her twin's murder had hit her until that moment. She had been on the run, being interviewed, forced to concentrate, swept up and preoccupied by constant movement, trying to accept the unacceptable, on automatic pilot. And now to discover that her sister's killer was Erik, a childhood friend, an old flame. She was still in the navy blue traveling suit she had worn when she arrived. Probably hadn't brought much else along. Sitting there at the table in the Greek's, it finally caught up with her. She sat there, straight-backed; her shoulders shook, and she wept.

"Ellie," she murmured. "Oh, my God! Ellie . . . oh One!"

I looked away and waited. What else could I do?

"How could a thing like this happen?" she cried. "One was only twenty-eight! My sister; more than my sister . . . me! Oh, Fitz!"

"What did you call her?"

"What?"

"You said . . . One."

She looked down at the table. "She was born first, by about two minutes. When we were kids, we used to call each other One and Two. I remember the last thing she said to me was, 'You've got to come for the wedding, Two.' "

Kit dabbed her eyes again. "I have to go home."

"Home?"

She nodded. "Grand Rapids. To . . . it's going to be on Monday."

So that was it. The impossible duty of going home to Michigan to bury her twin had triggered the reality of it for her.

"Sure."

"I talked to the medical examiner's office and Mom and Dad, and the bod . . . Ellie is on the way home now. I guess it's all over anyway. I'm flying out tomorrow morning."

"Shall I give you a lift to the airport?"

"Oh, you don't have to do that," she said softly.

"It's okay. I'm off the next couple of days."

"Oh," she smiled gratefully. "Well, that's very nice of you."

It wasn't mere altruism; I wanted to see her on that plane.

I picked her up at the Edison Hotel Saturday morning and drove her to Kennedy Airport. She sat beside me in the cramped Toyota the way she had in the cab, her bag on her knees, staring straight ahead. We went across town, through the Midtown Tunnel, and out along the Long Island Expressway.

"Thanks," she said at one point. "You've been a lifesaver."

At the American Airlines terminal she got out by herself,

gave me a quick look, nodded and smiled, and went quickly through the doors.

A ton of weight lifted off me as I drove back into Manhattan. As much as I empathized with Kit, it was an immense relief to be rid of her. At last I could get at the tall ships, get Ironhead off my back, and return to something more like my ordinary life. I was sure I'd never see her again.

I felt the tension leaving my shoulders, and realized I had been a coiled spring for days, muscles bunched into a collar of knots at the back of my neck. My brain also seemed to unclog, no doubt striving toward a condition of being worry-free. The last of the thirty-seven colliding troubles in my head began dissipating.

"Tranquility, I am sure, is nothing but a good ordering of the mind," observes Marcus Aurelius.

My mind was getting reordered. Almost lighthearted, I—and the Toyota—sailed back through the Midtown Tunnel into Manhattan.

THAT NIGHT IT SEEMED LIKE OLD TIMES AGAIN AS I stopped by Elaine's to yak it up with Kevin Duffy. Now that it was all over, I felt free to have a pleasant Harp and chew over some of the loose ends. I told him Kit had gone back to Michigan, and that Erik was probably downtown at central booking at police headquarters. And Duffy filled me in some, too.

"They pulled me into the station for a lineup," he said.

"Yeah?"

After Erik had turned himself in, Detective Jacobs brought Duffy in in his squad car, and there he was, looking through the two-way mirror at a lineup of cops and Erik Coleman, a tall, blond, ruffled young Viking with an attitude.

"I identified him," he said. "I guess that makes us both witnesses. That super from Riverside Drive, he identified him, too. Said he'd been in and out of Ellie's apartment."

"What did he have to say?" I asked.

But Duffy hadn't been able to find out anything much.

"Those dicks had him under wraps. He didn't look too good, though."

Detective Hanley had dropped a few tidbits, he said. He and Jacobs had gone to Erik's place, a garden apartment in New Jersey, after Kit gave them his address.

"They didn't find him, but they found a bloody shirt in a trash can," Duffy said.

"With Bobo's blood on it?"

"Got to be," Duffy said.

"That'll be enough for them to get a search warrant."

"What'll they do with him?"

"Book him on two counts of murder one and toss him inside The Tombs till the trial, I guess," I told him.

"Well, they got him, anyway," Duffy said, frowning. It was no great victory for him, either. "He must have snapped."

"Yeah," I agreed, sipping my Harp. "Now if I'm only rid of those two Chinese wackos, I'll be all right."

Duffy smiled. "Say what . . . Chinese?"

I laughed. It was beginning to seem like a hallucination to me. The cops had been right; they were a couple of passing muggers. I told Duffy about Dubbs Brewer's stories on the Chinatown gangs and the two Asian screwballs who had ambushed me on Riverside Drive to scare us off.

"At first I wondered if it had anything to do with Ellie's murder, since they were at her place," I said.

"Huh!" Duffy grunted. "That's funny."

"What?"

"There were some Chinese thugs in here one night."

"In here?" I said, surprised. Elaine's isn't the kind of place that attracts a lot of troublemakers unless you count Brit reporters or Australian journalists.

Yes, he said. He had forgotten all about it, but there had been some Chinese in one night. Three of them. One was all right, but the other two were something else. The image of my two pursuers swam up before me. Had they been at Elaine's looking for me? I was flabbergasted.

"Tell me!"

Well, he remembered, they had been thrown out.

"Why? What happened?"

He said it was because they acted like knackers, which is what the Irish call rowdies. "We eighty-sixed them."

That interested me. Chinese strangers in Elaine's causing trouble and being tossed out? Once again I was bothered by the unsettling thought that Ellie's apartment had been staked out. Could the men in Elaine's have been the culprits?

"What do you mean, Duffy? What did they say? What happened?" I was getting nervous about it. "Did they mention me, by any chance?"

Duffy gave me a startled look. "You? Why would they mention you?"

"I don't know. Tell me!"

Well, Duffy said, they were over in front of Bobo's piano, three of them.

"Were they talking with Bobo?"

"No." Duffy frowned, dredging it up. "They were at his piano, but I don't think they talked to him. He was playing."

Duffy paused to light a Marlboro, and stared into the past, back to that night.

"I don't think they were together," he said uncertainly. "The two toughs were, and they were meeting the other one, it seemed to me. I didn't pay much attention until they started shoving each other."

"What was it about?"

"I don't know! They were speaking Chinese, and then something set one of them off. Damned if I know."

"So what happened?"

Duffy frowned and looked away. "Some kind of dustup," he said. "They knocked some drinks and everything off the piano into Bobo's lap, all over him and onto the floor. He had to stop playing till the mess was cleaned up."

"What were they saying?"

His hands went up helplessly. "I don't speak Chinese."

"Did you hear them say anything like 'wagging tongue'?"

"What?" That didn't register.

"Never mind."

Anyway, there had been a confused squabble, a shoving and shouting match, Duffy remembered. "The two knackers were at the other one."

Bobo, he said, tried to pass it off, laughing and saying, "Hey, take it easy, I don't play that bad!"

About then, Duffy and some waiters closed in on them and doused the fire before it could go any further. The three were politely but firmly asked to leave, and ushered out onto the sidewalk on Second Avenue.

"The one, he didn't want to go with them," Duffy said.

But all three were ejected.

"I saw them outside, still at it," he said. "Screaming at each other. Then two of them walked the other one away."

"Walked him away?" I asked. "How?"

"One on each side."

Something jogged my head.

"Was one of them tall?"

Duffy stared at me, surprised. "Yeah. How'd you know that?"

"The other one short?"

He nodded.

"When did all this happen?" I pressed him.

"Well, it was before Bobo was . . . It must have been Thursday or, no . . . Friday night. Yeah, the night before Bobo . . . before it happened."

I sat back and sipped the Harp. Friday night. Bobo got it on Saturday night. One tall, one short. Mutt and Jeff.

I remembered one of Ironhead's dicta: "Willie Sutton doesn't go to a bank to make a deposit." He meant that he didn't believe in coincidence, and Willie the bank robber outside a bank was no coincidence. Those two Chinese men at Elaine's and at Ellie's were Willie Sutton outside the bank. I didn't believe in coincidence, either.

My beer suddenly tasted flat.

THIRTEEN

ON APRIL 17, 1524, THE FLORENTINE NAVIGATOR GIOVANNI da Verrazano guided his ship, *La Dauphine,* through the narrows between what is now Staten Island and Brooklyn into New York Harbor. Today the narrows are arched by the spectacular Verrazano Bridge. The navigator reported finding "the country very well peopled," the natives paddling canoes out to meet this strange, exotic winged craft. "They came toward us very cheerfully, making great shouts of admiration."

Giovanni's one-vessel sail-through to Manhattan didn't last long, I discovered from my tardy research. He had a look around and then sailed on that same day, leaving it to Henry Hudson to find the big river beyond. Actually, Giovanni may have planned a return trip, but, alas, he stopped off in the Caribbean where he was killed and eaten.

Such were some of the historic details I finally got around to reading up on during my days off. On Monday, I was back at it again as I raced around New York surveying the gallant armada: the *Sir Francis Drake* on South Street in Lower Manhattan, the *Amerigo Vespucci* at Pier 92 on West Fifty-fifth Street, and out in Brooklyn the *Fryderyk Chopin* at Pier 5, the Ukrainian *Tovarisch* at Pier 7, and the sleek, black Bulgarian *Kaliakra* at Pier 8.

All of them were breathtaking. In the Bible, the writer of Proverbs, chapter 30, verses 8 and 19, exclaimed, "There are three things beyond my comprehension . . . the way of an eagle in the air; the way of a serpent upon a rock; the way of a ship in the midst of the sea. . . ."

Making the rounds of the great flotilla, I could only agree that he got that right.

My problem was choosing one of these glorious vessels to ride on the sail-through up the Hudson to the George Washington Bridge next Sunday. The Parade of Ships, thirty-five strong, would sail past the Statue of Liberty, past a VIP reviewing stand on Governor's Island, and then negotiate its way through thirty or forty thousand small craft in the harbor while two or three million New Yorkers along the shores and the Battery cheered.

I began to understand Ironhead and Pippy McFadden's fascination. It actually was a pretty good story, and I was fortunate to be covering it. An embarrassment of riches, though. HMS *Bounty* sank because it was way the hell out in Brooklyn. The *Pandora*? A Brit ship. No, the proper choice, I decided, was one of Christopher Columbus's three ships. The *Nina*, the *Pinta*, or the *Santa Maria* would fly the flag of the New York *Daily Press*.

Rather pleased with myself, I wrote a long takeout on the armada, and when Ironhead gobbled it up, he glanced toward me with a surprised expression. Then he was across the city room to me.

"All right, Fitz," he enthused. "This is more like it! So which one flies our banner on its mast?"

"Well, that was just a little hyperbole," I said modestly.

"Haven't you talked to Pippy?" he asked then.

"Not yet."

"Listen, when you do that lunch with him at the yacht club on Wednesday, he's going to give you a flag to run up."

"Really?"

"Hell yes! Two flags. The New York Yacht Club and one he's made up that says *Daily Press*."

That was Pippy the Commodore for you.

"You ride the *Santa Maria*," Ironhead decided. "That was Columbus's flagship."

"Well, Ironhead, you know the *Nina* was the best sailer

of the three. She was a caravel. The *Santa Maria* was a nao, a broad-bottomed ship that wallowed around. Actually she didn't make it back to Europe. She ran aground off Hispaniola and stayed there."

Ironhead studied me, wondering at my nautical expertise. He beamed. I was out of his doghouse. I was beginning to get my sea legs on the story, sailing before a freshening wind without a cloud in the sky.

There was another story in the paper from Dubbs on Bobo's autopsy, which he had wheedled out of some source at the medical examiner's office. It was pretty grim. Bobo hadn't just been stabbed, but sliced all over like a fileted fish; and not by a switchblade, either, but by a long, slim, sharp dagger—a stiletto. No wonder Duffy the bartender thought Bobo had been hit by a sanitation truck. Dubbs had also gotten the source to tell him that the blood on Erik Coleman's shirt matched Bobo's blood type. I was still reading the article when I was hailed once more by Glenn the Switchboard.

I walked over, and he told me Paul had called again.

"Did you get a number?"

"He told me you had it."

"What?"

"Yeah. Isn't he a friend of yours?"

How the hell did I know?

"Hey," he said then, glancing at his board of blinking lights, "maybe that's him now. Your phone is ringing."

I went back to my desk, curious to find out who this close friend was whom I didn't even remember.

"Is this Paul?"

"Uhhhh?" came a voice. I thought at first it was one of the European ship captains.

"Fitzgerra?"

"Hello?"

"We must talk."

"What? Who is this?"

"You meet us. We talk."

"Pardon me?"

"You got it? We pay you."

"Who is this? Pay me for what?"

He was quiet for a few seconds. I could hear subdued voices in the background. Then he spoke again.

"Many dollars. Thousand dollars. You have the Phoenix? You meet us."

"Meet you? What do you mean? Meet you where?"

"Rest stop on Palisades Parkway. New Jersey. Ten clock tonight. The first one north George Washington Bridge. Call it Rockefeller Lookout."

I was trying to figure out the accent, and it sounded vaguely Asian. Chinese! I also tried to visualize the Palisades Parkway. I had driven north on it in the past a few times, and remembered that rest stops along it were pretty isolated. They weren't truck stops with restaurants and gas stations; they were just unattended scenic lookouts for viewing the Hudson River and New York beyond.

Meet a strange Chinese man at ten o'clock at night at an isolated rest stop? My head was trying to function. I didn't want to lose this caller, and tried to stall.

"For what?"

"You know."

And, of course, I did know. It was one of those two weirdos who had tried to walk me away between them, the same two who had been at Elaine's. What had he said? A Phoenix?

"Who are you?"

"You come, Fitzgerra. We know you. You got it. Many dollars. Or we find you again."

"Wait a minute!"

But the line was dead.

I pressed Star 69 to get a ring-back to the phone number and to whoever it was, but got the maddening announcement, "We're sorry. The call did not originate in the 212 area code."

Wonderful! Had the call come from New Jersey? Or from

the 718 area code, which covered Brooklyn and Queens? Or from some other area code?

Visions of Invisible Fist and Fu Manchu!

I couldn't make out what the maniac had said. A Phoenix? "You got it." It was beginning to get me crazy. What the hell was he talking about?

I phoned the Twenty-sixth Precinct. Detective Sgt. Thomas answered.

"Hey, Sarge," I said, "a street cop, Clancy, put in a slip about two Chinese muggers jumping me the other day near Ellie Cunningham's apartment. I don't know if you saw it, but I think one of them just called me."

"About what?"

"Damned if I know. A phoenix, he said. He seemed to think I've got it, whatever it is. Does that make any sense to you? I mean, somebody was looking for something at Ellie's and at Bobo's too."

"Hmmmm," the sarge pondered. "Well, we've consolidated both cases with Hanley and Jacobs at the one-nine."

I didn't much want to bother them again. They might not be too pleased that Dubbs had gotten that stuff from the medical examiner's report.

"Listen, Clancy mentioned a Chinese Squad," I told Thomas. "You know who runs that?"

"You mean Charlie Chan?"

"Who?"

"That's what everybody calls him. Jimmy Chen in the Fifth downtown. Yeah, maybe he can help."

The great armada vanished in the mists, and I was out of the city room, down to my Toyota, and down the East River Drive toward Chinatown. Charlie Chan? Typical of New Yorkers and cops, all right. I got off at the Brooklyn Bridge exit and parked in the NYP zone behind police headquarters off Foley Square. I had worked state supreme court there in the past, and generally knew the area, which includes Little Italy and Chinatown jammed together, straddling and sprawling above and below Canal Street.

The Fifth Precinct, I vaguely recalled, was on Elizabeth Street, up above Chatham Square, the heart of Chinatown. I hurried up Park Row past Chinese restaurants, Jimmy Wu's, and bake shops where they sell those delicious almond cookies. The streets are narrow, twisting, packed with Chinese. A lady fortune-teller sat on a stool mumbling over a paper, intently listened to by four Chinese women bending down to hear their futures.

I walked up to Canal Street and then across it and found Elizabeth Street. Upstairs in the squad room of the Fifth Precinct, I asked for Jimmy Chen.

A diminutive, smiling detective looked up and waved me to his desk.

"Detective Chen?"

"You got me."

He was neat and compact in a tan suit and with an offhand, casual manner that was both welcoming and unreadable.

"You head the Chinese Squad?" I asked.

Jimmy Chen smiled and leaned back. "I guess so. What can I do for you?"

"Ed Fitzgerald, *Daily Press*. I don't know what you can do for me, but something's going on that I don't understand. I seem to be in some kind of a mess."

"Aren't we all?" he tossed off. "So what kind of soy sauce is it?"

I gave him a quick rundown of the cloudy circumstances that had brought me to him.

"I thought it might be because of our stories about the street gangs, but they were up on Riverside Drive and at Elaine's."

"Sounds like something for uptown," he suggested.

"But they were Chinese."

"How do you know? Maybe they're Americans. Even New Yorkers."

"I saw them."

"You could tell that by looking at them?" he remarked rather slyly.

"The way they spoke."

"Ah! How was that?"

"Chinese!"

"Oh! You speak Chinese, do you?"

"No. They spoke English, but with an accent."

"Well, now, that's something else. People in New York with accents. Now, that does sound suspicious."

More obstruction! He was twisting me like a noodle.

"Look, Detective Chen . . ."

"Call me Charlie. Everybody does. Especially round eyes."

"What?"

"You say they spoke with accents? What kind?"

"Well . . . Chinese, of course."

"Yes, yes, of course. Fitzgerald, there is no such thing. There is the Mandarin dialect, which is the Pekinese dialect, the more or less official dialect. There is the Han dialect, and the Cantonese, Shanghaiese, and lots of others, but there is no Chinese accent. Could you identify them?"

Definitely a sideways jab at a bumbling Caucasian.

"They called me something weird—wagging tongue, or wagon man, or something."

"I see. Now we're getting somewhere. I don't suppose anybody else has ever called you something weird?"

"Well . . ."

"You should hear what some people call me."

"It was just strange for them to be up there at Elaine's and at Ellie's apartment."

Jimmy Chen grinned. "Chinese are allowed to go all over New York, you know. Even uptown. Irishmen, too."

"No, but . . . the cops up there don't get it."

Jimmy Chen nodded and doodled on a pad. "So they come into Elaine's and stop you on the street and call you up wanting something, but you don't know what it is?"

"A Phoenix or something."

"A what?" Now Jimmy Chen seemed to take notice.

"I don't know. That's what it sounded like."

"A Phoenix?" He gazed at me a moment. "Are you sure?"

Well, of course, I wasn't sure of any damn thing. Only that I needed to have those crazies found.

"You want me to round up all the Chinese above Canal Street?"

"I just don't know what to do," I complained. "I keep wondering if they're mixed up in those two murders somehow."

"I thought Hanley and Jacobs in the one-nine made a collar on that," he told me.

"Well, yes. But, these two are hassling me. Could you go with me to meet them?"

"What NYPD precinct is that?"

I could see that finding Charlie Chan was not going to solve my problem.

"I can't go over to New Jersey, Fitzgerald," he said. "Call the PIP cops."

"Who?"

"Palisades Interstate Parkway police."

"They're traffic cops. They don't know anything about this."

"Neither do I. But I'll keep an eye out for suspicious Chinese."

Was that a sardonic twinkle in his almond eyes? I had come there hoping Charlie Chan could explain away those two characters, but all I had gotten was that they could have been anybody.

I left.

I considered meeting Ching and Chang at Rockefeller Lookout, but thought better of going alone—at first. After a few minutes, though, curiosity was too much for my reporter's nose, and that night I drove uptown on the West Side Highway, crossed the George Washington Bridge to New Jersey, and headed up the PIP.

I got to the turnoff for the Rockefeller Lookout rest stop and slowed, still rolling, and searched the rocky cliff overlooking the Hudson River. I couldn't see much from the parkway, though. Trees and a parked car or van. Then some figures standing and moving around in the gloom, one of them taller than the other.

That was enough for me. I was dying to stop and talk to them, but not before I had some idea of who they were and what the hell they wanted.

FOURTEEN

I SAILED INTO THE EAST CHINA SEA THAT NIGHT AND UP the Yangtze River from Shanghai. Fu Manchu was the skipper, and Ching and Chang guarded me in the filthy hold crawling with cockroaches. Pursuing us was the tall ship *Christian Radich*, rigged as a police launch, Wolf Larson's cannon mounted on the foredeck and manned by Ironhead Matthews firing through the fog and howling over the water with each thundering blast, "Fitz, Fitz, Fitz!"

When I came jerking out of it, unkidnapped and safe from the river pirates, back in my apartment, it penetrated my distracted mind that I was supposed to be concentrating on America Sail.

I got up, embracing the tall ships story with a new urgency. Those shadows at the Rockefeller Lookout turned me into a dedicated fan of sailing ships. The Chinese mystery men had actually been there! Shadowy but nonetheless real. They were really after me.

There I was, a harmless ship reporter pursued by crazies I couldn't identify. It was not even my soy sauce. It was Ellie's and Bobo's and Kit's and the detectives'—maybe Erik Coleman's or even Dubbs Brewer's—but they all had the perspicacity to be either dead, in Grand Rapids, in police custody, or blockheaded. All I did was stop in for the last call at Elaine's, and now I was a hunted man hiding a priceless treasure and I didn't even know what the hell it was.

Walking back down through Chinatown along Mott Street

after my skewed meeting with Detective Jimmy Chen the afternoon before, I had spotted Ching and Chang everywhere—at every bean curd and shellfish store, bending insidiously over every bean sprout and water chestnut stand, looking out through the windows of Jimmy Wu's. But whether I met them in the gloom of a rest stop or in broad daylight, I wouldn't recognize them until they had both my arms and were walking me away toward who knew what.

I drove down to the *Daily Press*, adopting the mentality of a camel. I was determined to put it out of my mind. Those maniacs wouldn't venture into the city room, and as long as they didn't know where I lived, they wouldn't be able to find me. I would steer clear of the Riverside Drive apartment and Elaine's and Chinatown and the United Nations, too. Kit was back in Michigan and out of my hair, and I was out of the entire mess. With my head buried in the sand, I couldn't see them, so surely I was invisible to them, too.

Ironhead should be pleased to learn that I was finally, irrevocably, back on the tall ships story.

My plan to ignore my troubles worked wonderfully for most of the rest of that day. I chased the tall ships, scouted out the *Nina* at the *Intrepid* Sea-Air-Space Museum over at West Forty-sixth Street and the Hudson river, and arranged to sign on as a seaman before the mast for the gala on Sunday.

"Hey, great," the captain of the *Nina* said. "I was afraid we were going to be ignored completely."

"No other reporters have signed on?" I asked, surprised.

"We're a little old-fashioned for them," he smiled. "The really big ones came along a couple of hundred years later."

It was terrific. I'd have the *Nina*, Christopher Columbus's best sailer, all to myself.

But at the end of that day, the soy sauce bubbled over out of my telephone into the city room.

"Fitzgerald?"

"Yeah?" I squinched my ear into the phone, trying to pick up an accent.

"Charlie Chan."

"Who? Oh . . . Detective Chen?"

"What did you say those wackos called you? Wagging tongue?"

"That's what it sounded like."

"Could it have been *waiguoren*?"

The word resonated through my head. "Yeah! That's it! What is it? What does that mean?"

"Barbarian."

I was bemused at that. "They called me a barbarian?"

Jimmy Chen laughed softly. "It's what mainland Chinese call you round eyes."

"Mainland Chinese?"

"Can you come down here? We have to talk."

"Yeah, sure! Did something happen?"

"You said they were looking for a Phoenix?"

"That's what the guy said."

"Interesting. Come down here."

Interesting! I had thought Charlie Chan had brushed me off, but apparently he had been chewing things over. Finally, somebody was listening to me. I ran out to the Toyota, drove down to Chinatown, and hurried up to the Elizabeth Street station. Detective Chen waved me to his desk as before, and sat there staring at me.

"What's up?"

"Your opposition might have given us a lead here."

"The *Post?*"

"Yeah." He tossed a newspaper in front of me. "The *China Post.*"

It was a Chinese-language newspaper. Although by now I knew it was probably written in Mandarin or Han or something.

"There's a story in here about this?" I asked, confounded.

"Maybe." He picked up the *China Post* and glanced at it. "I've been working a case about a body found in the East River. No identification. The man is Chinese, so I asked our local paper, the *China Post*, to run a story for me asking for help to find out who he is."

"You think it's one of those characters who are after me?"

"Not if they called you yesterday. This body's been in the water for a while. I got a phone call about it, looking for a missing person. I took her to the Bellevue morgue medical examiner's office, and she identified the body. Lee Ying."

He watched me to see if that registered. It didn't, so he continued.

"She wanted to know if a Phoenix-head medal had been found with him."

"A Phoenix medal?" That interested me very much.

"She wanted to know if a Phoenix had been found on the body. Or inside it."

"Inside it?"

"Maybe something he swallowed."

"What?"

"I've been thinking about those Chinese thugs being up there at Elaine's," he said. He got up and paced around, pondering. "That piano player was found up there, too, near the East River."

"Yes."

"Hmmm," he said, and stopped pacing. "Interesting. I had at first assumed Lee Ying was murdered and went into the water down here around Chinatown. Now I suspect he went into the water uptown and floated down here after a while."

"You think he was killed up near where Bobo was murdered?" I asked. "You think they're connected?"

He sat at his desk again. "You see, Lee Ying was all sliced up. I saw that story in your paper about Watson's autopsy report. I checked out that report. He was all sliced up, too, in the same manner."

"The same people got them both?"

"I have to say yes. Lee Ying died of what is known as a thousand cuts, and so did Watson. It's a singular, most effective ancient Chinese method, once used in the Forbidden City by the emperor, or the empress dowager."

"Who is this somebody who identified him?"

"Anna Cheong of Taylor Lee Trading and Import on Canal Street. She told me Lee Ying had obtained the Dowager Phoenix medal from China and was supposed to deliver it to her company. She's understandably upset."

"What do you make of it?"

Detective Chen lit a dark, twisted cigarette. "Anna was waiting for Lee Ying to deliver a Dowager Phoenix to her. Lee Ying didn't arrive and neither did the Phoenix. He was intercepted and murdered, and now she's looking for the medal. You say there were three Chinese up there? Two walked the other one away against his will?"

"That's the way it looked to Duffy, the bartender at Elaine's."

"I believe that man in the middle was Lee Ying. Those other two met him there to steal the medal. There must have been a problem because he was tortured with those thousand cuts."

"And Bobo too?"

He nodded.

My head was spinning. He cocked his head and asked, "Have you eaten?"

I was a bit confused by the non sequitur. "No."

"How would the *Daily Press* like to spring for a meal? This is not a request. I cannot accept gratuities. But if you insist."

"Sure. You know a Chinese restaurant around here?"

He smiled at that. "Something else."

"Italian?"

"Done."

We walked out of the Fifth Precinct, and I led him down toward Foley Square. I knew just the place, Giambone's on Mulberry Street, across from the Chinatown playground behind the Criminal Court Building, where I used to hang out when I covered state supreme court.

Inside at the front table, as usual, I spotted Harry Reeves of the *Post*, my old colleague and opponent on the courthouse beat, sitting over an after-work silver bullet with lawyers and judges.

His florid face lit up. "Fitzboggen!"

He called me that because, he explained in his leprechaunish way, all Irishers came out of a peat bog.

"Harry, you old fart!"

"So, Fitzboggen, I hear you've turned into Moby Dick."

My fame was continuing to spread. I led Jimmy Chen to a back table, where a round of drinks soon appeared from Harry Reeves.

We ordered—I always got the lasagna, and Jimmy took calamari and risotto—and sipped our drinks.

Pretty soon, I realized why he had allowed the *Daily Press* to invite us to dinner. The matter of the Phoenix medal required some background, and I was an ignorant *waiguoren*. Different developments had jogged Detective Jimmy Chen's mind, he told me, and my visit was the latest of them.

First of all, I had to understand who Lee Ying was. He was a con man, a Chinese art dealer and smuggler who illegally brought in artworks and artifacts from China to peddle in New York.

"He's known to the department," he said, "but we haven't been able to nail him."

Lee Ying, he now believed, had smuggled a Phoenix-head medal out of China and brought it to New York to deliver to Anna Cheong. Somebody else must have known that, and gone after him.

"The way he and Watson died, an ancient Chinese way, and the fact that Madame Cheong was looking for him, identified the body, and thought he might have a medal on him, all came together, you see."

I didn't exactly see yet, but it linked the Chinese and Bobo.

A Phoenix-head medal, he explained, actually known as a

Dowager Phoenix, is a gold coin that was minted in the Forbidden City in Beijing upon the ascension of the empress dowager Tz'u-hsi, the last true ruler of China, to the supreme office of grand empress dowager.

"Rare and valuable?" I surmised.

"Extremely. There were only nine struck. Nine is the emperor's magic number, the largest single digit. And Tz'u-hsi was only the grand empress dowager for one day."

"What happened?"

The empress dowager, he explained, ruled China as regent over the emperor Kuang-Hsu, whom she took prisoner and starved until he died on November 14, 1908. With his death she became grand empress dowager, but died the next day. So her one-day reign as grand empress made the nine Phoenix medals stamped with the date of her ascension and death rare, unique treasures, priceless to Chinese experts.

"There are those who say she poisoned the emperor because she knew she was dying and didn't want him restored to the Dragon Throne. Anyway, she had her day, and the Dowager Phoenix medals were ready to be struck."

After the death of Tz'u-hsi, the last emperor, Pu Yi, ascended the Dragon Throne as a child of three, but was deposed during the revolution of 1912. Pu Yi stayed on as a sort of paper dragon under rule by *wai low*, foreign devils, until 1924, when the royal Ching Court vanished into history with the birth of the Chinese republic, itself not to have a long life.

"And so, you see, the empress dowager Tz'u-hsi, also known as the Venerable Buddha, is considered the last true ruler. And the Dowager Phoenixes, with her face on one side and the Phoenix, her symbol, on the other, are historic treasures, especially to those who revere the memory of the emperor and Tz'u-hsi."

As far as he knew, the remaining medals, or some of them, were in the Palace of Cloudless Heaven in the Forbidden City, or some might have gotten to a coin dealer in Hong

Kong. They could never have been gotten out of China legally.

"To certain Chinese, it may be enough to kill for," he concluded.

I blanched a little, nibbling at my lasagna.

Jimmy Chen had another piece of information. Two Han Chinese had jumped ship from the freighter *Neptune Jade* out of Shanghai at Port Elizabeth, New Jersey, and had presumably disappeared into New York. One was a former boxer, and the other was known as Quishi.

"Mutt and Jeff?" I asked, stunned.

"Could be."

"You think Bobo and Lee Ying's killers were Quishi and Invisible Fist, the two Han Chinese off the *Neptune Jade?*"

"Could be."

The quiet calm of NYPD detectives can be unnerving.

"I don't get it," I admitted. "If those two killed Lee Ying and stole the medal, why are they calling me about it? And why would they kill Bobo?"

Jimmy tilted his head. "I can't answer that, unless Watson saw something he shouldn't have. I only know that they got them both." He paused a moment. "And Eleanor Cunningham, too."

"What!"

He nodded slowly. "Lee Ying and Watson were both tortured and then finished off with a thrust of a stiletto up under the ribs and twisted. I checked out Ms. Cunningham's autopsy, too. They didn't use a thousand cuts on her, but they finished her off the same way."

I could only thank the Fates that I had not stopped at Rockefeller Lookout.

"Son of a bitch," I muttered. "But they seem to think I've got the Phoenix. Are there more than one floating around? Are these different Chinese? What the hell am I supposed to do?"

"Watch your step," he smiled. "And for now I don't want any story linking these murders, or any mention of the thousand cuts."

"Jesus, Jimmy, I'm a reporter!" I protested.

"You're also a witness."

"I can't sit on this!"

"You can say I'm working the Lee Ying case."

"And the Dowager Phoenix?"

"No! A Chinese artifact. I don't want the Phoenix mentioned. It could cause a stir in Chinatown among certain people, and I don't want anyone bothering Anna Cheong."

I sighed. Snookered again. I was getting deeper and deeper into a story that wasn't mine.

"Okay," I had to agree. "I'll tell Dubbs Brewer to call you, and you can fill him in."

Then another thought struck me. "What about Erik Coleman? If you're saying Chinese killers got Bobo and Ellie . . . ?"

He looked away uncomfortably. "Not my collar, Fitz."

"Well, but, this doesn't look like the work of an orchestra manager. Are you going to tell Hanley and Jacobs about this?"

He shifted in his chair. I recognized his body language. He didn't want to interfere in another detective team's collar.

"That's up to them and the D.A.'s office," he finally said. "I can't tell them to drop their case. They'll have to straighten it out."

"But, damnit, Jimmy, he's in The Tombs, and you're saying he didn't do it."

"I'm not saying anything about him," he replied. "That's not my case." He gave me a look. "Some soy sauce, Fitzgerald."

SOMETIMES I WONDER ABOUT THE CONCEPT OF MENTAL telepathy—thoughts leaping through the ether and hooking up with someone else's brain waves—because when I got back to the office later, who did I get a call from but Kathleen Cunningham in a troubled state.

"Fitz! It's me!"

"What's the matter?"

"Fitz, I've talked with Erik."

Oh, boy!

"Fitz, they've charged him with murder, and he's in jail up there. His lawyer called me and put him on the phone. Fitz, he's half-crazy. Fitz, I don't think he did it."

Something went thump inside me. After what I had just heard from Charlie Chan, it didn't look like it.

"Yeah," came out of me.

"What? You don't think so either?"

"Damnit, Kit, things have happened since Hanley and Jacobs busted him."

I filled her in on some of the things Chen had said.

"But that means he couldn't have done it!"

I conceded that I didn't see how. Hanley and Jacobs would have to kick him loose now, I thought, although cops don't like to back off after they've made a case, and Jimmy Chen certainly didn't want to tell them they were wrong.

"He wants to talk to you," Kit said.

"Why me?"

"I didn't know what other name to give him. It's got me crazy. Fitz, we practically put him in there!"

Hateful words that I didn't want to hear. Goddamnit, I had only mentioned him to the cops because it had seemed the obvious thing to do. Now all of a sudden it's my fault?

But Charlie Chan's words and my wild ride up the Yangtze had spooked me.

Shit!

"Who's the lawyer?"

FIFTEEN

IT WAS A NICE, DICEY SITUATION, ALL RIGHT. THERE WAS Dubbs's story in the *Daily Press* that Erik Coleman had been charged with the two murders. There was his story from the medical examiner's office that blood on Erik's shirt was the same type as Bobo's. There was the whole damned story, wrapped up, finished, and it wasn't mine to begin with.

So why was I on my way to The Tombs, the Manhattan House of Correction, to talk to Erik Tuesday morning? God knows, I didn't want to do it; what could come of it but shooting down our own story? It would outrage Hanley and Jacobs, who had been practically given the damned perp by me. It would bewilder Ironhead, who thought I was finally following the fleet.

But Kit's plea to please talk to Erik rang in my ears, and Charlie Chan's scary account rode on my consciousness. And I felt a little responsible, too. If Kit and I were right that Erik hadn't done it, where the hell were we? Back being chased by phantoms from Rockefeller Lookout.

I drove downtown, parked behind police headquarters, and walked over to The Tombs, the grim, stone monolith prison on White Street, where the lawyer, Wayne Owens, was waiting for me.

"Listen, I don't really know what I can do here," I told him rather defensively.

"He seems to think you can help him," said Owens, lean and angular in a three-piece suit. "You can tell his side of it."

We went in through a series of steel barred gates, first into the reception area, then through another steel gate, along a corridor and into a large, airy room with wooden benches and tables.

Owens dealt with the correction officer behind a thick glass wall, and after a bit Erik came in from the other end of the room and joined us at a wooden table. He was, as Duffy had said, a tall, blond Viking with a scowling face, and his eyes were clamped on me from the moment he entered. Erik Coleman did not look happy.

"Fitzgerald?" he asked, sliding onto a bench across from me. He stared at me for a long moment, as though committing my face to memory. "You're the one I have to thank for this?" he snapped pugnaciously.

"I wouldn't say that, exactly," I hedged.

"No? Well, then what would you say? You sicced the cops on me!"

"You were Ellie's boyfriend," I said lamely. "Bobo's blood was on your shirt. You turned yourself in." I was looking for some excuses, limp as they were, for having had any part in dumping him in here.

He leaned across the table at me, maddened. "I didn't turn myself in! Who told you that shit? That's a lot of crap!"

I examined his rather handsome, open, Midwestern face, and he appeared to be sincere, all right. Pretty burned up and desperate, but sincere. Which didn't improve my mood any.

"I loved Ellie!" he burst out, flushed and trembling, his eyes blinking, his shoulders shaking. "My God, how could anyone think . . ." He looked away a moment.

"Look," I finally dived in, "there may be a screwup here. Kit and I don't think you did it."

"What!" Pretty much a skyrocket burst of outrage.

"There've been new developments."

Wayne Owens leaned closer, and Erik's eyes were popping out.

"Is that so?" said Owens.

"They're going to drop the case?" Erik asked anxiously.

I let out a breath and lit a Tiparillo. How the hell did I get into this? "It's not up to me," I finally muttered. "Why did you give them a statement?"

"I didn't give anybody a statement!" he complained. "Sure, I told them everything I could! When I heard about Ellie, I was crazy! I went to the police station to find out what happened, and instead of telling me anything, they started questioning me. I didn't know it was a statement! I was just trying to help them; I wanted whoever did it more than they did!"

So that's what Hanley called turning himself in. I could imagine the grilling Erik had gone through.

"One of them, Jacobs, kept knocking my chair, yelling at me," he said. "They said they had witnesses! You and that bartender. He threw my bloody shirt on the table in front of me. There's nothing against me but blood on that shirt!"

I felt pretty sick about the whole thing.

"So can you get me out of here?" he demanded.

"Look, I'm only a reporter," I retreated.

"Aren't you also a witness?" the lawyer asked.

There it was, the hook upon which I wriggled.

"Nothing I said tied you to the murders," I insisted. "They built their case later on."

"What are these new developments?" Owens asked.

"Well," I hesitated, "I'm not writing about them. See, it's not my story."

"You can get me tossed in here, but you won't help me get out?" Erik was furious.

"Look, counselor," I told Owens, "talk to Detective Jimmy Chen, Hanley and Jacobs, and the D.A.'s office. There's nothing I can do!"

"Oh, you only tell lies to lock people up!" exclaimed a steaming Erik Coleman.

"Couldn't you at least tell his side of it?" Owens the lawyer asked, leaning across at me intently. "I'm pushing for a bail hearing. I'm trying to get him out of here."

I walked out of The Tombs in a state of numbed misery, trailed by Wayne Owens. Write his side of it? Wouldn't that be cute. I was supposed to be a witness against him.

"Any help you can give," he said, and strolled away toward Centre Street.

I went slowly back to my Toyota behind police headquarters and felt myself clamped into a double bind. Kit and Owens wanted me to write a jailhouse interview giving Erik's side of it, meaning a sob story in which he could deny everything. I wanted to write a story about Detective Jimmy Chen finding Lee Ying's butchered body in the East River and saying it had floated downstream.

What I really wanted to write was that Lee Ying's murder was connected with Bobo and Ellie's murders and with Quishi and Invisible Fist and that missing Dowager Phoenix medal. But how the hell could I do it when I was being gagged on one side and blamed on the other, and it wasn't even my story?

I sat in the Toyota, lit a Tiparillo, and mulled things over. Detective Jimmy Chen's scenario—Lee Ying at Elaine's with that Phoenix medal meeting those two Chinese men, who later tracked me down at Ellie's and called me by name—connected things for me, at any rate.

I tried to organize it into my own scenario.

Okay, Lee Ying, the art thief smuggler, steals this priceless medal out of China and brings it to New York for Anna Cheong of Canal Street. Invisible Fist and Quishi come after him, slip off the *Neptune Jade*, and find him in New York.

Why they all ended up in Elaine's, I couldn't imagine. But, anyway, they did. So what happened during that shoving match Duffy had described?

"It looked like two of them were at the other one," Duffy had said.

Okay, so Quishi and Invisible Fist were at Lee Ying shoving him around. It had to be about the medal. Why would Lee Ying even meet these guys if he was supposed to deliver it to

Anna? Was he double-crossing her, trying to sell it to them instead? Apparently they weren't there to buy it, but to take it.

Then what happened? Quishi and Invisible Fist dragged Lee Ying off into the night, tortured him, and took the Phoenix, and he ended up dead in the East River. Nice and neat and probable. But why did they come back for Bobo? Why go after Ellie and then me?

"You got it, *waiguoren,*" one of them had told me. "We pay you."

That phrase kept dancing through my head. I had it? But they had to have stolen it from Lee Ying. Was there another one floating around? Then it occurred to me that maybe they had not succeeded in getting the Dowager Phoenix from Lee Ying. Maybe it had gotten lost in the scuffle, and they thought one of us had ended up with it.

It made sense. Whatever had happened, the whole thing was wide open again, and I was being pursued by Lee Ying's and Bobo's butcher killers.

A double bind, all right. Or maybe even a triple one. Here I was into the second week of America Sail, with all the tall ships presumably in port, and I was going to the *Daily Press* to tell Ironhead that a story that wasn't even mine was all screwed up; that Chinese wackos really were chasing me. That didn't calm my nerves any, but I did have Detective Jimmy Chen of the Chinese Squad to back me up.

I drove uptown, practicing my explanation, hopeful that this last detour from the tall ships would be acceptable, and that it would finally solve this mess.

But I should have remembered my mother's wise counsel, delivered when I got ahead of myself:

"Don't calculate your juvenile poultry before the proper process of incubation has fully materialized."

SIXTEEN

IRONHEAD COULD NOT—OR WOULD NOT—UNDERSTAND what I was talking about when I tried to explain why I couldn't seem to get free of the Bobo Watson case.

"What the hell is it all about?" he frowned.

I filled him in on the Chinese looking for the Phoenix head and calling me and about my visit to Detective Chen. "I'm not working the story; the story's working me. Those Chinese seem to think Bobo or Ellie had that damned medal or that I have it."

"Goddamnit, what about the tall ships?"

"I'm signed onto the *Nina*," I ventured. "But the thing is, if those two Chinese sliced up Bobo and Lee Ying and got Ellie, too, then Erik Coleman is the wrong guy."

"What!?" A bubbling, molten snort. "Are you telling me that the guy the cops want to make you a witness against is a bad arrest?"

"That's the way it looks now."

"You practically handed this guy over to them!" he said.

"I just mentioned him. He was a logical suspect, Ironhead. The cops thought so, too."

Ironhead stood up. Shot up, you might say. Blasted off like a NASA rocket heading for orbit around Mars. His face went red, like a cannon emanating fire and smoke. The vein in his forehead stood out and throbbed.

"You found the body! You're a witness against this guy! The *Daily Press* has practically convicted him on your say-so, and now you're trying to tell me you have disgraced this newspaper?"

"Ironhead," I protested, "for crissake, I didn't understand it before, but after talking to Charlie Chan, it looks like this is all about these Chinese who have been chasing me. I've been trying to tell you that."

"Chinese . . . *sailors?*" he wanted to know. "Chinese . . . *ship captains*?"

Finally he sat down again and stared into space.

I sat down too, lit a Tiparillo, and plunged in.

"I might as well tell you I talked to Erik in the Tombs."

"What the hell were you doing down there?"

"Detective Chen called me in. After what he said, I had to wonder about Erik."

"A jailhouse interview?"

"Yeah. I didn't want to open up this can of worms again, but after Jimmy Chen gave me all that stuff, I thought I had to."

He spat something vile.

"What do you want me to do?"

"Well, shit, I guess we'll have to skin back on the story," he muttered. "Give your notes to Toolen. I'll have Dubbs call Jimmy Chen, and we'll put something together. And then call Pippy. He says he can't reach you. He's breaking my balls."

"Okay."

I walked away. The damned Brand X murder story kept growing, and I was still shut out of it. It was the first time I had been involved in a growing story that I wasn't allowed to write.

At my desk, the phone was ringing.

"Ed Fitzgerald?"

"Yeah." I didn't recognize the voice.

"You're a hard man to track down. Paul McFadden here."

Who! *Paul* . . . McFadden! Pippy!

"I've left two messages. I've been expecting your call. Where have you been?"

"Oh, uh, I was just going to call you!"

"You'd better shape up that switchboard operator! I expect to have calls returned!"

"Yeah, sure!"

"Now, just to let you know, we're lunching at the club tomorrow. One-thirty. You can come at one, if you like."

"The New York Yacht Club?"

"I've promised them a good fill-in. How're you doing?"

"Oh, fine. Making the rounds of the ships."

"All right, then. Don't be late."

I went up to Sam Graff, the mustachioed assistant city editor. "Sam, did you know Pippy's real name is Paul?"

He cocked his head at me, eyes over the rims of his glasses. "Where do you think 'Pippy' came from? Paul Patrick. P. P. Pippy."

Actually, going down to the sea in ships again was rather a relief.

SEVENTEEN

I WISH I COULD TELL YOU I WAS ABLE TO STEER CLEAR OF any more entanglements with the Bobo and Ellie murders after that and was able to work at helping Pippy McFadden get his commodore's cap. But I couldn't seem to get loose. Finding Ellie's body had made me a witness, an unwilling one, and those Chinese hound dogs on my trail wouldn't let up. Now Charlie Chan was in the picture, and he was back on my phone that afternoon.

"Fitz," he said, "can you come back down here?"

"What's up?"

"Well, I'm expecting a visitor, and I'd like you to be here."

"I'm not supposed to be on this, Jimmy," I dodged.

"That's too bad. This thing has landed in my lap, part of it anyway, and I need some cooperation."

"It's not my story."

"Listen, Fitzgerald, this isn't a story. It's a homicide investigation. I didn't get you into this soy sauce; you did."

He hung up.

So I went down the FDR Drive again. I parked in the NYP zone behind police headquarters and walked up through Chinatown to the Fifth Precinct. When I went in, Jimmy was sitting behind his desk in a brown-striped seersucker suit, and across from him was Kathleen Cunningham.

"Kit!" I blurted out.

"Hi Fitz." She looked a lot more together than on her first visit, alert in a green suit. I realized she must have returned right after Ellie's funeral.

"How'd it go back home?"

She looked down into her lap a moment. "How could it go? It was terrible. I couldn't stand sitting home waiting, not knowing; and if Erik's not the one, everything's up in the air again. I couldn't get much information calling from Grand Rapids. I flew in this morning. I'm back at the Edison.

"I saw your story about Watson and the Chinese art smuggler and called Detective Chen," Kit said.

"It's not my story."

"Well, it's in your paper. Detective Chen was just telling me that the murders might be connected with some Chinese people."

We sat at his desk across from him, and he finished telling Kit what he had told me, about Lee Ying at Elaine's, his body floating down the river, and the Dowager Phoenix.

"Is that what it's all about?"

"We shall see, Miss Cunningham."

"Who's the visitor?" I asked him.

"A new suspect?" Kit wanted to know.

"Anna Cheong of Taylor Lee Trading and Import of Canal Street. She was expecting delivery of the Dowager Phoenix that was stolen, so she has a keen interest in this."

Detective Chen's dark, almond-shaped eyes glinted with anticipation. There he sat on a hot day with his jacket on. Usually, cops are in shirtsleeves in the squad room, their Glock pistols in shoulder holsters or hanging on a hook behind them. This visitor had to be a somebody.

"Did this Anna Cheong know she was buying stolen goods?" I asked Detective Chen, and then answered my own question. "She must have."

Chen gave me a look but didn't answer. Then his phone rang, and he picked it up. "Okay," he said. "Send her up."

He stood up, buttoned his jacket, and walked to the squad room door. He opened it and waited, and then greeted Madame Cheong.

"Nice of you to come by," he said, and added something in Chinese that sounded polite and formal.

Into the squad room stepped Anna Cheong, a slim, aristocratic, magnificent pillar of uncertain age, forty or fifty, in a brilliant yellow silk suit, a beehive of ebony, lacquered hair tightly swept back around her head, dark eyes peering out commandingly. Pearls on her ears and a gold pin—a bird of some kind—on her left shoulder. Madame Cheong was a piece of work.

She smiled and answered Detective Chen in Chinese, also sounding very polite and formal. After a few moments of greeting, Detective Chen waved his hand at Kit.

"I would like you to meet Miss Cunningham," he said.

Madame Cheong tilted her aristocratic beehive and glanced, and then stiffened, her face chalky, her eyes burning, and she flung out an excited burst of Chinese.

"Yes, the resemblance is striking," Chen said gently. "But this is her twin sister, Kathleen."

Madame Cheong quickly recovered her dignity and spoke softly. "Miss Cunningham, my apology. Having a slight interest in this matter, I had seen a photo of your precious sister in the newspaper. You have my deepest sympathy."

"Thanks," Kit managed to say, clearly overwhelmed by the impressive presence.

"Well," said Detective Chen, "I asked you to come by because Miss Cunningham and Mr. Fitzgerald here are interested in the unfortunate death of Lee Ying, as well as in the lost medal. You have each suffered loss, some deeper than others. Perhaps we have a nexus here?"

Madame Cheong stared intently at me, and then at Kit.

"Lee Ying's path and Miss Eleanor Cunningham's path may have crossed," said Chen. "It may have been unfortunate for both of them."

"I have only a slight interest in Lee Ying, because of a trifle that may have been misplaced," Anna demurred.

"Ah, yes, the Dowager Phoenix."

Madame Cheong reacted, but only slightly.

"Yes. A trifling artifact was to be delivered to my firm by Lee Ying, and it has somehow gone astray. Perhaps one of you may know of it?" She searched my face and then Kit's. The eyes of a dragon.

"No," I assured her. "I don't know a thing about it! But somebody thinks I do."

"You see, Madame Cheong," Detective Chen said, "Lee Ying was at a restaurant, Elaine's, and perhaps had the medal with him. Later when the department came in contact with him, you inquired about it. He did not have it. We are unable to determine what happened to it."

"The interest of my insignificant firm merely concerns a trinket mislaid," Madame Cheong observed. "Miss Cunningham, your precious sister was there, I understand."

"My sister?" Kit's head seemed to be spinning by now, trying to put things together. "Yes, Ellie was there. Bobo Watson was there. Lee Ying was there, and now they're all dead! Do you have any idea what happened?"

The question brought a flush to Madame's high cheeks.

"I don't understand," she flared. "Why do you ask me this?"

"Well," she went on, "you seem to know this Mr. Ying, and it looks like he was mixed up with Ellie's murder!"

"Mr. Lee," Madame Cheong corrected her, her face a mask.

"Come, come," Detective Chen interrupted. "I do not say who was mixed up with what. We are seeking information here. Perhaps an exchange of information might assist us."

"You say he was bringing this dowager medal to you?" I said.

Madame smiled. "The Phoenix was to be delivered to my firm. If Lee Ying had it at that café, I only wondered what had happened to it."

"You mean, you think Ellie got it?" Kit asked.

"Please, precious daughter. I do not know. I only wonder.

Mr. Fitzgerald, you were there, too, I understand."

"I've been at Elaine's, yes."

"It is of minor importance," Madame Cheong said lightly. "Don't concern yourself. It will turn up."

"Listen, Mrs. Cheong," I asked her, "do you know a couple of Chinese sailors—one tall and one short?"

"Pardon me?"

I realized it was rather a broad question.

"Two Chinese guys stopped me, and I think one of them called me later. He seemed to think I had that Phoenix, which I didn't understand. Maybe they didn't get it from Lee Ying."

"No?"

"Maybe not. Maybe it got lost somehow, and they're still looking for it. Why else would they think I had it? Maybe they thought Bobo had it. Or Ellie."

"What do you mean?" Kit asked impatiently. "What has this to do with Ellie?"

I had an idea fleetingly by the tail, and tried to hang on to it.

"Kit, that Dowager Phoenix is worth a fortune, I gather. Isn't that so, Mrs. Cheong?"

"An insignificant trinket that might have value to some," she said coolly. "It would not be important to a *wai low*."

Where had I heard that before?

"It hardly seems insignificant to somebody," I told her. "What it looks like is that they murdered Lee Ying to get it, but they're still looking for it. Then they got Bobo, and Ellie . . ."

Chen turned to Madame Cheong. "Is there anyone who knew that Lee Ying was bringing the Phoenix to you?"

She gestured uncertainly. "Not that I'm aware of," she said. "Word sometimes gets around. My firm deals in exotic artifacts. It would not be important to a *waiguoren*."

I looked into deep, dark, penetrating eyes. Definitely a piece of work.

Detective Chen smiled his way between us. "Well, let us

all be on the lookout for this Empress Dowager's Phoenix medal," he said. "Perhaps it will provide the answer to this business."

Not much more came out of that strange meeting, and Madame Cheong eventually excused herself and left.

"Wow!" Kit breathed, sinking into a chair at Chen's desk. "What did she mean, my sister was there? Is that why she was murdered?"

"It would seem so," Detective Chen said thoughtfully. He walked to his desk, took off his jacket, and sat down. He stared at us for a long moment.

"Let me explain what I think this is all about. Yes, the Dowager Phoenix medal. Lee Ying was murdered by people trying to get it. I now believe they did not succeed. He was tortured to persuade him to say where it was. I assure you, he told them what they wanted to know. His answer sent them to Mr. Watson, who was treated the same way. Then to your sister, I'm sorry to say."

"Lee Ying said Bobo had it?" I asked.

"Or Ellie?" Kit added.

"I do not know, exactly, but, yes—they were led to believe that Watson or your sister had it. Now they think Fitzgerald has it, or they might think you have it, Miss Cunningham. It appears they will not stop searching until they have it."

"But she said it's just a trinket," Kit said with annoyance.

"It is the Chinese way to denigrate things of great value so the spirits will not become envious and take them away," he said. "The Phoenix is an item of immeasurable worth to certain people."

He knew of at least two Dowager Phoenixes, he said, one in the British Museum and one that he had actually seen once in the Wan Chi Tong office in Chinatown. The tongs, associations of Chinese businesspeople, pretty much controlled Chinatown as though it were an independent fiefdom, like Hong Kong, he explained.

"Some of them are criminal enterprises," he said, "and we

have to watch them. Chinatown gangs do their bidding, and in turn they look the other way when the gangs shake down stores and restaurants in protection rackets."

I remembered that a few years ago the head of one of the tongs, a prominent restaurateur, had gone to prison for such activities.

"I went to see Wei Wang, head of the Wan Chi Tong, to show the flag, to warn him about associating with street gangs," Chen went on. "Of course, he said he's only a businessman, and he showed me a Dowager Phoenix on display in his office as an emblem of his community spirit and patriotism. It was his proudest possession, handed down, he said, through his family for generations. How he got it, I have no idea, and I had no jurisdiction to inquire. Maybe what he said was true. But it is no trinket."

Detective Chen pushed his chair back and opened a drawer in his desk. "Madame Cheong was waiting for delivery of a Dowager Phoenix, possibly stolen from the Forbidden City itself."

He took out a large, red book decorated with a golden dragon and laid it on the desk, open to a page.

"Here," he said. "A photograph of the Dowager Phoenix in the British Museum."

We bent over and looked at it. It showed a medal somewhat larger and thicker than a quarter—not quite the size of a half-dollar—stamped with the likeness of the dowager empress, a squat, ugly, elderly Chinese woman on a throne holding a small scepter in each hand. Beside the photograph was a photo of the obverse side, a depiction of a Phoenix bird. It was stamped with Chinese characters.

"That's what they're looking for?" Kit asked, peering at the Dowager Phoenix.

"It is the last relic of the empress. It is not a trinket to them. I did not fully understand before, but now I begin to, a little," he mused. "When I met Anna at the morgue, she was wearing a long coat. Only today did I meet the real Madame

Cheong. She called you *wai low* . . . foreign devils. *Waiguoren* . . . barbarian. You are round eyes. You have no idea what this is all about."

Detective Chen leaned back and lit one of his thin, twisted, dark cigarettes. "You have just met a woman who fashions herself in the image of the Empress Dowager Tz'u-hsi, the last true ruler of China in the Forbidden City."

"She was gotten up like I don't know what! Madame Butterfly!" Kit said. "And that pin she wore, a peacock full of diamonds and emeralds."

"A Phoenix, Miss Cunningham."

"That was a Phoenix?"

"The symbol of the empress."

"What did she say in Chinese when she saw Kit?" I asked.

"When she saw you, Miss Cunningham, you were a bird of ill omen. Your dead sister. A returned spirit. She spoke Mandarin at first. She is an educated Manchu of the highest class, or has made herself so. When she saw Miss Cunningham, she fell back into her own dialect . . . Hunanese."

"She got excited there for a moment," Kit said.

"She said, 'Lord of Ten Thousand Years, she's alive.' She swore by her god, the emperor."

I must have been looking rather dubious.

"If you wish to understand what sort of soy sauce you two have stepped in, you must understand Madame Cheong and the people she is fighting with over that medal," Chen said.

Madame Cheong, he now told us, wore imperial yellow, the color of the emperor. She wore a Phoenix pin, the symbol of the empress. She spoke court Mandarin, and when startled swore by god, her god, the last emperor.

"He was Pu Yi, the Lord of Ten Thousand Years. She sees herself as the empress dowager Tz'u-hsi, a woman so formidable that she would say, 'If anyone causes me a moment's sorrow, I shall give him a lifetime of misery.' And she meant it, too—in spades."

The whole thing spooked me. Crazies after a priceless

Chinese medal apparently had killed three people and now were after Kit and me.

"What about Madame Cheong?" I asked him.

"What about her?"

"She's in the middle of this," Kit said.

Detective Chen stared at us. "Exactly. Property that might have been stolen was supposed to be delivered to her. Even if she had received it, I could not say it was stolen. I have no jurisdiction over thefts from China. She identified a body, that's all."

Plainly, Charlie Chan had his doubts about the dragon lady and so did I. I took it that he was telling us this to caution us. Kit was even more insistent.

"Well, could you at least question her about my sister?" she pleaded. "That man, Lee Ying, worked for her!"

Detective Chen let out a breath. "Miss Cunningham, since it was your sister, I will tell you this in confidence." He flung a look at me. "And not for publication. Of course I checked her out."

After Madame Cheong identified the body and asked about the Phoenix, he said, he traced her movements at the time of the murders. She was in her shop on Canal Street, and when Ellie was murdered, she was dining at the Golden Goose Pagoda restaurant on Mott Street with the owner, Wei Wang.

"Wei Wang?" I said. "The head of one of the tongs?"

"Yes. The Wan Chi office is on the top floor of his restaurant."

"You mean Anna is a member of the tong then?" Kit wondered.

"She is a Chinatown businesswoman," he came back, and paused to light one of his dark, twisted cigarettes. Kit glanced at it curiously.

"Golden Monkeys," he said. "They help me think."

I lit a Tiparillo for the same reason.

"You should know who Madame Cheong is," he said, "but

I have no reason to go after her." He gazed at us and spoke seriously.

"Until the killers get that Phoenix," he said soberly, "anyone who might have it, or have any knowledge of it, is in extreme danger."

EIGHTEEN

KIT AND I CAME OUT OF THE FIFTH PRECINCT ONTO ELIzabeth Street a lot less jauntily than we had gone in, and we walked back down through Chinatown, each with our own thoughts. It was dusk as we angled over and went down Mulberry Street, and there were Chinese lanterns twinkling in some of the stores. Once again, moving along through the Asian tide, I spotted Quishi and Invisible Fist everywhere and nowhere. I had walked these Chinatown streets for years as a reporter and had never felt any anxiety here, although in truth I had hardly noticed most of the scene except in passing. Even then, surrounded by people, I couldn't imagine any danger in this throng.

"I don't understand the whole thing," Kit muttered as we went along.

We went down Mulberry Street alongside the iron fence of the Chinatown playground behind the Criminal Court Building, and ahead of us was the metal canopy of Giambone's, where Jimmy Chen had explained the Dowager Phoenix to me. I suddenly realized I couldn't remember when I had eaten last.

"Come on," I told her. "Let's eat."

We went into Giambone's, which, like so many other long-established places taken over by the latest wave of immigrants, was now run by an Israeli. They used to say there are more Jews in New York than in Tel Aviv, more Irish than in Dublin, more Italians than in Naples. Maybe those people who call New York the capital of a foreign country are right; except that it's the City of the World.

I remembered Salvatore, the previous owner of Giambone's. He and his father before him ran the place for seventy-five years. Salvatore told me that a Chinese woman owned the whole block, and that each month his father and then he went to her personally and paid her the rent in cash. They never had a lease.

I never heard anyone say that New York has more Chinese than Shanghai or Beijing. It occurred to me that even though I had worked around Chinatown for years, I knew almost nothing about the Chinese in New York. Let's face it, they lived among us in a sort of foreign capital of their own in the City of the World. I hadn't thought much about what I didn't know about them until I met Quishi and Invisible Fist.

Inside Giambone's, I said hello to a couple of lawyers sitting at the bar.

"Fitzgerald, where ya been?" asked Mickey Silberman, the negligence lawyer who always reminded me that his name was spelled "with a B, not a V."

Right away, he pulled me over to tell me he had a hot story for me, meaning one of his lawsuits. That's the way it is with people you cover on a beat. You move on, but as far as they're concerned, you're still the courthouse reporter.

"Naw, Mickey," I told him. "I'm not at the courthouse pressroom anymore. We've got a reporter there, Tony Burton."

"Nah! He doesn't do much on divorce cases."

I suggested Jed Starnes of the *New York Times* or Harry Reeves of the *Post*, if they were still on the beat.

Mickey made a face. "Reeves doesn't think it's a story. I tell you, he's getting old!"

I could imagine my old *New York Post* opponent, Harry Reeves, the poo-bah of state supreme court, snorting, rolling his head around, and telling Mickey the story was "a piece of shit." I didn't see Harry at the front table, where he usually held court during lunch and sometimes after work.

Kit and I sat at a table in the back. I ordered a Rheingold, and she wanted scotch and water. We sipped the drinks, and she looked down in the dumps.

"Oh, Fitz," she moaned.

Yeah.

"We've got to try to make sense out of this," I finally decided.

"Sure. How?"

Yes, how? I've heard that Chinese puzzles are supposed to be the most intricate, and we certainly had one of our own.

There was an image in my head of a game we used to play as kids, where you put a toothpick on the mouth of a bottle, then another, and another. You build up this toothpick tower on top of the bottle's mouth as high as you can until one of them unbalances the tower and it collapses.

There were Bobo Watson and Ellie at Elaine's, two toothpicks across the bottle's mouth. Then Lee Ying, Ching, and Chang: three more toothpicks across the first two.

"The first time the five of them were all there was on a Friday night," I told Kit.

"Why would those Chinese go to a place like Elaine's?" she asked, puzzled.

That had confused me, too, but now I decided it had to be because either Lee Ying or the other two wanted a neutral site, someplace outside Chinatown, some location where they weren't likely to run into anyone they knew. Like Wise Guys picking an obscure bar for a sit-down.

"I think they picked a place at random, and Elaine's is very well known and they'd have no trouble finding it."

Kit's face went red, and she stared straight ahead, her back straight as a board. I had come to recognize that posture and that stare. It meant internal explosions.

"I can't think of any other explanation," I told her.

"What a city," she muttered.

"So, Duffy and the waiters eighty-sixed the three Chinese guys." I continued with my toothpicks.

Okay, so Mutt and Jeff hustle Lee Ying away, and the next we know of him he's floating down the East River.

So why was Lee Ying at Elaine's meeting the other two Chinese guys?

"Chen said this Lee Ying was a smuggler and a crook," I went on. "So maybe he decides not to bring it to Madame Cheong, but to sell it himself."

"He's at Elaine's trying to sell it to these other two?" Kit considered.

"Maybe so."

So what had gone wrong? The two buyers shove Lee Ying around in front of Bobo's piano. Lee Ying wanted too much?

"Maybe they decided to just steal it instead of buy it," Kit offered, and I thought that sounded right. "Then they could sell it to Madame Cheong or somebody else."

Our toothpick tower climbed precariously.

The next development was the final toothpick. How did Bobo's murder figure into this? The tower wobbled and crashed.

"I can't figure the Bobo thing in yet, but it's got to be connected. Because then they went after your sister, and then me."

We were nibbling our food by then, my lasagna and her shrimp scampi, but the nourishment didn't seem to rise up and stoke our brains. It occurred to me, though, that whatever Lee Ying was forced to tell Mutt and Jeff, it had sent them back after Bobo. They must have been told that Bobo had the Phoenix.

"They thought Bobo had it," I said between bites.

"How could he have gotten it?" Kit complained. "Or Ellie?"

I munched the lasagna and pondered. More toothpicks on the bottle. But it had to be something like that. Lee Ying told them something that made them believe Bobo had it.

They went after Bobo and killed him trying to get the damned thing. That's why they cut out his pockets and took his jacket. They were ripping his clothes apart, looking for it. When they couldn't find it, they went after Ellie.

"But if they came after you," Kit considered, "and if Madame Cheong went to the police looking for it, then they still haven't found it."

"No."

"And now they're after me, too? But that's crazy!"

"You heard Madame Cheong. She said I was there. Somebody wants that damned thing very bad. They're not going to stop till they get it. Anybody who might know anything about it is on the spot."

I wish I could tell you we solved our Chinese puzzle that evening, sitting in Giambone's as dusk turned to night over Chinatown. About the only conclusions we reached were that the Dowager Phoenix was still out there somewhere, and there were people willing to do almost anything to recover it.

We sat over another round of drinks, but Kit was wilting, her lovely blue eyes tired. She'd had a long day, beginning with the flight from Grand Rapids and then the session with Charlie Chan.

"I'm beat," she murmured.

"Where are you staying?"

"Back at the Edison. It's nice of you to help me."

"Well, what the hell." I wanted to tell her I hadn't planned on it, and didn't really know how I could help anyway.

She laughed at that. "Wow! Saying nice things to Mr. Hard-Boiled Reporter makes him blush."

If I hadn't blushed before, I wouldn't be surprised if I did then.

"Well, you know . . ." I trailed off.

"Yes, I do now. But, boy, it takes some close study to look into that stone tower and see the marshmallows."

"We'd better go," I told her, and paid up.

She was still smiling to herself, and when we walked out

her hand was in mine. The nearness of the willowy, Grand Rapids beauty insidiously invaded my reason, and as we went down Mulberry Street I heard the song about the pavement always staying beneath my feet before. It was strange, in a way. I had been improperly attracted to her twin, and now here was the same, identical vision with her hand in mine, her scent enveloping me.

I don't want to hear a lot of snide chuckles about a reporter getting too chummy with a news source. I was only trying to comfort her, and listen, it had been months since Audie fled West. And I'm not a monk, either. Besides, Kit wasn't just a news source anymore. We were in this thing together. And if that's not enough of a rationalization, then blame it on Audie McMillan for deserting me.

We angled across to Park Row and down along the wide, two-lane avenue toward police headquarters and my Toyota. It's pretty wide open there and desolate at night, even though you're in the shadow of the huge mustard-colored police headquarters. As a New Yorker I instinctively watch my ass on the street. When I glanced back toward Chinatown, I saw them.

One tall and one short, crossing Park Row.

The tug of my hand in Kit's alerted her, and she looked at me, startled.

"What?"

"I think they're behind us."

She jerked her head to look back, and we walked faster.

They followed us.

"Oh, my God!"

Then we were running. Down Park Row, along the back of police headquarters. There could hardly be a safer location in Manhattan, except that there were no cops around. And then I spotted Mutt and Jeff again, and they were between us and police headquarters.

"Hey!" I yelled. No cops in sight.

I dragged her on a run toward the Toyota, and we scrambled inside and locked the doors. I kept looking for cops, and saw some across the intersection at the side door. But they were too far away to hear me.

Whamp! There was a crash against the driver's-side window.

I started the car, and my head jerked to look.

Quishi and Invisible Fist!

Blam! Invisible Fist was at Kit's window, slamming it, trying the door, shouting.

The Toyota lurched into flight.

NINETEEN

I BOLTED AWAY FROM THE CURB, AND KIT WAS CRANING her neck, looking back out through the rear window, squinting frantically into the darkness.

"Do you see them?"

"No!"

There wasn't much light, despite some illumination around the rear of police headquarters. I swung around the triangle parking lot lined with NYP parking zones, and circled back around toward headquarters, looking for our two pursuers or a blue-and-white police car. I wanted a cop, and would ram one if I had to.

"What are you doing?" Kit cried. "You're going back toward them!"

"They're on foot," I said, and careened around and back along behind headquarters, looking for them. Still no police cars in sight, except parked, unoccupied vehicles with lights off. It was like dashing around outside the high, impregnable walls of King Arthur's castle; the knights were all inside at the Round Table having a banquet, or out scouring the countryside for highwaymen, or seeking the Holy Grail. What about the damned peasants right under your walls!

I swung a left and zoomed back across Park Row, driving like a maniac, trying to get arrested, and found myself in Foley Square. It's a huge, broad expanse, surrounded by immense courthouses—the towering U.S. District Court for the Southern District of New York, the state supreme court, the gloomy, blackstone, flat-fronted family court, the Federal Building housing the FBI, a regular gigantic facsimile of the Roman Forum. And it was deserted. By day, it is thronged with lawyers, judges, cops, defendants, and hot dog wagons, but at night you could fire a cannon through Foley Square and hit nobody and nothing, particularly not a police car.

"Let's get away from here!" Kit pleaded, and I decided it was a good idea.

I looped around and headed toward the entrance ramp to the FDR Drive under the Brooklyn Bridge, the way back uptown to civilization. It was a blunder. When I hit Foley Square, I should have gone north uptown toward Canal Street. But when I curled around back down Park Row, a car pulled out of a spot, and its lights went on.

A police car? No. A dark-colored Mercedes. I had seen that damned dark shape once before at the top of Central Park! The lights flashed in the rearview mirror. Apparently, my brilliant tactic of circling around the deserted Foley Square streets in a white Toyota had let them keep us in sight and had given them enough time to run to their car.

"Shit!" I muttered.

"Oh, Fitz!"

That again!

"Oh, my God!"

"Shut up and let me drive!"

I drove, all right, and the lights of the dark Mercedes blazed in the rearview mirror. I wanted the uptown ramp again, but they had other ideas, as well as a monster vehicle that treated my little Toyota with considerable disrespect.

Scrunch! The damned, dark juggernaut sideswiped us, sending the Toyota careening down a side street leading I didn't know where.

"Fitz!" Kit squealed.

Racing ahead, I was on local streets, going through a housing project, past a gigantic stanchion of the Brooklyn Bridge, now towering high above us, down another street, and there were iron pillars ahead under an elevated highway.

"South Street!" I told myself.

At least I knew where I was again. It wasn't far from Mutchie's, the waterfront bar we used to frequent when I worked the lobster trick. Determining my location was but of minor value, however, because South Street was a wider thoroughfare and there was more room between the iron pillars. I had only been staying ahead of the Mercedes by speeding through narrow streets and around corners. Driving frantically along South Street under the elevated highway in and out of the pillars, the damned German main battle tank closed in on us.

Wham! We were bumped from behind. The Toyota wobbled.

Kit howled.

It suddenly occurred to me that the one thing my little space capsule had over the arrogant dark monster was maneuverability. Like the Red Baron, I could turn inside the wider arc of the Mercedes, and in a second I swung violently into a tight curve around a pillar and zoomed back in the opposite direction.

Kit spilled halfway across my lap, yelling crazily.

"You'll kill us!"

But I had a few seconds on them now, and I knew where I was going. Ahead through the pillars along South Street was a ramp to the FDR Drive, uptown, a lighted roadway, and maybe safety.

The Mercedes got itself turned around, though, crashing through some wooden flats, and it was soon after us again. It was like an F-16 fighter jet pursuing a weekend Cessna. Passing Sloppy Louie's where I once had whale steak, the gap closed. I drove through the Fulton Fish Market, deserted like the whole damned area! Passing the old New York Post Building, the gap narrowed more. They were tailgating us.

I jerked the Toyota to the right, shaving an iron pillar, and hit the brakes. The Mercedes swerved, tires squealing, and went by us like a Greyhound bus.

I backed up furiously.

I went ahead again, but they apparently had lost patience with this cat-and-mouse game, and rushed alongside. They had cornered us under an elevated highway in the dark and desolate lower depths of the bottom of Manhattan.

Scrunch! Wham!

Their second, more determined sideswipe sent the Toyota on a sliding, crazy slant, and half-sideways against an iron pillar; the Mercedes was jammed cheek-by-jowl against my driver's-side door. Kit and I were trapped between the Mercedes and the pillar, the face of Quishi glaring at me through his window, yelling something.

Quishi was yelling and gesturing at the driver, Invisible Fist, and with a scrape and a screech the Mercedes backed up. I realized that Quishi wanted to get the monster free from the Toyota enough to open his door, and then ours.

The passenger-side door of the Mercedes apparently was stuck a little though from the impact, and he was shoving it.

"Let's get out of the car!" Kit yelled.

I didn't like our chances on foot, and gunned the engine. The Toyota moaned in protest, and stuttered forward, scraping free from the pillar, something falling off the side, hubcaps or chrome or maybe a wheel. But it got free of the pillar, and I drove on.

If you can call it driving. Lumpety-lump and squealing, metal on concrete.

"Goddamnit," I cursed. "We've got a flat tire or two. We're riding on the rims!"

The Toyota had been reasonably perky before, but now we crawled, scraping the street, limping along. Ahead was a ramp leading upward. I crept toward it like a damned snail. But by the time they were on our tail again, we got onto the foot of the ramp, and the ramp was so narrow that it took only one car at a time. Surprisingly, we picked up speed. The Toyota was coming back to life.

Then I understood that it wasn't my foot on the pedal that was hurtling us up the ramp, but the shove we were getting from behind. The Mercedes was ramrodding us like a locomotive. The Toyota's bare feet screamed in metallic agony.

We went around the curving ramp, and we were on the Brooklyn Bridge! Even the damned Brooklyn Bridge had only a few cars crossing it, and our waves and shouts at passing cars resulted in nothing. New Yorkers don't stop for strange cars at night. And maybe they thought we were being aided by good Samaritans, giving our pitiful wreck a helpful push. They were, all right, but they weren't good Samaritans; they were the savage Sarmatians Marcus Aurelius fought on the Danube.

They kept pushing us out across the bridge, and I couldn't coax the Toyota into enough speed to free us and outrun them. I didn't know where they were pushing us, but I didn't like the idea of the darkness of a Brooklyn street across the East River.

But then they disengaged. We were rolling free. Barely.

"They're letting us go!" Kit cried hopefully.

I wondered about that, but not for long. In a moment they had passed us up, and I hoped to see their taillights heading into Brooklyn.

Instead, the Mercedes swerved in front of us, angling in toward the bridge railing, and cut us off. We slammed into the side of them.

Now the dark streets of Brooklyn seemed more inviting. We were marooned and trapped at night in the middle of the bridge, which is about three-quarters of a mile long. And still there was damned little traffic.

"Fitz!"

I reached over and shoved open her door.

"Run!" I ordered her. "Find the cops!"

She scrambled out and took off along the roadway back

toward Manhattan. I climbed across the passenger seat and scurried after her. But Invisible Fist had had enough time to get out, too, and as I came around the rear of the Toyota, a hard fist battered my right ear.

"Pig!" he shouted.

I was on my knees, so the only place to hit him was his own knees. I lit into him, my head spinning, driving him backward. Thank heavens he was the short one.

Cars halted on the Brooklyn Bridge normally don't cause anyone crossing the bridge to stop, especially at night, because breakdowns happen all the time, and you never know who's in that stalled car. But a fight and an outbreak of road rage will slow some rubberneckers. And there we were, sprawled on the bridge behind the Toyota, rolling around on the pavement.

I got untangled, and we were on our feet again, and another explosion of heat staggered me. With this short, wiry character, you never saw the blow coming. I went sprawling again, and managed to shove him with my feet, and we were against the side bridge railing.

"I haven't got it," I yelled at him, but it didn't register.

He was at me again, delivering an unseen whizzing smack, ringing bells and stars, and I was halfway down against the bridge railing. I kicked him again, banging him backward.

"Stop it, you maniac!"

"You will come with us, *waiguoren*!"

"In a pig's patoot!"

He came at me again, and I was so battered and bruised and disoriented that I virtually collapsed, sinking into a squat, my back against the railing. He was on top of me, his head and shoulders over my head, and when I instinctively reared up into him, he tilted forward, over my back, and was gone.

I was bewildered. My head jerked around, and I darted a look over the side, over the rail. There was a dark, silent, flailing silhouette and then, a hundred feet or so down in the dark waters of the East River, a tiny speck of a splash.

"Jesus!"

I sank down again, stunned, shocked, frozen.

Some of the stars zinging around my head dissipated, and I glanced around, trying to get my bearings. Oddly enough, Quishi seemed to have been unable to get out of the passenger-side door, apparently because it had jammed when we crashed into that pillar. I saw his face staring out, his eyes huge.

Our fight had halted some rubberneckers, and once a car slowed and stopped, others slowed and stopped behind the first one.

Somebody in the first car had rolled down the window and was yelling at me.

"What happened? Did he go over?"

He had, all right. I glanced down again, but there was nothing to see but the swirling, eddying black waters. Steve Brodie staged a celebrated leap from the Brooklyn Bridge soon after it opened, and lived to tell about it. Not many others ever did.

Groggily, I struggled to my feet, hopelessly confused.

Then it caught my eye: flashing lights, coming across the bridge from Manhattan. At last, the cops.

Quishi, trapped behind his mangled car door, must have noticed them, too. He slid across into the driver's seat and pulled away, heading on over to Brooklyn. Never had I seen a fairer sight than his disappearing taillights.

I staggered away from the bridge rail, gasping, hanging on.

A good number of cars had halted by now, and the honking started.

And here came a uniformed cop out of the sector car, walking toward me, his arms outstretched.

"Now, listen, buddy, no matter how bad it seems, this ain't the answer."

I stared at him, exhausted and speechless.

"You want a priest to talk to?"

I finally found enough voice to answer. "What?"

"A rabbi?"

I sank down against the railing, utterly spent.

He approached cautiously, speaking sympathetically. "That's better. What happened, pally?"

"A guy went over the rail."

He reacted to that, staring out over the railing into the river.

"Somebody already jumped?"

"He fell."

"Who was it? A friend of yours?"

"Invisible Fist."

"Who?"

"I don't know his real name."

Rubberneckers were out of their cars now, edging up behind the cop, peeking past him at me.

"They were fighting!" one of them, a fat guy in a plaid golf hat, said. "I tried to stop them!"

"What?" The cop asked.

"Yeah, I said, 'Hey, whatta ya doing to that little guy?' "

The cop's partner came over and told the plaid golf hat to get the hell back into his car and get moving. By now the line of cars was stretched halfway back to Manhattan, and rubberneckers were building in the Brooklyn-to-Manhattan lanes. There isn't as much traffic at night as during rush hour, but there's always traffic in Manhattan.

I breathed deep, rubbed my face where red welts were blossoming out, and lit a Tiparillo.

The abiding truth about New York held: cops may not always be interested in a mere murder, but they won't stand for anybody stopping traffic.

TWENTY

I DON'T KNOW HOW LONG I SAT THERE IN MY HALF-DAZED swoon, both utterly exhausted and so wired that everything popped and flashed inside my head, jerking in an uncontrollable cycle, replaying distorted, disconnected, surreal images in a kaleidoscopic fugue.

Dash along South Street . . . *SCRUNCH, WHAM* . . . Quishi glares through two canted windows like Quasimodo . . . rise up and a flailing, falling, silent figure . . . the dark waters of the East River.

Back on South Street. Unseen blows. Eddying waters.

And again, and again.

Until a terrified but relieved Kit came close, and she slumped down beside me, her head in my shoulder, shuddering and crying.

"Areyouallright, areyouallright!?"

"Some soy sauce, Kit," I mumbled.

Kit drew back and gazed at me nose to nose, her eyes wide, like somebody in a lifeboat from the *Titanic*, safe for the moment but still at sea, bobbing precariously on rolling swells.

"Oh, Fitz!" She kissed my face all over convulsively.

Well!

She held me rather desperately, arms around my back like iron bands, head buried against my chest, as though fearful that we would go over the rail, too, and her words came out in a flood.

"Fitz, oh, you're a hero! Oh, my God, I don't know how we got out of that. I don't know how you did it! How did you do it? I've never been so scared in my life! Oh, Fitz!"

She was asking the wrong person, because I had no idea. If that desperate flight was the stuff of heroism, it was driven by terror, panic, confusion, and chance. Some sense of time and place gradually came back to me, and I looked back and down at the river again. Moving lights below on the water. A police launch had been dispatched to make a search below the bridge, I surmised.

"What happened to you?" I asked Kit.

She had dashed wildly toward Manhattan, she said, and then met a police car coming toward her. It passed her and she had to run all the way back, and they would hardly let her through the police line.

"I'm afraid I called a policeman some names I didn't think I knew," she blushed.

I found myself chuckling at that, releasing tension. She was turning into a New Yorker.

There were four police cars there by then, two from each side of the river, with flashing lights and cops with flashlights in the roadway waving traffic on in both directions. Then a fifth cruiser pulled up, and a sergeant talked with the uniformed cops, and then came over to us. He leaned down.

"You're the jumper?"

I let out a breath. "Ed Fitzgerald, *Daily Press.* There was no jumper. There was a fight with this guy trying to kidnap us, and he went into the river."

The sarge frowned, glanced over the side, and then looked at Kit.

"Who are you?"

"Kathleen Cunningham from Grand Rapids. This man deserves a medal!"

The sarge nodded briefly and went back to the uniformed cops.

Apparently they decided there was no immediate emergency anymore. One guy was in the river, and the police harbor squad was on that. I was not going to jump, so that was okay. That brought them to the problem of the moment.

The first cop came back to me. I was on my feet by then, though still a bit wobbly.

"Is that your Toyota?"

I told him it was, what was left of it.

"Got to get it out of here."

I told him I didn't know if it would still run, but I'd try. He examined my face intently, and I thought he was going to hold up fingers and ask me how many I saw.

"Drive it?" he said. "You're on the rims, pally. You want to tear up the the bridge surface?"

"I don't want to do anything except go home and soak in a tub," I told him abruptly.

"You don't want a doctor?" he said, examining the blooming welts on my face. "What were you guys fighting about? He cut you off?"

"They were trying to kill us!" Kit yelled at him. "Don't you understand! I want Detective Charlie Chan!"

"Who?"

"Son of a bitch!" Kit smoldered.

Well, well. The trembling fawn had become a raging tigress. That's what New York and a murder will do to you.

Well, the most important order of business was to get my mangled piece of junk off the bridge, and along came a tow truck with more flashing lights. The tow-truck operator winched the Toyota onto a flatbed, and talked to the cops, and then they came back to us.

"That's gonna be one-fifty for the tow," the cop said.

"I didn't call any tow truck," I complained. "You did."

"That vehicle can't stay here."

"It wasn't my fault! I'm not paying for this."

The tow-truck driver tossed his head. "I don't know nothing about that."

"I've got Triple A," I told him.

"No good on the bridge. We got authorization here."

I rubbed my face. Terrific! You have Triple A, but wherever your car breaks down, it's someplace where Triple A can't go. I gave up. "All right, all right. Take it."

"Who's paying?" the driver wanted to know. "You got NYP plates."

"He says *Daily Press,*" the cop said.

"Yeah? You write sports?"

"No!"

"I can't haul nobody without I get paid. The boss won't take it."

"Don't you trust the *Daily Press*?"

"I don't trust nobody."

You may not believe this, but there we were in an attempted murder and kidnapping, with a dead man in the river, and nothing mattered except a hundred and fifty cash for the tow truck.

"How much have you got?" I had to ask Kit.

She looked worried, but dug out some cash, and I put in the rest, and finally the wounded shell of the Toyota went trundling off back to Manhattan to the tow-truck driver's garage. He wouldn't take it to Second Avenue John's near my place.

Of course, the night wouldn't have been perfect without the arrival of four more detectives, two teams of them, from Manhattan and Brooklyn. Our demolition derby had occurred in the middle of the Brooklyn Bridge, so who had jurisdiction?

One of them approached us, looked us both over, and said, "What happened here?"

I sighed. "Officer, I'll tell you what. Could you contact Detective Jimmy Chen at the Fifth Precinct in Chinatown? He knows the whole case."

"Case? This is a case?"

"Oh, yeah."

"I understand there may be a body in the river."

"There is," I assured him.

"You saw him go over?"

"He was on top of me! I came up, and he went over."

"You put him over?"

"I stood up! He was on me!"

"Is that so?"

I'm damned if he didn't make notes in his logbook. But, then, I guess he had to. It was true, there was a body in the river, and some kind of crime must have been committed here, either against us or by us. Dead bodies and traffic jams; that's police work.

We slumped back down against the railing again, and the detectives and cops all conferred with each other. I didn't know if any of them had listened to us, but finally two detectives came back and told us to get into their squad car.

"Where are we going?" Kit blurted, frightened.

"You have to come with us."

We fell into the backseat, and the squad car took off back to Manhattan. Up through Chinatown again, and we were deposited at the Fifth Precinct. We sat in the squad room, both of us barely functioning. I don't know how long it took, but finally Detective Jimmy Chen walked in. He stared at us a long moment.

"What the hell have you two been up to?"

It was one of those endless, distended, agonizingly weary conversations where you have to think but can't, where you're under water and languid and can hardly move your body or your brain. You hardly know what you're saying but you'd better not say the wrong thing. Not if there's a dead body involved.

We told Charlie Chan the doings of the evening and night as best we could, in fits and starts. He listened patiently, taking notes and with a tape recorder whirring.

"Okay, that will do for a preliminary statement," he said. "I don't think you're in any condition to go back over it right now."

He had that right.

"You'd better stick to stories, Fitz," he suggested then. "And Miss Cunningham, I suggest you return to Michigan."

"What's going to happen?" I asked wearily.

Detective Chen considered it carefully.

"A man is dead, Fitzgerald. It will have to be dealt with."

"But it was self-defense!" Kit wailed.

"Not even that—an accident," I insisted.

"I have no choice," he replied. "The D.A.'s office has to be notified. It will have to go to a grand jury."

"I'll be indicted?" I managed, shaken.

"That will be in the hands of the district attorney. Under the circumstances, I'm not going to recommend any charge now. But you must consider yourself in technical custody. I'm going to send you home. You'll be contacted."

I smiled at him gratefully.

"Thanks."

"An assistant D.A. will want to talk to you, probably tomorrow. Meaning today, since it's now after three. I have to caution you not to discuss anything about this until you finish with the A.D.A."

"Okay."

"Some soy sauce, Fitzgerald."

Finally, sometime after three in the morning, we got out of there. We walked in a daze to Canal Street, hailed a cab, and rode uptown to Times Square to drop Kit off at the Edison Hotel.

"Fitz," she said, getting out. "Are you all right?"

"Later," I managed to say.

Then the cab took me across town to my place. I barely remember the ride or arriving home. My last official act that endless night-morning was to pull the telephone jack from the wall so I could get some sleep.

TWENTY-ONE

BLAMMING, BLAMMING, AND SOMEBODY CALLING.

Sometimes you can come awake disorganized, adrift in the frightening sensation of not remembering where you are. That morning when the pounding and calling came, I was in the opposite condition; I remembered everything in a nanosecond and wished I could forget it, or that it had been a nightmare.

I felt myself gripped with an overwhelming urge to flee, to hide, escape. I was a prairie dog on an arid, open plain, and the sky was full of swooping, hungry birds of prey.

I slid to the apartment door, not ready to let the world in, but then heard her voice.

"Fitz? Are you all right? Fitz?"

I opened the door, and Kit dashed in, looking pretty crazed.

"I called, but . . . are you all right?"

"Not yet."

I fled to my gopher hole, pulled the door shut, locked it, and sank into the bathtub. All I wanted to do was soak there forever. Kit Cunningham might have been crazed, but I was in no better shape. She would have to wait for me to resurface.

"Fitz?" The bird of prey called out curiously.

I turned the water on full to drown her out. I was safe in my burrow. Nobody could reach me here. I was trying to fight off the sensation of a vast net closing around me. I had been involved in the violent death of Invisible Fist, and there would be consequences no matter how it turned out.

"Easy, Fitz," I told myself. Come down to earth. Find something to hold onto. I desperately needed some calming wisdom from my mentor. My copy of *Meditations* was in my hands.

"Nature brings you nothing that you cannot bear," Marcus Aurelius counseled me. "Nothing can happen to you which is not a human accident; nor to an ox which is not according to the nature of an ox; nor to a vine, nor to a stone, which is not according to the nature of each."

Was what had happened to me according to the nature of a reporter, or of a New Yorker, or perhaps of a mere idiot? I was forced to agree with Marcus, as usual; what had happened to me was certainly according to the nature of a reporter who gets his nose caught in a murder.

"Stick to writing stories," Charlie Chan had advised me. He was correct, also.

But, Marcus and Charlie, I ask you: when you get dragged into the tail of a story and it turns into a snake with a venomous head at the other end, and it turns on you, what then? When a story that isn't yours starts chasing you, what are you supposed to do? Run if you can, but if the snake story runs faster and catches you . . .

A knock on the door. "Fitz?"

"Nobody home."

"We're on TV!"

"What?" I stayed in the tub, but Kit's voice penetrated to my burrow.

"There's a story about that man going off the Brooklyn Bridge, and that a *Daily Press* reporter is being questioned!"

I slid down deeper into the water. The tub wasn't deep enough for me to disappear, but I tried. I was facing arrest, possibly on a charge of accidental death, manslaughter, or even murder.

After a few moments, there was more banging on the bathroom door.

"Fitz! The phone's dead."

"Don't touch that phone!"

"What?"

"I pulled the jack. Don't touch it!"

"Are you all right?" She was getting nervous talking through the door to my cell.

"Go away!"

"Go . . . where? What? Have you heard any more?"

There was tingling in my scalp, an electric buzz up my spine. Had I heard something last night? The distant echo of vague thumps reached me, somebody tapping on the outside bulkhead of my sunken submarine.

Bam, bam, bam!

"Come out! I can't talk to you like this!"

"I'm in the tub! We'll talk when I get out."

When a mess gets big enough, you want to be an ostrich or a turtle, or a gopher. The sweep of the Bobo–Ellie–Lee Ying–Invisible Fist–snake story–murders buried me under a ton of earth. Trying to add up my troubles, I built another toothpick tower but it collapsed before I had gotten anywhere near its inevitable destruction.

I smoked a Tiparillo and soaked. Let the world with its Kits, Ironheads, Hanleys, Quishis, and tow-truck operators go to hell. Marcus and I and the snake were in conference. I knew I couldn't really hibernate there forever, although it was tempting. But at least for the moment I was out of everyone's reach. The bathtub is the last refuge of a fugitive.

Help me think, Tiparillo and Marcus. Which of the swarming devils confronting me must I tackle first? They say it's better to deal with the devil you know rather than the devil you don't know. I wasn't sure about that. I didn't want to deal with any of the devils I knew.

Bam! Bam! Bam!

"Fitz!"

"Set the alarm clock," I told her.

"What?" She was confused.

"One hour! Until then, shut up!"

"Are you crazy?"

"Just about."

The bam-bamming stopped, but I could hear Kit's restless footsteps pacing around and the murmur of the TV. I blotted it out. I was in my underground war room in the London blitz like Winston Churchill, sifting intelligence reports.

What the hell had happened? was the repetitious fugue clanging around inside my head. How had Quishi and Invisible Fist found us on the dark streets of Chinatown? I wasn't going to get out of the tub until I figured it out. I was out of patience with toothpick towers, and so I tried a tic-tac-toe game. Arrange a line of O's or X's, and get some idea of what was going on.

Okay, we walked through Chinatown on their turf, which maybe wasn't too smart. One O. They were waiting for us to come out of the meeting with Charlie Chan. Two O's. There was no way for them to know that we were there. An X.

I tried X's. They knew we were seeking out Detective Chen because it was a Chinese case. One X. They waited for us to come out. Two X's. How the hell could they know when we would be there? We had gone there virtually on the spur of the moment. An O.

Where the hell was Marcus? Didn't they have tic-tac-toe in ancient Rome? For the love of Jupiter, it's like a syllogism! But Marcus had spoken, and the rest was up to me.

I kept coming back to the fact that they were waiting for us. It couldn't have been an accident. It was an ambush. Who would have told them we were there and would be coming out? Had we been followed there? I didn't think so. Charlie Chan blabbed to somebody? No way.

A lacquered, ebony beehive and darting, penetrating eyes skewered me.

Anna Cheong, the yellow pillar!

She had been there with us. One O. She left before we

did. Two O's. She contacted Quishi and Invisible Fist and sent them after us. Three O's!

Madame Cheong! Taylor Lee Trading and Import of Canal Street. The dragon lady who wanted that Phoenix. My head whirled a bit. I had thought that those two Chinese at Elaine's were trying to intercept that delivery to her, to get that medal for themselves from Lee Ying. What if they were working for Madame Cheong?

My tic-tac-toe line crossed the square on a straight diagonal angle. They had to be in on this together. Kit had been right when she instinctively asked if Madame Cheong was a suspect.

Another scenario built itself in my fevered imagination. Madame Cheong is in the Chinese art import business, and what would she love to have more than a priceless Chinese artifact, which Charlie Chan said could be worth millions? Of course, such a national treasure would be unobtainable in the Forbidden City in Beijing, as imprisoned as the Mona Lisa is in the Louvre. And even the Mona Lisa had been stolen one time.

Okay, here's Lee Ying, the art smuggler, telling Madame Cheong he can get her one. Or maybe she sends him after it. In any event, Lee Ying gets a Phoenix and brings it to New York.

There he is with an item worth a fortune. But instead of delivering it to Madame Cheong, he meets Quishi and Invisible Fist at Elaine's. Why? To sell it to them?

My scenario sprang a leak. If Lee Ying, Quishi, and Invisible Fist all worked for Madame Cheong, what was the problem? Was Lee Ying double-crossing her, looking for other buyers? If so, the last people he ought to have tried to sell it to were Madame Cheong's own two murderous henchmen. Why would he go to them, of all people?

There was another crack in my scenario, too. How had that damnable thing gotten into Bobo's hands, or Ellie's, if it in fact did, and left them both dead? There was a third crack, actually. Where *was* the bloody thing?

It wasn't all clear by any means, but my O's and X's converged and pointed at Madame Cheong. I had to start somewhere. I rose out of the tub.

Ideas and plans were chasing themselves around inside as I shaved, went back into the bedroom, and dressed. Kit, in a dark sheath dress clinched with a gold belt and medallion, looked more like her twin than ever. At the table in the kitchen nook, she was crouched over coffee, staring at me warily. I grabbed a mug, poured some coffee, sat across from her, slurped it, and pushed down the button on the alarm clock.

"What were you doing?" she asked, looking concerned.

"When I was a kid, the bathtub was the only place in the house where I could be left alone."

"You scared me. I kept calling you, and when I couldn't reach you, I finally decided to come over here."

"You were right about Anna Cheong. She sent those two after us."

"What?"

"Had to be. They must have followed us and waited outside Giambone's until it was good and dark. When we went for the car, they went for us."

She looked troubled, nodded uncertainly, and stared at me hopefully.

"What are we going to do?"

"I want to talk to Anna."

"Charlie Chan wants us to come in and talk to an assistant district attorney, too."

"Of course." And I had to talk to the paper, too. All the devils I knew were lined up with thumbscrews. But before I met the devils I knew, I had to meet the one I didn't know—Madame Cheong. If I went to the office or to meet an assistant district attorney, I didn't know if I'd ever emerge again.

I walked to the table beside the sofa, shoved the phone jack back into the wall, and a bumblebee chorus immediately sprang into the *1812 Overture. Wraaaaaaannnnnng!*

"Shut up," I snapped, clicked till I got a dial tone, and called Frank the auto insurance guy at Allstate.

"Listen, I had a fender bender, and I need a rental car from Triple A," I told him. "Can you cover that?"

Frank was all cautious concern. "Cover it? What happened? How bad is it? Any injuries?"

"A bump or two," I hedged. "Two flat tires. And, uh . . . maybe somebody should go have a look at it." I dug out the card from the tow-truck driver and told him where the Toyota was.

"Hey, we don't do that," he said. "Get a couple-three estimates, and call the claims adjuster. You want to file a claim and kick up your rate for two flats?"

"There might be a dent in the door."

I called Triple A, and a sympathetic lady there said I could pick up a rental on Second Avenue. I told Kit we had to get going. As we went out, the *1812 Overture* sounded a new salvo of cannons.

We walked toward Second Avenue, Kit a step behind and hesitant. "What are you going to say to her?"

"Why is she trying to murder us!" I blurted.

It was pretty much the thrust of what I wanted to know, although I wasn't really sure how to go about it.

"Maybe we should talk to Detective Chen first," she suggested cautiously.

I had considered that, but felt that he would tell us not to go to Anna's. And I was determined to face down the dragon lady. This damned thing had to be about that Phoenix, Lee Ying, and those two crazed killers. Only one of them was left now, but he was as big as two of them.

The rental car was a maroon Dodge Daytona, a step up from the Toyota. Driving it, I felt quite important, and decided again, as I had many times before, that it was time I got myself a decent set of wheels. The auto rental office was only a block from Second Avenue John's Chevron station, so I stopped there first. I gave him the card from the tow-truck driver—J. T. Rogers, Automotive, Worth Street—and told him that's where the Toyota had been towed in.

"She broke down?" He looked surprised, because he always told me the little Toyota would run forever.

"Fender bender," I said, not wanting to go into it. "Can you go down there and rescue it and tow it in?"

Both hands up before him. "Yes! Don't worry about it. She'll be fixed up right now."

With the Toyota in the hands of my paramedic and headed for intensive care, I aimed the Dodge Daytona downtown again. Kit shifted in her seat and watched me anxiously.

"If she sent them after us, the other one might be around Madame Cheong's place," Kit said softly.

"I know," I admitted. "But if they're after us, it's time we accepted it and went after them!"

"Oh, Fitz!"

Brave words from the souped-up reporter, but I knew it was true. There was no way around it anymore. Detective Chen had said he had nothing on Madame Cheong and could not go after her. Somebody had killed three people, and they had been brazen or desperate enough to pursue us in the shadow of police headquarters. I had to believe they would not stop until they had that medal, or until we solved this puzzle or stopped them. Quishi was still out there. It was Quishi or us. Or Madame Cheong and Quishi or us.

I drove along Canal Street until we spotted Taylor Lee Trading and Import, and then curled around back down through Chatham Square along Park Row to the NYP parking zone behind headquarters.

I stuck a slip of paper from my reporter's notebook under the windshield wiper with the words, "Daily Press Vehicle," and added my NYP plate number. Then we walked up to Canal Street and Taylor Lee Trading and Import.

A bell tinkled over the door as we went in. Inside, the store was two stories high, crammed with Chinese artifacts and gewgaws of every description. Long tables held stone Buddha statues, dragons, lamps, jade beads, fans, bells and chimes, photos and drawings of the Great Wall, and an array of imitation Chinese wands inscribed in vermilion and black.

Along one side rose a wooden staircase, and at the top I saw Madame Cheong. She stepped out of an office, and stood looking down at us.

Kit's hand squeezed mine, and she caught her breath.

Madame Cheong descended down the long staircase, slowly, watching us. She still wore a yellow blouse and the Phoenix pin at her shoulder, but her slacks were black. At the bottom of the steps, she halted and smiled.

"Mr. Fitzgerald. Precious sister. I have been expecting you."

"Oh, you have!" I got out rather truculently.

"We have things to discuss, haven't we?"

She walked to a desk toward the rear, and we followed.

She had seemed tall, but as we moved behind her I realized she was rather petite. When she reached her desk and sat facing us, she seemed tall again. It was the ebony, lacquered beehive hairdo and her manner that made her seem so.

"Now, listen," I told her, "this has gone far enough! You're behind this or mixed up in it. And if you're not, this may be your last chance to help us."

Her face flushed slightly, but she did not lose her composure.

"Mr. Fitzgerald, please, let us understand each other."

"Damned straight!" I was ready to reach across her desk and grab her by the throat.

"I do not understand why you say I am mixed up in something," she said coolly, "unless, of course, you mean that something that was supposed to be delivered to me is a source of confusion."

"That goddamned Phoenix medal or whatever it is! We haven't got it! We don't want it!"

"Here today," she said, "we may be able to talk more freely than in the presence of strangers."

"Strangers? You mean the police?"

"Perhaps, as you say, I can help you. If you help me."

Kit sat forward, "How? My sister was murdered! I'll do anything to help anybody who can tell me who did this."

"That was tragic, precious sister," Madame said gently. "If you could only tell me, did she have the Dowager Phoenix?"

My head turned to fire. "Goddamnit, we don't know anything about it!" I raged. "We want a killer, not that damned thing!"

"Yes. You want something; I want something. Let us help each other. I believe Lee Ying left it with that piano player or your sister."

"Why would he do that?"

"I don't know. Perhaps to hold it for him."

"They didn't even know the man! Why would they hold it for him?"

"Perhaps they didn't know they had it," she considered. "Those two you have mentioned . . . they came back looking for it."

"Wait a minute," I said. "How do you know they came back? The cops don't know who killed Bobo Watson, but you seem to."

"I can only surmise, Mr. Fitzgerald. You say they are still seeking it from you; I can only surmise they sought it from the piano player."

"Yeah, well, I surmise something else! Those two work for you."

There was a flittering of her dark eyes, but she made no response.

"And I think you know what happened up there, but the damned Phoenix got lost in the shuffle somehow. You think

Bobo or Ellie got it, or I did. Well, we didn't, so call off your henchmen."

Madame Cheong tilted her head. "Mr. Fitzgerald, the Phoenix must be found. Finding it may answer many things."

"How?" Kit pleaded.

"Whoever got it perhaps realized its value," she said. "It would be like a winning lottery ticket. Whoever has it now may plan to cash it in."

She was staring curiously at me. "If you know who has it, I would be willing to be generous."

I got up. "You are insane! This thing must be worth a fortune! Who were you going to sell it to—some Hong Kong billionaire?"

For the first time, she got angry. Her eyes narrowed.

"Foolish *waiguoren!* Do you think anyone would sell the Dowager Phoenix?"

That caught me. She didn't want to sell it? Then what was it all about?

"Well then, why do you want it so desperately?"

"There is no way for you to understand the return."

"What?"

"I leave you with this, Mr. Fitzgerald. I will have the Phoenix!"

There was no sense in holding back anything anymore, and I let her have it.

"You sent those two madmen after us!" I accused her. "One of them is in the East River! Do you know that?"

Not a blink. The burning eyes of a fanatic.

I pulled Kit to her feet. It was impossible. Madame Cheong would admit nothing, and I couldn't make her. But certain things were settled now between us. She knew she was my target, and I knew we were hers.

TWENTY-TWO

THE BELL OVER THE FRONT DOOR OF TAYLOR LEE TRADING and Import tinkled as I slammed it behind us, and stalked along Canal Street, leading us to I didn't know where. After a few steps, I realized I was heading toward Elizabeth Street and the Fifth Precinct, and halted. I stood there a moment, Kit beside me, and lit a Tiparillo. My compass spun. I couldn't face Detective Chen or some A.D.A. yet. I knew it was time to face the most urgent devil I know, the Mephistopheles of Forty-second Street.

"I've got to check in at the office," I said.

"Okay. I'm going to see Detective Chen," Kit said, her face set. "I want him to know what she said. She practically admitted she knows those two Chinese men killed my sister!"

I had to agree and wished her good luck with Chen. But I had to get to the office and tell Ironhead what was going on. Kit hurried determinedly across Canal Street, and I walked back down Park Row to the Dodge Daytona. I grabbed the reporter's notebook slip from under the windshield wiper. I couldn't see the words I had written on it because of the parking ticket covering it.

I drove up the FDR Drive to Forty-second Street, and parked in the NYP zone on Fortieth Street. I stuck the note under the windshield again, with the ticket on top of it, and walked up to the *Daily Press*.

As had happened often during the last several days, I had completely lost track of the time. I glanced at the wall of clocks in the *Daily Press* lobby that tells the time in London, Berlin, Tokyo, and Bombay, any of which locations appealed to me at the moment.

It was almost two o'clock. Ironhead would be in full gallop.

I got off the elevator on the seventh floor and walked into the city room, and it was as though I had walked in stark naked. Blipping computer keys fell silent. Everything stopped. A hush fell over the room. Glenn the Switchboard watched me as though I were an alien from the Andromeda Galaxy.

The sensation that something had happened reached Ironhead, who was bent over the city desk, and he looked up. I walked toward him, and he stared dumbly at me as though I were a ghost.

"Fitz?" he said tentatively with what almost appeared to be concern. "Are you all right?"

"I guess so," I managed, surprised and pleased at this warm welcome.

"We didn't know what had happened to you," he said, looking relieved. "The cops said you'd gone home. You weren't there. We checked the hospitals, police precincts, the morgue."

"You thought I was dead?"

"I didn't know what to think! Dubbs called in to say the cops had you, that somebody went off the Brooklyn Bridge! The cops said they'd kicked you loose. We called your place and sent Bobby up there! You scared the bejesus out of us!"

"I'll be damned," I said. It was a pleasant surprise to realize that Ironhead was worried about me.

He got up and leaned toward me, examining my face, which was red and welted like somebody who has gone three rounds with Evander Holyfield.

"Your face looks like hamburger. You sure you're all right?"

"The guy coldcocked me before he went off the bridge."

He reacted to that, all right. "My God! What was that all about?"

"It's complicated," I sighed, and took out a Tiparillo.

"That dick at the Fifth Precinct," he started.

". . . Jimmy Chen . . ."

". . . told us you left there about 3 A.M. What time is it now? Two in the afternoon? Where in the hell have you been? What's this about somebody going off the bridge?" he asked. Having assured himself that I was all right, a note of annoyance crept into his voice.

"I can't get free of the damn thing, Ironhead."

He relit his slime stick. "Why do I have to find out these things on television? Who is this Chinese man you dumped into the East River? Do I have a reporter or a goddamn one-man crime wave!"

"Where'd you hear all that?"

"Where? *Where?* On TV! From the cops! From the D.A.'s office! From every-fucking-body but my own reporter! What the hell happened?"

"I told you some Chinese thugs were after me!"

Ironhead's head shook like a wooden doll's, his eyes bouncing around.

"*Chinese* . . ." The word apparently was incomprehensible to him. He addressed the big, four-sided clock on the ceiling over his head for some reason. "I send him on a story in Manhattan, and he ends up being chased by Chinese guys!"

I noticed some of the reporters were edging around listening to this, apparently curious or fascinated. Fitz was turning on Ironhead's spit, and it seemed to be the worst jumble yet.

Ironhead peered intently at me. "Is there anything else I should know? Did anything else happen? Are there any more bodies out there, any Japanese or Mongolians?"

"No. Why would you think that?"

"Why? Because you disappeared for twelve hours! When you're out of my sight, who knows what can happen!"

"No. I was home."

"You weren't home! Nobody answered!"

"I had to think," I explained. "I was in the tub."

Ironhead blinked, his head jerked, and he stared at me from an angle. "You were what?"

"I had to figure out what was going on. Nobody would let me think."

I was confronted by a blast furnace. Ironhead in a florid-faced, sputtering rage. He popped to his feet, leaning on the desktop, his head leaning toward me like a frothing hyena.

"You've got dead Chinamen in the river, cops grilling you, us ringing your phone off the hook, Bobby driving up there pounding on your door and checking hospitals, and you're in the goddamn bathtub playing with yourself!?"

So there had been a thumping that had only distantly penetrated my sunken submarine: Bobby, the head copy boy, ringing my bell and banging on my apartment door. I had slept through it, and would have been of no use if he had awakened me. I could only thank my automatic reflexes that had caused me to unplug the phone.

"Is this more about the Watson murder?" he asked, frowning.

"Yeah." I sat down and explained the whole thing as best I could.

"I finally figured out that this Madame Cheong is behind it."

"*Who . . .* ?"

"A Canal street art dealer. She'll do anything to get that Phoenix medal."

"Madame Cheong? You threw a woman off the bridge?"

"No, no. That was Invisible Fist. Anna's too damned smart to have anything connected to her."

The city editor's rage spiraled down into something approaching helpless confusion. His head wagged like Inspector Clouseau's Parisian Prefect of Police. I hurried on to clarify things.

"The thing is, I have to talk to the D.A.'s office, and I didn't want to until I got instructions from you."

"From me? *From me?* When the hell have you ever listened to instructions from me? Only after you've disgraced my newspaper and didn't even phone in a goddamn story when you were in the middle of it."

"There were cops all over me. It was after three in the morning," I pleaded.

A gray-headed hulk shoved through the ring of eavesdropping reporters and stuck his face against me.

"There you are!"

"Corcoran, look, I'd better warn you. The D.A.'s office might call you."

"Oh, they might, huh? You think they might call me?" The flustered newspaper lawyer flapped a sheaf of telephone message slips at me.

"They were chasing us," I launched in, "and pushed us onto the bridge, and then Invisible Fist came at me. All I did was stand up, and he went over the railing!"

My colleagues hovering around buzzed at that.

"Jeez, Fitz, you really offed a guy?" Bike asked, impressed.

"I didn't . . . it was an accident," I protested. "Anyway, I have to call that detective. Corcoran, I guess you'd better help me out on this."

"A murder suspect!" Corcoran breathed. "For the first time in the history of the *Daily Press,* a reporter has this newspaper in a homicide case!"

"Wait a minute," Ironhead snapped. "He says it was an accident!"

He wasn't pleased with me, but you had to give Ironhead credit for standing up for his staff when things got sticky.

"He may be a pain in the grumper," he flung at Corcoran, "but he's no murderer."

Then, Ironhead turned to me. "What are you doing being chased by Chinese?"

"They're behind these murders," I said.

"You never gave me a statement for those other detectives, either," Corcoran complained. "Now the D.A.'s office wants another statement?"

"I found that body, and it hasn't stopped since," I muttered defensively.

"Which you were not supposed to do!" Corcoran complained.

What could I say to that?

"All right, never mind that crap," Ironhead snapped. Then, looking at me, he asked, "Can you write the story?"

"I don't see how," I had to say. "I'm part of the damned thing."

"Yeah, well that's great. One of our own reporters in the middle of the damned thing, and he can't write it. All right, never mind. We've pretty much got it. This thing keeps getting in the way of that ship story. How are you doing on that?"

The ships? Various half-forgotten details swirled up and around my head. What day was it? What time was it?

"Did you ever get squared away with Pippy?" he asked then.

Pippy!

"Oh, my God!"

"What?"

"I've got to run!" I was supposed to be at the New York Yacht Club for Pippy's lunch at one-thirty.

"Go on, get the hell out of here!"

I bolted for the door, glancing back at the four-sided clock hanging from the ceiling. It was two-thirty.

TWENTY-THREE

WHERE THE HELL WAS THE NEW YORK YACHT CLUB? RUNning across Forty-second Street, I tried to remember. I recalled noticing it one time when covering a hearing at the Association of the Bar of the City of New York. It was right across the street from it, too close to drive to, and you can't park there anyway.

I hurried across Third Avenue, then Lexington, past Grand Central Terminal, and then uptown on Vanderbilt, over to Fifth Avenue. It's one of those annoying things in the news business—you're sent out on a story on the spur of the moment when you don't know where you're going. Reporters are supposed to know where everything is even if they've never been there before.

I remember the day I walked into the city room and Ironhead yelled, "Fitz, don't take your coat off! Go with Danny!"

There went Danny Murphy the photographer, out the door and me after him, sprinting to a *Daily Press* radio car in front. We were whisked to the East Side heliport a few blocks away near the Queensboro Bridge, and Danny filled me in on the way.

"A bank robbery in Brooklyn," he said. "We're gonna chase them in a chopper!"

Into a helicopter we climbed and off we fluttered, over the East River, over Brooklyn, to zoom along over the roof of the bank robbers' getaway car speeding through Brooklyn streets. We were going to scoop everybody. The desk was monitoring the police radio and giving directions to the chopper pilot.

"They're passing St. Matthew's Church!"

We scanned the streets below us. St. Matthew's? Brooklyn is not called The Borough of Churches for nothing. There are churches on every corner—St. Matthew's, St. Cecilia's, St. Everywhere's—and we had no street map nor any way to read one if we had. Whether the cops caught them I don't remember, but we never did.

When you're sent on an assignment, you go, and you figure it out on the way. A reporter's supposed to know where everything is, even if he's just moved to New York from Knoxville, Tennessee.

Anyway, I angled up Fifth Avenue to Forty-fourth Street and ran along, and there it was. The New York Yacht Club is a wonder. The front of it has all these sculptured concrete billows up and down the sides, and the entrance looks like the stern of HMS *Bounty.* I burst in through the doors into the lobby. Inside, there were colorful portraits of past commodores on the walls; a glass case that held the America Cup when the Australians didn't have possession; oak trim; deep carpet; and a uniformed flunky guarding entry.

"Uh, Pippy McFadden!" I said.

"You're not Pippy McFadden."

"Fitzgerald, *Daily Press!* I'm having lunch with him."

His guard-dog demeanor changed in a flash at the magic name of Pippy, and he waved me in.

"In the bar, I believe."

I swept along the carpet past more commodores and into the bar, which was another wonder; it was all traditional old New York brass and oak.

"Pippy?"

He was standing at the bar in a navy blue captain's blazer with a double row of brass buttons and white duck trousers. He shot a look at me.

"Fitzgerald?" He frowned.

"Yes, sir. I, uh, got caught in traffic."

"Traffic?"

He glanced at his watch. "The lunch is over! Didn't I tell you one-thirty?"

"See, a hot story broke, and . . ."

"But aren't you covering America Sail?"

"Yes! Of course. I'm signed on for the sail-through."

Pippy glanced at the guy standing beside him, another yachtsman by the cut of him, and then back at me.

"Well, I told all the guys you'd be here, and would give us all the skinny. I'm going to have to have a word with Arnold!"

Oh, boy!

"It wasn't his fault ! It's a big *Daily Press* scoop!"

Pippy sipped a dark, smoky drink, and made a face.

"You want something?" he asked grumpily.

"Maybe a Rheingold."

"A what?"

"Anything. Budweiser."

He waved at the bartender. Getting me a drink helped quiet his annoyance. I'll say this for the rich and privileged: they don't easily lose their cool or forget their manners.

"This is Stan, our commodore," Pippy said then.

"Yes, yes. Welcome aboard," said Commodore Stan, sticking out a big paw and crushing my hand. These yachtsmen might look a little goofy in their shipboard regalia, but some of them have hands like seamen from yanking ropes.

"We'd like you to run up our flag," said Pippy, shoving a cardboard box at me on the bar. "And I've had one made for the *Daily Press*, too."

"Hey, great."

He opened the box and held it up for me. A blue triangle with a yellow border and the proud words, "America Sail—New York *Daily Press*."

"Smart looking!" I complimented him.

"She ought to whip in the breeze quite nicely," he smiled,

mollified. "Our members will be on their vessels in the harbor and along the river as you go by. Pete's going to have some photogs stationed along the way."

I sipped my Budweiser. Ironhead was right. Pippy was organizing a regular maritime gala.

"Got to run along," Commodore Stan said then, and offered his big paw again. I avoided it with a brush of my hand, and he went out jovially.

Pippy's face went stern. "You embarrassed me here today, Fitzgerald! What the hell do you mean, getting here an hour late! More than an hour!"

"Sorry. It was unavoidable, and I know you put the paper first."

"Yes . . . well . . . !"

"I know we're going to play the sail-through big," I added hopefully.

"All right, then. What ship will carry our flag?"

"I thought the *Nina,* Columbus's best sailer."

He nodded knowingly. "The *Nina.* Okay. The *Santa Maria,* you know, wasn't much of a ship. That's not bad, Fitz. Are you a yachtsman, by any chance?"

Don't you love it when you meet somebody like Pippy, who owns a gleaming, sleek white yacht worth who-knows-how-much, and he casually asks about yours?

"Oh, no! I'm afraid we landlubbers have to leave that to commodores like you."

Pippy beamed a little, smiling modestly.

"Oh, I'm not the commodore yet," he said shyly. "But, you never know."

It occurred to me with a tinge of fright that he was counting on my coverage of America Sail to help him win that commodore's cap.

I finished the Budweiser and told him I had to get moving. He surely understood that busy New York *Daily Press* reporters couldn't hang out in the middle of the afternoon.

"Yes, sure, you run along. We'll be posted along the Parade of Ships route. Give this your best effort, Fitz. Ironhead tells me you're one of his best writers, and I'm counting on you for a good yarn."

"Sure."

I left.

Walking back from the yacht club, I felt myself pondering a host of imponderables. I found myself on Vanderbilt at the side door of Grand Central Terminal, and I went in and strolled into the Oyster Bar. I felt the need for another Budweiser and some time alone to figure out where I was.

In the soup, all right.

On Sunday I would ride the *Nina* on the America Sail up the Hudson. Until then, I could try to get to the bottom of things. I sat at the bar and took a sip. The story about Invisible Fist going off the Brooklyn Bridge, I felt, was going to rattle some cages. The damned story and the murders were about to blow up.

Madame Cheong's burning eyes glaring at me.

Quishi's taillights disappearing into Brooklyn.

An assistant D.A. calling Corcoran, bugging Detective Chen.

And if they found the body in the river?

I lit a Tiparillo. At least you could still light up in a bar. I was experiencing the sensation that I had to do something, but didn't know what.

The Chinese puzzle lacerated my nerves. That frustrating Dowager Phoenix floated before me. The image of Anna Cheong's sly puss made my brain simmer, but I was tantalized by what she had said, that finding the Phoenix might produce the answer to all of this. Where the hell was it? Marcus Aurelius advises one to not be "whirled around" by events. Okay, so stop whirling, and examine this situation.

The last place where anybody seemed sure the medal had been was with Lee Ying. I'm back at Elaine's on the Upper East Side again. Lee Ying is met there by the two Chinese butchers, who I now believed had been sent there by Madame Cheong.

I pondered that imponderable. Lee Ying apparently was trying to find other buyers for the medal, but he met with Madame Cheong's own two henchmen? Why? It was absurd. The only possibility had to be that he didn't know they were sent by her.

So there's Lee Ying with the Phoenix, ready to make the score of his life, letting the word out to Chinese art buyers. Madame Cheong hears of it through her contacts, and tells Quishi and Invisible Fist to get in touch with Lee Ying and arrange a meeting. Lee Ying picks an out-of-the-way place, as far as Chinatown is concerned, Elaine's, but well-known and easily found.

Does that fly? Lee Ying thinks he's meeting with possible buyers at Elaine's? But instead he meets Anna's boys, and they aren't there to buy it but to demand it from him. He balks. They shove him around, get kicked out, and hustle him away.

That happened on a Friday night. They drag Lee Ying away and use their stiletto to inflict their thousand cuts, and he is forced to tell them what they want to know. Either they went too far in their questioning and he died of his wounds, or they killed him afterward and dumped him into the river.

Then they come back on Saturday night and wait outside Elaine's for Bobo. They must have felt they'd be unwelcome inside. It always led back to that. Lee Ying must have told them he gave that elusive medal to Bobo at Elaine's.

I sipped the beer and puffed the Tiparillo. They cut Bobo's clothes to shreds, left him for dead, and then ransacked his apartment up in Inwood, still looking for the medal. Then they go to Ellie's apartment to search some more, and they murder her, too. And come back later to look again.

I hadn't been back to Ellie's apartment, which was now a

crime scene and sealed off by the police. I hadn't gone up to Bobo's and searched his place, either.

Was it possible that Bobo knew what he had? Or that Ellie did? Could they have heard the Chinese talking about it? I couldn't figure that one.

I got on the pay phone in the Oyster Bar and called Jimmy Chen.

"Fitz? Where are you? Kathleen was here."

"I know. What do you think about what she told you?"

"What do I *think? What do I think?"* He sounded annoyed. "I can't believe you went to see Anna. You're a damned witness! What the hell's the matter with you?"

"Jimmy," I said, "people keep shoving me across bridges, and they work for Anna Cheong. You won't go after her! What am I supposed to do?"

"You don't know they work for her!"

"The hell I don't! Maybe the NYPD can't say so officially, but I can't wait for you to make a case. By then I'll be in the river, too."

"Goddamnit, I've got nothing on her!"

"Or Quishi either, I guess?"

"Only your say-so. I'd bring him in if I knew where to find him."

"Watch Kit and me! He won't be far behind!"

"Fitzgerald, you're asking for trouble! Trudy Oppitz is looking for you."

"Who?"

"The A.D.A. assigned to interview you."

Terrific! They want to find me! How about finding Quishi and hauling in the dragon lady?

"How about the *Daily Press* springing for another meal?"

"What?"

"I want to talk to you before I talk to her."

A pause. "Fitz, I'm NYPD assigned to investigate this."

"Listen," I said, "have you checked around uptown?"

"Well, sure. Some. Over by the river, trying to figure

where Lee Ying went into the water. Not much help."

"I mean at Elaine's."

"Not my turf, Fitz. That's Hanley and Jacobs's scene."

"Lee Ying was there, too."

"What are you driving at?"

I told him that as far as I could see, it was all one case and it started at Elaine's. Wouldn't it make sense to go back there and try to figure out what happened to that Phoenix that everybody was chasing?

"You said you always like to know the motive. You might find it worthwhile to drop in there."

"When?"

"Tonight."

Another pause. "The *Daily Press* still goes? This is not a request. I cannot accept gratuities."

"If Trudy asks, you can say I'll be in eventually."

"How can I tell her anything when I haven't heard from you?"

"Okay."

I walked back across Forty-second Street and down to the Dodge Daytona in the NYP parking zone on Fortieth Street. Putting that earlier parking ticket under the windshield wiper hadn't worked, because it obscured my note that this was a temporary *Daily Press* vehicle. I had a second parking ticket on top of the first one.

I headed up to Forty-second Street, across to the West Side, and then uptown onto Riverside Drive and to Ellie's apartment building above 113th Street. I had the key to her apartment from Kit, and didn't have to get buzzed in this time. I took a look around on the outside, in case Quishi might be staked out again.

I rode on the bumping elevator to the sixth floor, and I let myself into 6-B, ducking under the yellow tape that said CRIME SCENE: DO NOT CROSS. I was in too deep to worry about such details.

Inside, the place was still as before, torn up and ransacked. But I went over it again, checking behind picture frames, removing Bobo's smiling photo from the bulletin board, even checking the toilet tank where people have hidden things ever since they saw Al Pacino take a gun from one in *The Godfather*.

No luck. Just a bigger mess than before.

I came back out of the apartment and was locking the door when along came Syrian Jack hurrying along the hall, his feathers ruffled.

"Why do you come here? No more bodies, no more burglars!"

"I lost my watch."

I got on the elevator just as Missus Hooper's door opened and her head stuck out.

I headed around onto Broadway and north again, up past the George Washington Bridge, past Dykman Street, beyond Baker Field where the Columbia Lions play football, and all the way to Inwood on the upper tip of Manhattan. Bobo's place wasn't an apartment but a basement room in a two-story rooming house on 222nd Street off Broadway. I found his name written in pencil with the word "back" beside it, and went around the back and down some stairs.

No crime-scene tape this time, but no sign of life. I tried the door without success. Nobody was around, so I took off my jacket, wrapped it around my hand, and broke a window by the door. I let myself in and searched the place, checking inside Bobo's piano, the piano bench, a book of music crammed with extra sheet music, the cupboard, his bedroom, and under the mattress.

After that, I went back out to the Dodge Daytona and headed back downtown. I don't think I had expected to find the medal at Ellie's or Bobo's, and both places had been pretty well gone over, but I guess I wanted to satisfy myself that they hadn't taken it.

I hadn't wanted to think that either of them were thieves

and felt a little sheepish. But I wanted to make sure, or as sure as I could.

In the business, we say, "touch all bases." I felt I had, but I still didn't have the damned medal.

TWENTY-FOUR

I DROVE BACK DOWNTOWN, AND WHEN I GOT TO MY PLACE, there she was, sitting outside on the stoop.

"Well," I said, "hello." She looked pretty shaken. "What's the matter?"

"Fitz, I'm sorry to bother you again, but . . ."

"What happened?"

"I think they know where I'm staying."

"Anna and Quishi?"

She nodded, her eyes blinking, trembly. "I think she called the hotel."

"Come on." I took her inside and up to my apartment. She wasn't in much condition to talk sitting there on the stoop in her condition.

She sat at the kitchen-nook table and stared at me.

"Did you see Quishi?"

She quickly shook her head no. "After I left Detective Chen I called the Edison to see if there were any messages. My Mom had called from home. But then the hotel told me there had been another call from somebody but she left no message."

"You don't know who it was?"

She frowned. "Fitz, the only people who would call me at the hotel, who even know I'm in New York, would be my folks or one of the detectives. Or you, or maybe Erik. Any of them would leave a message."

"Yeah, probably."

Kit didn't like it, she told me, and was getting as jittery as I was. But that wasn't all. She had then called back her mother in Grand Rapids.

"Mom told me a policewoman had called out there trying to locate me."

"A policewoman?"

"Because of the accident on the bridge, the woman said. She needed to reach me, and my mom told her I was at the Edison."

I didn't like it either. A policewoman? There was no policewoman on the case as far as I knew, unless it was Trudy Oppitz, the A.D.A. And she would have both of our addresses from the statement we had given to Charlie Chan.

"I just got a funny feeling, you know," she said. "I didn't want to go to the hotel and find him waiting for me." She looked away and then back. "I'm probably imagining things."

"You did the right thing," I told her. "Until we find out if that really was a policewoman, you'd better stay away from the hotel."

"I keep wondering if it was Anna," she said.

I had the same suspicion. Quishi had already found Ellie's apartment and Bobo's, I reminded myself. Kathleen would be the obvious next target.

"I shouldn't be bothering you with this," she murmured, "but I didn't know what to do."

I couldn't blame her. Who else did she know here except the cops, who couldn't baby-sit her, or Erik, who was in The Tombs?

"How did it go with Detective Chen?" I asked her.

She made a face. "Hmmp! Fitz, he acted like we're the criminals, bothering people! They're bothering us! I told him Anna practically admitted everything, but he said he has to follow procedure and can't act on somebody's guesswork or suspicion."

"Yeah. I talked to him, too."

"Did you get anywhere?"

"He's going to meet me tonight at Elaine's—unofficially."

"He is? I'm going, too! I want to see that place. Maybe we can figure out what happened there."

"That's what I'm hoping. We know a little more now."

"You think it's still there?"

"I don't know, but maybe if we could find it—if the cops had it and announced they had it—maybe those crazies would leave us alone."

I sank down onto the sofa, feeling rather beat, and lit a Tiparillo. We had a little time before we went to Elaine's.

She looked around my apartment with curiosity. "Have you eaten?"

"No." We hadn't seemed to have fit that into our schedule much since we'd met.

"Shall I make us something?"

"I don't know if there's much here," I managed.

"Well, let's have a look." She picked up the tall stack of *Daily Presses, Timeses*, and *Posts* on the table and put them on the floor beside the sofa. Then she noticed the books lying around, a shirt tied around some laundry on a chair, a tie hanging from a doorknob.

"Maid's day off?"

She bustled to the kitchen nook and got out the frying pan, which she gave a quick clean. Bacon was soon crackling.

"You're pretty low on supplies."

She was being kind. There was virtually nothing in the fridge except the bacon, an almost empty milk carton, the butt-end of a roll of braunschweiger, half a jar of Gulden's mustard, a jar of pickle juice with a couple of pickles, a tomato, and a few shreds of lettuce. The pantry boasted half a loaf of Levy's Jewish rye, a box of Ritz crackers, some cans of Campbell's bean-and-bacon soup, and some pancake mix.

"Come and sit and talk to me," Kit said.

I moved to the kitchen table and watched her busily making bacon, lettuce, and tomato sandwiches out of those few leftovers.

"I talked to Mr. Perry, and he said don't worry about hurrying back."

Mr. Perry, she explained, was her boss at American Seating Company, which manufactured and installed seats for sports stadiums and arenas.

"What do you do?"

"Executive secretary," she said cheerily. "I'm sort of his left-hand man. I'm in line for the color office, though."

"Color office?"

"That's what they call it. Creating and working out the color schemes for the seats."

"Aren't they all standard?"

"*What?* They used to be, in the old parks, green or blue. But now—this one owner let his wife pick the colors. Listen, when you're dealing with fifty thousand seats and they had all better match and look right and . . . it's a big operation."

I saw from the way she dressed that she had an eye for color, all right. And style, too. It was the first time we had actually had a chance to talk, and the first time she was able to mention Eleanor without crying. They had been inseparable in their teens, paraded as a matched set, twin cheerleaders at Mackinack High, pert, pretty, and smart.

"Nobody really knew us," she sighed. "We were decoration. The Cunningham twins. She was One, and I was Two.

She stared off into space, probably picturing herself and One cheering at a football game. After high school, they had gone separate ways, she said. She had attended the University of Michigan at Ann Arbor, while Ellie went to Indiana University at Bloomington. They hadn't wanted to be Siamese twins forever.

"Ellie was all for New York," she said.

"Not you?"

"Well. There was Greg."

In fact, there still was Greg, it turned out, a salesman at American Seating. They were pretty much an item in Grand Rapids, but somehow had not yet gotten engaged. It seemed he was waiting for that necessary promotion to vice president.

"I don't know. He's very nice."

Poor Greg, I thought. She didn't know? Very nice? He certainly hadn't set her head on fire.

The toasted sandwiches appeared, cut in triangles and on plates on the table. Kit sat down across from me.

"I called him. He said don't worry, either."

"Is he coming out here?"

"He's working on a stadium project and had to go to Florida. It's a big chance for him."

I munched and let that pass.

"It's been pretty wild here," she said, her face alive, keyed up. "You never stop! I keep wondering what it would be like to live here. I rode the subway today. They're really great."

What a charming, open person. Full of enthusiasm, eager to help; she certainly must be an enterprising and valuable left-hand man to Perry the seating exec.

She ate and watched me. "Fitz, I hope I haven't caused you too much trouble. I know I have, though. I couldn't help it!"

"I know you couldn't."

"You've been really wonderful." Her face went impish. "How come some smart New York woman hasn't hooked you?"

I had to smile at that. "Well, it almost happened."

I could have gone on to say that the job seemed to get in the way—either mine or Audie's.

"I'll bet you would have been here."

"What?"

"But I know that promotion is important."

I thought Greg the very nice would-be V.P. was going to find a different Kit when she got back to Grand Rapids.

I drove us up Third Avenue and around onto Second Avenue at Eighty-eighth past the yellow ELAINE'S sign out front. I found a parking spot on Eighty-eighth, and we walked across to the café.

Duffy was behind the bar and immediately put up a Harp for me. Then he froze and his face seized. I had forgotten that he had never met Kit, and here was Ellie back from the dead in front of him.

He caught himself quickly, though, and put out his hand. "Kathleen?"

"Hi! You must be the famous Duffy."

The big bartender blushed and smiled. "What'll it be? Nice to have you here."

He served her a scotch and water, and she looked around Elaine's curiously, spotting the piano across from the bar.

"That's where Ellie stood, by the piano?" she asked softly.

As with Bobo, the mention of Ellie's name stopped our mouths for a moment.

"Anything on the . . . situation?" Duffy asked, glancing at Kit.

I shook my head, not wanting to go into it.

"Can we look through his piano?"

Duffy shrugged. "I guess so. What are you looking for? We've got a new guy now. I don't know if anything of Bobo's is still in the bench."

"Have you got his stuff?"

Duffy thought so, but Ellie had taken a lot of his music for the funeral service. We walked over and sat at the little table by the front window, near the piano—Ellie's table. Kit stared around with interest.

"Some place! Doesn't Woody Allen come here?"

"And the world."

"You used to hang out here?" She was impressed.

"Only late, last call. After finishing the night trick sometimes. That's how we met Bobo and Ellie."

She scrunched up her nose. "Bobo. What a name."

Duffy brought a paper bag with Bobo's things, but there was nothing much in it. More sheet music, a daybook, two bow-ties, some pencils and pens, a few scraps of paper with notes on them. Nothing much of Bobo was left. It was like looking over dog tags.

I got up and walked to the piano, Kit following me. We opened the front and the top and looked inside. Nothing but piano keys.

The place began to fill up. Kit watched each new arrival with lively interest, nudging me and hissing, "Who's that?"

I pointed out the writer of "Law and Order," an actress from "One Life to Live," an independent film producer from London, a director from "the coast," and columnists and editors from *Harper's* and Sid Zion from the *Daily News*. The original name of the movie *Casablanca* was "Everybody Goes to Rick's." In New York among the literary and show biz glitterati, you could say everybody goes to Elaine's.

"Do you know all of them?" she asked.

"Not all of them."

This was a dodge. Of course I didn't know all of them, or even many of them, and those I knew, I knew only in passing. People are that way about New York reporters; they think you know everybody. But an obscure general-assignment reporter can be a very small fish in the big pond of New York. Bruce and I had been last-call guys, relative nobodies in this fast-track oasis. I barely knew the hotshot columnists on my own paper.

And then Charlie Chan walked in wearing his brown-striped seersucker suit. He glanced around, came to our table, and sat down.

"Just happened to be in the neighborhood," he smiled.

"Any arrests yet?" Kit jumped right in, leaning forward.

Detective Chen looked away, annoyed. You'd think a detective would get used to being always badgered, but I guess they don't.

"Who do you want me to arrest?"

"Madame Cheong!"

"On what charge?"

"Quishi!" I suggested.

"Sure. Where is he? And how do you know that skel who chased you is Quishi off the *Neptune Jade* anyway?"

"Who else? He worked for Anna."

"I don't know that, either!"

"But it's obvious!" Kit complained.

Detective Chen ordered a Pepsi, and sighed. "Everything's obvious to you, and I'm not saying you're wrong. But there's nothing on Anna Cheong."

"She was working with Lee Ying! She said so!" I explained.

"So?"

"He's dead!"

"So? Ordering a delivery isn't murder just because her delivery boy gets killed. I can't put Quishi, if it's him, or the dead one with her. She's an art dealer doing business."

"I'll flush her out, by God!" I simmered.

"Oh, yeah? How?"

"By finding that Dowager Phoenix! If I can get my hands on that, she'll crack. She'll give up her pals quick enough then."

Detective Chen's eyes swept the café.

"You think the Phoenix is here someplace?" he asked.

"It was here at one time, that's all I know."

We had a couple more drinks. Jimmy Chen stuck with Pepsi, apparently because he was on duty or didn't want to drink in front of a reporter. He was getting up to leave when the new guy strolled to the piano and sat down.

Detective Chen sat down again.

I sensed we were both thinking the same thing. We were sitting where Ellie had sat. The piano was where Bobo had played. The game board was set up before us.

The piano player, a jovial, chubby fellow in a jacket, sat down on the bench, nodded to us, and plinked on the keys, warming up. Right away, I didn't like him. I resented his presence in Bobo's space. All right, so it was unfair and unreasonable, but there you are.

I remembered Bobo and Ellie one late night sitting at the piano and playing together. I didn't realize at the time that she was an educated pianist. Bobo had called me and Bruce over to the piano, and he looked up at us shyly and brightly and mysteriously.

"Catch this," Bobo smiled, and played a song he had written for Ellie, "You Turned My Life Around." It was lovely. Ellie helped him play it, and she blushed when he sang the words in his croaky, captivating Hoagy voice.

"You turned my life around, I didn't know it,

You turned my life around, I was below it . . ."

Later I found out that Ellie had helped with the arrangement, put it into professional format, and sent it to a music publisher.

One of the waiters came in from the back room and put a large brandy snifter—the tip bowl—on top of the piano.

Detective Chen and I got up, both with the same idea, and without saying a word to each other, we stood in front of the piano, facing each other. The big glass tip bowl on the piano top was beside us, between us.

"Is this where they were when they were shoving each other?" he asked.

"I think that's what Duffy said."

The piano player kept plinking, glancing up at us, and smiling genially, as though telling us he'd be playing in a minute.

Detective Chen put his hands on the lapels of my jacket, and made swaying motions, as though we were shoving each other. I feigned a slow waving chop of my hand toward the tip bowl, but didn't touch it. We weaved around in a sort of slow-motion dance.

The tip bowl.

TWENTY-FIVE

WE SAT AT THE TABLE AND STARED AT EACH OTHER.

"What?" Kit was looking back and forth at us.

"If he was standing by the piano, between them," Chen considered. "And the tip bowl was next to him . . ."

"He had to ditch the medal somewhere," I added. "He could come back later and retrieve it."

I tried to envision the scene. There's Lee Ying being crowded by the two killers, with no place to run. What if he dropped the Dowager Phoenix into the tip bowl?

"Are there usually coins in the tip bowl?" Chen asked.

My vision of the scene blurred. No, not at Elaine's. Maybe not anywhere in New York anymore. Singles, fives, tens, an occasional twenty, but I had never seen any coins.

"Maybe it nestled among the bills?" I suggested.

"Maybe," he said. "But it might have clinked, or slid down to the bottom. They could have seen it."

"Maybe not if the tip bowl was knocked off the piano and everything spilled onto Bobo and the floor," I suggested.

"Is that what happened?" Kit asked.

I got up and asked Chen to come to the end of the bar, near the front window. Kit followed, and we sat in the corner. I waved Duffy over and ordered another round.

"This is Detective Chen, Fifth Precinct," I told Duffy. "Tell him about the night you eighty-sixed the Chinese."

Duffy ran through it for him.

"So they struggled right in front of the piano?" Detective Chen asked.

"Yeah."

"When they knocked their drinks off the piano, did they knock the tip bowl off, too?" I asked him.

"Sure. Bobo and Ellie crawled around on the floor gathering up all the money," he said.

She would, I thought. It was her hope chest.

Jimmy and I exchanged glances.

"You think he had the Phoenix in his hand and dropped it into the tip bowl?" Kit asked excitedly.

"Could be," said Chen, giving his usual cautious response.

"Bobo or Ellie could have picked it up?" Kit said faintly. "Bobo really had it?"

"Kit," I said, "it was Ellie who kept the tip money."

"Oh my God!"

We looked at each other and sipped our drinks. The Chinese puzzle started to fit together. Quishi and Invisible Fist hustle Lee Ying away and force him to tell them where it is. He finally is persuaded to say he dropped it into Bobo's tip bowl. It must have been too late for them to come back that night. Elaine's would have been closed. They would have to return on Saturday night and wait for Bobo.

"I believe they grabbed Mr. Watson when he left early Sunday," said Chen.

My flesh crawled as I imagined the scene. They follow Bobo to his car, parked on the dark deserted street, grab him, and demand he hand over the Phoenix. If he had it or knew where it was, he would certainly have been forced to tell them. He met their stiletto, bewildered, either unable to tell them or forced to say that Ellie must have it. They must have gotten his I.D. and his keys and gone up to Inwood to ransack his basement room.

"So then they went after Ellie?" Kit shuddered, her face red.

"You must remember, Miss Cunningham," Chen said gently. "The tip bowl went onto the floor, and your sister helped Mr. Watson gather up the money."

I asked Duffy if he thought the two Chinese had seen Ellie on the floor gathering up the money.

"They could have," Duffy said.

"Listen," I said, getting worked up, "this shows our innocent Madame Cheong had at least some guilty knowledge. She knew what had happened up here with Quishi and Invisible Fist!"

"That's a reach, Fitz."

"Okay, I'm reaching."

"Who did you say?" Jimmy asked, puzzled. "Invisible Fist?"

"The short one. That's what I called him. I don't know his name, but his fists came from nowhere."

"We checked some more on that. The other one off the *Neptune Jade* was Yuan Zhang."

"By the way, have they found him yet?" I asked, not really wanting to know. He shook his head no.

Kit was keyed up. "You mean to tell me this is the first time you've figured this out?" she challenged Detective Chen.

Jimmy leaned back on his bar stool, and his face went flat.

"Miss Cunningham, please remember this is not my precinct, not my case."

"You're all cops!"

"I must work with Hanley and Jacobs. Lee Ying's murder is my case, not the one up here. Yes, we work together, but . . ."

"You've got to arrest Madame Cheong and bring in that other one!" she insisted.

His almond eyes got black. "We are doing everything we can."

I could understand Kit's frustration. It drives people crazy when they think they know what happened but the police, forced to follow police department procedure, have to make a case.

"What do we do now?" I asked carefully.

Not carefully enough, though.

"Get yourself to the D.A.'s office and unload to Oppitz," he said sternly. "This is police work. I am here tonight, shall we say, unofficially, but I warn you that any more interference is going to be trouble."

"Interference?" Kit asked.

"Yes, ma'am. I don't think that you realize the danger you are putting yourself into."

"The bastard is after me," I protested, "so I'm going after him!"

"You will do nothing of the sort!" He glared at me. "You want me to take you in?"

"We're not the criminals!" Kit exclaimed. "Where are Hanley and Jacobs, anyway? Do they know all this? I want you to tell them about this!"

Detective Chen stood up, and he wasn't inscrutable this time.

"I came up here as a favor to Fitzgerald here," he said angrily. "This is not my turf! By rights, I should run him in!"

I understood Chen's dilemma. He was in Hanley and Jacobs's precinct up here, meddling in their case. They might not be pleased to find out he had not gone through channels. Detectives can be territorial, too.

"I don't care whose turf it is!" Kit complained. "I want whoever killed my sister!"

Chen's only reaction was to stiffen.

"I have to go. This was a mistake! Trying to cooperate with some people hangs your ass out! Fitzgerald, you know better than this even if she doesn't! Now, I'm telling you, and this is official: get yourself down to the D.A.'s office and unload!"

"But, Jimmy, listen . . ."

"Detective Chen!"

Oh boy! We had rubbed him the wrong way.

"I can't be put in the deep freeze now, when we're really going on this."

I thought he was going to ignite.

"Going on this? Didn't I just tell you to stop interfering? I let you go home! I held off on a charge! I told that A.D.A., Oppitz, that you were coming in! Are you trying to make me look like a horse's ass?" He was steaming.

"We're not interfering; we're helping," Kit wheedled.

"We don't want your help!"

"But our story has to shake them up!" I said.

He blinked. "What story?"

"Didn't Dubbs Brewer call you about the bridge thing?"

He relaxed a little. "Yeah, I gave him what I could without jeopardizing the case. But you didn't write anything, did you? You have to see that A.D.A."

"I will. How much did you tell Dubbs? Did you mention Madame Cheong and Quishi?"

I had to wonder at the preposterous situation. Here I was, a reporter caught inside a story I couldn't write, asking a cop what another reporter was allowed to write about us. That's what comes from finding a body.

And never mind what I knew; Detective Chen was giving out the story, and he hadn't mentioned Madame Cheong or Quishi or the Phoenix. As far as he and the NYPD were concerned, this was officially an investigation by Detective Chen of an attack by unidentified assailants on a *Daily Press* reporter and Kathleen Cunningham of Grand Rapids, whose sister had been murdered earlier, possibly because the reporter had been a witness in the case.

"But, Jesus Christ, Jimmy," I sputtered, "I told you it was Quishi and Invisible Fist, and they're working for Anna!"

"You know more than we do," he declared stiffly.

"Goddamnit, you told me who they were!"

Detective Chen's mouth pursed. He shook his head. "Fitzgerald, I attempted to make sense of this. It's all speculation. I don't know if they're the ones off the *Neptune Jade*, I don't know if they're the ones who chased you, and I don't know if they work for Anna."

"You know whoever got Lee Ying and Bobo got Ellie!"

"That is my opinion, based on autopsy evidence. But I don't know who did it, and I don't want it printed. I don't want these murders linked up, and I can't put Anna in any of this."

Kit was distraught. "You can link the dragon lady to Lee Ying," she interjected. "You can place Lee Ying and my sister here at Elaine's! The same people killed them both!"

Jimmy closed his eyes. "You two have it all figured out. Well, the department needs evidence! Goddamnit, we have only the sketchiest idea of what happened to you two! We need a full statement."

"It was all there, basically," I dodged.

"Yeah? Well, based on what you said, and if it isn't interpreted generously, you just might find yourself facing a charge of murder, or manslaughter!"

"Come on, Charlie! You know that's crap!"

"You talk to Oppitz! And don't shoot your mouth off that I was up here! Goddamnit, if I wasn't on the wrong turf, I'd take you in right now!"

He turned and stalked out.

I looked out and saw him storming across the street. I had done it, all right. Pissed off the only cop in New York who had been willing to help us.

TWENTY-SIX

THE *DAILY PRESS* STORY THE NEXT DAY WAS A BLOCK-buster, all right. I was still in it but not in the byline. It was written by Thomas Toolen, Betty Applegarth, and Walter Brewer.

REPORTER'S PROBE SPURS
BROOKLYN BRIDGE PLUNGE

Twinned side-by-side under the headlines on the front page were photos of Ellie and Kit, and there was even a one-column mug shot of me inside; it was the photo from my press card where I resemble a Kmart security guard.

"A *Daily Press* reporter digging into the murders of a celebrity pianist and his fiancée was chased onto the Brooklyn Bridge early yesterday, and one of the unidentified pursuers plunged into the East River," it began.

It went on from there, and whether Jimmy Chen liked it or not, the story linked up all three murders. Kit and Ellie became prominent Grand Rapids society debutantes; Ellie, the tragic, brilliant pianist two steps from Carnegie Hall; and Bobo, the next Bobby Short.

Unfortunately, Tommy Toolen had not been able to drag Madame Cheong or the empress dowager's medal into the story. Only that a reporter's digging into the murders of Ellie, Bobo, and art dealer Lee Ying had sent unknown assailants after him and Kathleen Cunningham, a rising executive at American Seating Company.

The only reference to the dragon lady that Tommy could shoehorn in was that Lee Ying was reportedly delivering a Chinese artifact to a Chinatown art dealer.

It blew things apart, all right. Mostly me. Because most of what I had been warned not to divulge—except in a confidential statement to Assistant District Attorney Gertrude Oppitz—ran riot through the columns. Any good reporter could put the pieces together, and they hadn't needed anything from me. The only angle missing was what it was really all about—Madame Cheong, the Phoenix, Quishi, and Invisible Fist.

I read all this at my place late that night after leaving Elaine's with Kit and picking up an early edition on the way home.

Not only had Tommy, Dubbs, and Applegarth managed to do an end run around the stuff Detective Chen tried to withhold, but Dubbs Brewer, probably pissed off that I was sticking my nose into his story, got Tommy to drop in this little jab: "Sources at police headquarters said that detectives investigating the murders were at a standstill, with neither evidence nor suspects."

That would please Detectives Chen, Hanley, and Jacobs, all right. Because they did have some evidence and some suspects, but they just didn't want to reveal it. They even had a suspect in The Tombs. That's what happens when the cops and the press get into a pissing match, when the cops sit on facts and the paper has to fill in the blanks as best it can. And there I was in the middle, a half-cop witness and a half-gagged reporter, unable to please either of them. I knew damned well Jimmy Chen would raise hell with me about the story, even though I didn't write it.

I was on my feet, pacing, and Kit came to me, mewing apologetically, her face in my shoulder. "I'm sorry I bugged

Chen like that. Everybody trying to help, especially you, and I go off like that."

"Well . . ."

She looked up at me fearfully. "Will all this cause you trouble?"

Oh, no, I thought. I didn't dare show my face at the paper, at any of the precincts, or at the district attorney's office. Other than that, I could go anywhere, maybe to some dim, out-of-the-way saloon like Mutchie's where nobody would recognize me.

"You've got to help me, Fitz. Don't let me go off like that. I know it doesn't help. Nothing like this has ever happened to me before."

I held her and knew it wasn't her fault. What else could she do? What else can you do when someone close to you, someone who is your very double, half of you, is murdered, and you're helpless and can't get it out of your mind, when you sit up panic-stricken in the middle of the night and feel a dagger under your ribs? How can people not drop everything and solve this? How can people ride sightseeing buses to St. John the Divine, watch a parade of tall ships, or go to Elaine's for drinks and music when Eleanor Cunningham, dead on a blood-soaked mattress, is not the name of a stranger but your own sister? How can the world not stop? Who is there to rage against but the personification of help—Detectives Chen, Hanley, Jacobs? And even me.

People read of the murderers of an Ellie or a Bobo, and turn to the sports pages. It's only names, words, and not what a detective or a reporter sees. Uncaring killers murder more than their victims. Those left behind will never be the same, will never forget. It is not just a news story or a crime statistic to them.

And what else could I do? Reporters write too many such stories and develop a hard shell against most of them, in self-defense. But sometimes that passing name in a story you write is your bar pal Bobo or his girl, and sometimes a name in a story gets on a plane and jets to New York and to you, and turns from a few printed letters into a frightened, wilted, lovely young woman in a gray traveling suit with red trim with large, bewildered blue eyes begging for help. You try not to get involved, not because you don't care but because there are too many of them. Too much caring and you can crack, too. What else could either of us do? We were both being washed along on a raging river, going we didn't know where.

On top of everything else, I had Kit staying in my place now. She didn't want to go back to the Edison Hotel until we could find out if that "policewoman" who had called was in fact Madame Cheong.

Then the phone rang. I walked to it and yanked the plug from the wall. Kit didn't say anything, and I saw that she understood it was necessary sometimes.

I sank onto the sofa, and she quickly joined me and cuddled against me.

"I'm sorry, Fitz. Really I am."

What a kid. Blown about by a hurricane and sorry for others.

"Hey, listen. You've been terrific."

"I haven't."

She snuggled against me, and my arm was around her. We both needed some escape and some comforting. We're in this thing together, she had said.

"I wasn't going to do this," she murmured. "You may be stuck with me till tomorrow."

At the moment, that was fine with me. She looked up at me, absolutely adorable, and her mouth was near mine.

"You've been so good to me."

"It was easy."

"I'm going to be better from now on."

I didn't see how.

I suppose it was inevitable. Sharing dangers throws you together, and at that moment we were both a little shell-shocked. Neither of us had anyone else, and we both needed someone.

She reached down and took off her high heels. Is there anything more deliciously inviting than red lacquered nails on slim, white fingers slipping off heels?

I AWAKENED AND REALIZED I HAD ESCAPED THE NIGHTmare that often rode my back through the night after such an evening. I had also found an antidote to Marcus Aurelius. It was a black-curled head on the pillow beside me. I slipped out of bed and let her sleep on. God knows we had both needed it, she perhaps more than I.

But if I had escaped nightmares, I now faced day-mares, if one may use such an expression. Those thirty-seven urgent matters that I had to attend to but had avoided now coalesced into one tangled star-chamber proceeding.

I made the coffee, and sat there sipping from my Harry S. Truman mug. I glanced at Harry's dictum inscribed on the mug, "If you can't stand the heat, get out of the kitchen." Another mentor. But, Harry, what if you can't stand the heat but can't get out of the kitchen?

I showered, shaved, and dressed and came back for another mug.

There was news on the TV about our doings, too. The murmur stirred Kit, and she sat up and stared out at me. She was probably experiencing that eerie sensation of waking up and wondering where she was.

She slid out of bed and closed the bedroom door.

I contemplated Harry's unflinching face on my coffee mug, and accepted my fate. I would have to stand the heat, because I could not get out of the kitchen. I plugged the phone back in.

Wraaaannggg!

"All right, already," I snorted, and clicked the receiver to cut off the caller and get a dial tone.

"Daily Press." Always so calm and untroubled, like those

ditzy radio disc jockeys who spout smoothly about nothing while the city is on fire.

"Hey, Glenn, Fitz."

"How you doing, Fitz? I see you made the paper."

"You could say that. Say, by the way, why didn't you tell me that that 'Paul' who was calling me was Pippy McFadden?"

"Is that who it was?"

"Never mind. Give me Corcoran."

A blip, and the *Daily Press* lawyer was on the line, considerably dour. "I just called you."

"Look, you've got to help me. I've got to go down to Hogan Place and see that A.D.A."

"No, you don't."

"What? Did you get me off the hook?"

I was beginning to entertain warmer thoughts about our newspaper counsel. He *was* our shield and protector. This was premature.

"No!"

"You're supposed to be our mouthpiece when little accidents like this happen," I complained.

Something clattering. An exhale. A barely heard, half-suppressed moan. "*Little accidents* . . . !"

Then the real Charles W. Corcoran materialized.

"I can handle minor blunders, I can finesse you idiots misquoting the cardinal or the mayor, even screwed-up semi-libels, but goddamnit, I can't get maniacs out of vats of tar!"

Oh.

"She's coming up here."

"The A.D.A. is coming to the office?"

"That's right! I smoothed it over that much. She's tired of waiting for you. She'll probably bring handcuffs. Get your butt in here! And get that phone fixed!"

Kit was up and into the shower. I lit a Tiparillo and knocked on the bathroom door.

"Kit, I've got to go to the office. I'll call you."

"Wait, Fitz!"

But I didn't want her dragged any deeper into this mess than she was already, and I went out the door. I drove the Dodge down to the *Daily Press*, parked in the NYP zone, and left another hopeful note under the windshield wiper.

"ASSISTANT DISTRICT ATTORNEY GERTRUDE OPPITZ," SHE said, all business. "This is a tape recorder." She set it on the table. "I'm taping this statement. Is that acceptable?"

She seemed taller than she actually was, and she wore minimal makeup, a single gold chain, and a black suit with a white blouse. Her face was strong, with large dark eyes that clearly broadcast that she was a no-nonsense prosecutor.

We sat around the big wooden table in the conference room, and Corcoran told her that taping was fine.

"You may proceed," she said. A regular automaton.

I told her all I could about what had happened, and she listened stolidly and took notes.

"You can't identify the two men pursuing you?"

"I can speculate. Quishi and a Mr. Yuan."

"It was Mr. Yuan who you believe went into the East River?"

"Has he been recovered, by the way?" I ventured.

She didn't react, and she didn't answer.

"Mr. Fitzgerald is an authorized staff member of this newspaper," Corcoran said officially. "He was on assignment."

"He was on the 3 A.M. shift?"

"Well, a newspaper reporter is on call at all times."

I was pleased to hear Corcoran defending me like that, after his earlier intemperate words.

"Can you give us any idea how this matter will be disposed of?" he asked.

"We shall see. I have to confer with Detective James Chen and other officers who were at the scene."

"We would expect consideration," Corcoran went on. "We would oppose any formal charge."

"I understand you would. We shall see what we shall see."

"Is it going before a grand jury?" I chimed in. That was the main point as far as I was concerned.

"That's standard in such cases. Detective Chen will give us his recommendation."

I didn't like that. Jimmy Chen could decide? And this no-nonsense legal machine? It's a fact of the criminal justice system that a prosecutor can get anyone indicted for anything. They like to say they can indict a ham sandwich, and it's true. Rarely does a grand jury oppose the D.A.'s office and vote a no-bill, and when they do they're often treated like dangerous radicals or traitors.

Miss We-Shall-See gathered up her notes and the machine with my fate inside and walked out. At least I hadn't been arrested or taken into protective custody.

Corcoran leaned back, put his hand over his eyes, and wagged his head.

"Listen, thanks," I told him.

"You're suspended!"

"What?"

"We can't be responsible for any more of your antics. Until this matter is disposed of, you're on vacation."

"But this thing has finally blown open! I have to go after Madame Cheong!"

"That's just what I mean!"

"What about the tall ships story for Pippy?"

Corcoran peeked out from under his hand and smoldered.

"Your suspension will be effective after you complete that assignment. You will not work on any other story!"

"Is this from Ironhead?"

"You don't question me! Arnold is an employee here! There are some situations beyond his control!"

Suspended! Wasn't that cute? And what would it mean after the tall ships sailed through? Getting your newspaper dragged through the courts is bad news. They have to defend you until you're out of hot water, but after that it leads to only one conclusion.

I contemplated my life in New York without the *Daily Press*. There was nothing there.

TWENTY-SEVEN

I WENT INTO THE CITY ROOM AND OVER TO IRONHEAD AT the city desk.

"Ironhead," I complained, "Corcoran says I'm suspended."

Ironhead glanced up at me, and leaned his head into his hand.

"Shit!"

"Is that so?"

"You should be suspended, you damned doofus!"

"But I was chasing a story!"

Ironhead wagged his head and wouldn't look at me. "Yeah. The wrong story."

"But we got it, and I'm all squared away with Pippy."

He stared at me, his mouth working, his head bobbing. It was a lovely tangle, but there was our story on the front page. All the shouting and madness and danger and uncertainty added up to the kind of vintage *Daily Press* adventure he had grown up on.

"I'll do what I can," he spouted then, "but goddamnit, stay away from the Great Wall! Are you all set for the sail story? Did you talk to Pippy?"

I told him I was on top of it.

"Fitz," he said, looking tired, "it's a new world out there. The days when you could swipe a woman's stomach from the coroner's office to prove she was poisoned are gone. We're all goddamn journalists now. We're a couple of dinosaurs."

I was astounded to hear Ironhead open up like that. I knew perfectly well that his juices started bubbling when a good story happened, and that he loved real hard news compared with the kind of soft stuff he had to send the ponytailed reporters out on. Here he was, the once all-powerful city editor of the New York *Daily Press*, overruled by the front office. The tail, as we saw it, wagging the dog.

"I'm still alive for the ships?"

"Get the hell out of here!"

I went to my desk and looked over the America Sail handouts, not unhappy to be back on the uncomplicated nautical puff piece. What day was it—Thursday? According to the gala schedule, the *Nina,* the *Pinta,* and the *Santa Maria* were going to sail away from Pier 86 today and work their way down the Hudson to take their place in the reviewing stand off Governor's Island in the harbor. I would ride down on the *Nina.*

I came out through the lobby onto Forty-second Street prepared to follow the fleet. But the Fate that spins our thread of life wasn't through jiggling me.

"Fitz!"

Across the street, in the front window of the Greek's, there was Kit, waving at me. I crossed over and went inside and sat down at her table.

"Anything new?" she asked eagerly.

"Yeah. I've been suspended."

"What?"

"At least on the Chinese story."

"What do you mean! That's crazy!"

"I'm practically a suspect, so I can't work the story."

"What are we supposed to do?"

That "we" didn't apply to me any more. I should have been happy about that.

"I have to go over to the Hudson and catch up with Columbus's ships."

"I know you have to," she said, resigned. "I can't keep

nagging at you. You go ahead." She stared out over the street, lost.

"What are you going to do?"

"Fitz, I know I ruffled Detective Chen and got him upset. I'll call and apologize."

"He'll get over it."

"But I've got to keep him on the case."

I let out a breath. "He told us to stay out of it."

"I know. But I can't!" She looked away. "You go ahead. I'll keep after him." She got up. "Thanks for everything."

She got up and walked to a pay phone and punched in numbers. I sat there feeling helpless. Of course she couldn't stop. But I had to sail! Then she waved me over to the phone.

"He wants to talk to you," she said apologetically, holding the phone out at me.

Oh boy!

"Did you talk to Oppitz?" he wanted to know.

"This morning."

"Okay." He sounded relieved. "What did she say about you going to see Anna?"

"I don't think that came up. It was all about the bridge accident."

"Well," he said, "good. Stick to that for now."

"Anything more on that missing medal?" I asked.

He sighed. "No. It's probably been sold somewhere by now."

"You know, Charlie, she doesn't even want to sell it."

"What?"

"No. She said nobody would sell T'zu-hsi's Phoenix."

"What did she say she wanted it for then?"

"She said that since I was an ignorant round eye, I wouldn't understand the return."

Jimmy was silent for a moment. "The return?"

"Yeah. What do you think she meant?"

I detected interest. He was turning it around in his mind.

"Does that mean anything to you?"

"I'll be damned," he muttered. And then, "Why didn't you tell me this before?"

"I don't know. I didn't think of it. It didn't mean anything to me."

"All right, you've got to come down here."

I thought my heart was going to stop. "Jimmy, I can't! I'm on another story."

"That's too damned bad! You're part of this investigation."

"You told us not to interfere!"

"That's right, but when there are new developments, you're a material witness."

"What new developments?"

"Have you got ears, Fitzgerald? But, listen, I'll come and get you. I don't want you walking around down here. He has been seen."

"Who? Quishi?"

"Wait in front of the paper."

"No, Jimmy, listen . . ."

Bang! Errrrrrr!

I was getting dizzy from this push me–pull you tug of war between the *Daily Press* and the cops. Was I in this damned thing or out of it? Once again, the *Nina* was sailing away into the sunset.

Kit and I sat at the front window of the Greek's and watched until his squad car pulled up and he got out, looking around. Then we ran across the street. I seemed to be hiding from the *Daily Press* uptown, and was only safe in Chinatown with a bodyguard.

He drove us downtown in silence, looking at me a couple of times and shaking his head. In his squad room, he strode to his desk, picked up the red covered book with a golden dragon on the cover, then dropped it. We sat across from him.

"Anna Cheong told you she wanted the Dowager Phoenix for the return?" he said meditatively.

"That's what she said."

"Interesting."

"Does this have anything to do with the murders?" Kit wanted to know, always keeping her eye on the goal.

"I don't know," he admitted. "You should never have talked to her."

"But we had to!" Kit pleaded.

"Miss Cunningham," he retorted, "*I* will talk to her, at the proper time! It can't be helped now."

Detective Chen sat back and lighted one of his thought-helping, dark, twisted Golden Monkey cigarettes.

"But through your absurd bungling, you may have stumbled upon something that might show us a way. I always like to know what the motive behind a crime is. That Phoenix may have provoked these matters. Now we hear that the reason behind it may not have been merely for money."

"What did she mean?" I asked him.

"Fitz, not to be patronizing, but it is true that you are an ignorant *waiguoren*. And why wouldn't you be? You have no reason to know China, which was a center of civilization when ancient Rome was a mud hill."

Marcus Aurelius would like to hear that, I mused.

For thousands of years, China was the all-powerful, all-knowing Middle Kingdom, and the peoples beyond were all barbarians. Only with the fall of the Manchu dynasty and the emperor Pu Yi in 1912 did China fall under the despised control of *wai low*, foreign devils, he explained.

"In a history such as China's," he said, "this was only yesterday. The communists, currently in charge, are but a passing breeze. There are those who yearn to see the emperor once more seated on the Dragon Throne in the Palace of Cloudless Heaven in the Forbidden City. There are those who wish for and plan for his return."

"They want to put the emperor back on the throne of China?"

"There are those who consider it inevitable."

"You're not kidding?" Kit said.

"Not at all. China is constantly changing, never more than

now. The communists are hanging on by a thread."

He stood and walked around. "I do not say that this is inevitable, as others do, but there are those who believe it and will move heaven and earth to make it so."

"Madame Cheong wants the Dowager Phoenix to bring back the emperor?" Kit asked, confounded.

He tilted his head. "She links it to the return. I have already told you she fashions herself as the empress dowager Tz'u-hsi, the last true ruler of China."

He returned to his chair. "I had wondered about something like this, but couldn't put it together. Now I believe it. Madame Cheong wants the Phoenix for the return."

"But how would she use it?" I asked.

He didn't know that, he conceded. Perhaps to help fund a movement, perhaps as a talisman, a bona fide that would positively identify the bearer as a servant of the emperor.

"A holder of the Venerable Buddha's medal would be honored, respected, obeyed as her descendant; perhaps she would even be provided with funds, and she would certainly be accepted as a leader, or one of the leaders, of such a return."

Madame Cheong's fanatical burning eyes flitted before my face, and it sounded plausible. Throwing off the communist yoke had become fashionable as it had become possible. We were not dealing with a mere art smuggler or thief, but with a patriot who served the revered memory of the Lord of Ten Thousand Years.

"There may be other Phoenixes in other hands that are working toward this, too," Detective Chin surmised. "We know Wei Wang has one. The return would hardly be the work of one woman from Canal Street."

"But what does this have to do with my sister's murder?" Kathleen persisted.

"Only that we may guess why the search for it has cost so many lives."

"If you're right," I said, sobered by his explanation, "nothing will stop them until they get it. And it's still out there somewhere."

"I fear you are correct, *da bizi*."

"Who?"

He grinned. "It's what the Chinese call you *wai low*. Big nose. And now that we have a better idea of what we are up against, I caution you yet again, to keep out of this business! If this is all true, they will not be pleased about what happened to Yuan Zhang."

"Any word on that?" I asked.

He shook his head. "The river is big, Fitz, and the harbor bigger."

"Did you say Quishi has been seen down here?"

"A mainland Han Chinese man speaking Shanghaiese, who is six-feet-four or five, has been seen at Wei Wang's restaurant on Mott Street, the Golden Goose Pagoda, and entering and leaving the Wan Chi Tong office," he offered quietly. "There are not many that big, and I have somebody who watches the Wan Chi office for me."

"So Madame Cheong is part of the tong!" Kit said, her eyes fluttering nervously.

"As a merchant, she would be connected, even if she is only a woman. She may only be a *pai ma pi*."

"A what?"

"A minor player, a functionary. It means . . . 'those who pat the horse's rump.' We know she never was shaken down by any of the gangs."

"This is too much for me," I said softly.

"That's what I've been trying to tell you."

TWENTY-EIGHT

"CAN YOU DRIVE US BACK UPTOWN?" I ASKED CHEN. "I have to get moving."

Before he could answer, Kit interrupted.

"Jimmy," she said, "don't you think it's pretty clear by now that Erik Coleman didn't do anything? The paper says they're going to arraign him today. Couldn't we at least get him out on bail? His parents are going to be here, and they're frantic."

"Erik's parents are here?" I asked.

"I'm sure they are," Kit said. "When I left, they told me they'd be flying out for the arraignment."

I was feeling pretty guilty about it, too. "Could you check with Hanley and Jacobs?" I asked. "The case against him has to have fallen apart."

Detective Chen was reluctant, but we all knew that if this was about Madame Cheong, Quishi, and that damnable medal, then Erik was a little lost sheep who had strayed into the wrong meadow. Chen called the Nineteenth to see what the situation was, but hung up fast.

"They're in criminal court right now," he announced. "Come on."

"Wait a minute," I said, "I've got to get uptown."

He turned on me. "You want him out? You helped get him in? If you want my help, you're coming along."

"But, damnit . . ."

We hurried out of the precinct and down Mulberry Street through Chinatown to the grim, monolithic Criminal Court

Building at 100 Centre Street, only a few blocks away. And there in Arraignment, Part One, the proceedings of *People* v. *Coleman* were already under way.

At the defense counsel's table in the well of the courtroom sat Erik, the tall, blond, bewildered Viking with his lawyer, Wayne Owens, and in the second bench were his parents, George and Helen, leaning forward intently.

". . . a bungled travesty, Your Honor," Owens was orating, "without a scrap of evidence! Mere supposition! The police admit they do not have a murder weapon. We ask for dismissal of these charges or, at the very least, for reasonable bail."

Kit hurried up to the front and slid in beside George and Helen Coleman. Detective Chen sat in the first bench, which is always reserved for cops and lawyers.

For a moment, George Coleman turned and looked back at me, scowling. He was fairly bald, had a mustache, and his eyes were like twin howitzers. I found out later he had been a marine and was an executive at Amway Stores, and that Helen was a schoolteacher. Not the kind of people who usually end up at murder arraignments.

Well, there was a good deal of legal orating by a prosecutor, and then who stood up at the prosecutor's table but the imposing Trudy Oppitz, who told the judge the case "was in some disarray."

"Are the People asking for a dismissal?" the judge wanted to know.

"An adjournment, Your Honor, until we can clarify this matter," Oppitz said with a trace of annoyance. "The People agree to hold these charges in abeyance. We may D.T.P. this case."

D.T.P.—decline to prosecute! I was relieved. The case might never go to a grand jury.

Since the People's case seemed sketchy, not to say wobbly, the judge decided Erik could be released on bail. I ducked out into the courthouse corridor, and breathed a sigh of relief.

I was feeling charitable and magnanimous about helping to rescue Erik, and ready to congratulate him.

After the Colemans posted bail—they had to put up their house, it turned out—they all spilled out of the courtroom, Kit hanging onto Erik and half-blubbering with relief.

"And you remember Fitz!" she smiled, indicating me to Erik as if I were his savior. I smiled modestly.

Amway executive George Coleman, the former marine, who on his feet was as tall as his son, gave me a look that might have once sent a grunt to the stockade. He didn't seem pleased at all.

"You!" Erik pulled loose from Kathleen and stepped toward me. "You're the asshole who got me into this!"

"Well, see," I began, but . . .

Wham!

A fist caught the corner of my mouth, and I went tumbling down in the courthouse corridor with a split lip.

Hanley and Jacobs came out in time to see this, and grabbed Erik between them. Erik was still lunging forward, trying to kick me. He was also letting off steam, referring to me in uncomplimentary terms, including "goddamn moron" and "fucking busybody." Alas, there was not a lot of forgiveness in him.

It seemed to please Half-Dome Hanley, though, and I wasn't sure if it was because he enjoyed seeing a nosy reporter get his comeuppance or that he was able to arrest Erik again.

"Okay, pal," he told Erik. "That'll let us keep you for a while longer! I'm arresting you for assault!"

"Wait a minute," I told him, getting up. "I'm not signing any complaint. Let him go."

"But he coldcocked you!" Jacobs noted.

"Well . . ."

I had to admit I understood Erik's outburst. I guess I had it coming.

Erik pulled loose from the two cops, not bothering to apologize, and he and his parents walked quickly away, anxious to put the Criminal Court Building behind them. I couldn't blame them.

Kit and I walked out more slowly with Detective Chen.

"I'm so sorry, Fitz," Kit clucked. "I guess he was angry."

You could say that.

We walked back up to the Fifth Precinct, and Detective Chen had a cop drive us back up to the *Daily Press,* leaving another stern warning in our ears to stay out of things we didn't understand and that were too dangerous for amateurs and *waiguoren*.

I intended to heed his advice. I had had enough of invisible fists and split lips to last for awhile.

We got out in front of the *Daily Press*. Kit was silent, shaken, disheartened. We may have gotten Erik Coleman loose from this mess, but the whole thing seemed to have spun out of our galaxy into the mists of the Middle Kingdom.

"I'm going to the *Nina*," I told her.

"Oh." She stood there, immovable.

"You want to come along?"

We walked down to the Dodge Daytona on Fortieth Street, where I removed another parking ticket from the windshield and put it in the glove compartment with the others. I drove her across town to the *Intrepid* museum at Forty-Sixth Street and the Hudson River, and was allowed to park on the pier.

"There you are!" the captain of the *Nina* said jovially as we walked up. "Just in time. We're shoving off."

We clambered up the gangplank, and off went the *Nina* out into the river and then downstream. A fine, fresh breeze in our faces, we stood on the raised quarterdeck near the captain's cabin, out of the way, and enjoyed the ride. They were right about the *Nina*; she led the way, the *Pinta* following smartly and the *Santa Maria* wallowing behind.

"She was a staunch and well-founded craft, the *Santa*

Clara was," the captain said fondly. "Columbus's favorite. And his flagship on later voyages."

"I thought she was the *Nina*," I said.

"Ahh! Right you are! But that was a nickname, after her owner, Juan Nino."

Kit got interested as the captain filled us in on the old ship. For a few minutes, she took her mind off her troubles.

"It's so little to have crossed the Atlantic," she said.

"About sixty tons, as they said then," the skipper said. "Not what we'd call tons, you know. A ton meant a *tonelada,* a cask of wine equal to a couple of hogsheads of port. You figured her tonnage by how much wine she carried in her hold."

He noticed my split lip and inquired what had happened.

"I ran into a Viking."

"One of those squareheads off the *Christian Radich?*" he remarked. "Yeah, some of them are tough cookies."

Then the skipper got busy maneuvering the *Nina* downriver. The crew was all over the rigging, working her sails, and the *Nina* had an engine to help, too, something Columbus could have used. It was a pleasant afternoon cruise down the Hudson, past the immense twin towers of the World Trade Center, with the Statue of Liberty off the starboard bow in the distance, glinting in the sun.

The only gloom in the occasion was Kit's face, still lost in anguish and uncertainty.

The *Nina* was worked around and tied up at Governor's Island, and we got off.

"See you on Sunday, then, mate!" the captain called, waving.

There was a good deal of activity already, with all sorts of small craft slipping into the harbor, jockeying for position, sliding between buoys floating in lines to control the ship traffic.

The America Sail organizers had press and VIP boats running from Governor's Island to the Battery by then, and we rode across. It all looked shipshape for the Parade of Ships, and I was feeling smug that I had made all the necessary preparations and was on top of things, despite the confusion of the murders. I even knew *Nina*'s real name.

We took the subway from South Ferry back up to Times Square to retrieve the Dodge, and Kit didn't pay much attention to this ride underground; it was routine already. She was still feeling frustrated, and who could blame her? We came out of the subway at Forty-fourth Street and Eighth Avenue, and ahead I spotted the green sign of Sardi's restaurant.

"Come on," I said, and led her along to Sardi's, still trying to dispel her funk.

Her walk quickened a little as she took in the theater where *Phantom of the Opera* was playing, and looked across at Shubert Alley. Inside at the bar, José, the bartender, smiled as always.

"Fitz! We haven't seen you for a while."

"This is Kit from Grand Rapids."

"Hello, Kit from Grand Rapids."

We sat in the bar and looked out the window. Kit sighed, sipped her drink, and said defeatedly, "I'd better go back." That's the decision she had been making aboard the *Nina* and the subway.

What could I say? She sat there, adrift, her lovely blue eyes troubled. The wonders of Manhattan weren't enough to heal the pain she could not escape.

"Well, you've had a look at the two hottest joints in New York," I said lightly. "Elaine's and Sardi's. You're a regular New Yorker."

She smiled wanly. "It is an amazing city. Living here . . . wow!"

I lit a Tiparillo. She wavered between wonder and flight.

"But it's time to go home, Fitz. Could you go to the Edison with me so I can get my things and check out? It ought to be okay now."

"Yeah, okay."

We walked the two blocks north to the Edison, where she asked about any messages. Only her mom. No policewoman. I went up to Kit's room with her to get her bag, and then we walked back to the pier to reclaim the Dodge. I didn't see anybody tailing us. I drove her back across town to my place.

"You'll keep at them, won't you?" she pleaded, her eyes tearing.

"If I can."

"Because, I don't know how I'm going to go on not knowing."

Yes, the agonizing uncertainty. The lacerating mental images about Ellie's last moments. The desperate need to know what happened, to find who had done it, to see them caught, and to make them pay—the need for what the media likes to call closure. As if there could ever be any.

"I feel so bad for Ellie," she said softly. "And I've failed her."

"You tried."

At my place, we carried her bag in. She would have to pack, call the airline, get to the airport. It was as though she were already going through the doors of the American Airlines terminal at Newark Airport.

At the door to my apartment, the key wouldn't go in, and when I turned the knob, the door swung open freely. The world turned upside down.

Everything was thrown around; the sofa pillows were on the floor, books were tossed, and the place was a shambles.

"Fitz!"

"Get away from here!"

Not stopping to wait for the elevator, I dragged Kit down the stairs and into the front entrance hall. We ran out onto the street.

"They were here!" she cried.

I ran, pulling her behind me, to a pay phone on the corner at Second Avenue, looking back over my shoulder for a giant pursuer. There was nobody except strollers and a woman pushing a baby carriage. I called 911 to report the break-in, and asked the police dispatcher to find Detective Chen. Then I called him at the squad.

"He's on the air," a voice said.

I asked the dispatcher to reach out for Chen and tell him to come to my place.

Kit and I stood across the street and down a couple of doors and watched the window of my apartment on the second floor. There was no sign of anything.

"They're still looking for it!" Kit whispered.

I had to think she was right. They had hunted for that damned thing at Bobo's and Ellie's, they'd tried to find Kit at the Edison, and now they had been at my place. I guess it figured. I was the next stop, and if they were engaged in something as chancy and huge as trying to restore an emperor, they could find the apartment of a mere reporter.

A police sector car arrived first, and two uniformed cops went up to my door, Kit and I following cautiously. The door was still standing open. We went in after the cops.

My apartment was more burglarized than Ellie's or Bobo's had been, it appeared to me. The hangers in the closet were denuded of suits, jackets, and trousers. There was a spaghetti tangle of ties. Drawers in the bedroom had been thrown out and dumped, and the pantry had been tornadoed. Nothing was left in its usual place.

"Anything missing?" one of the cops asked casually.

How the hell could I tell?

Jorge, the super, looked in.

"Did they get it changed?" he asked, and then halted. "What happened?"

"Did they get what changed?" I asked him.

"My goodness!" he said, staring around. "Did they do this?"

"Who?" I asked.

"The locksmiths were here, but I don't get this." He waved his head around.

"Locksmiths were here?" I asked.

"Well, they came to change the locks. I saw in the paper you had some kind of trouble. But, if I were you, I'd call them and raise hell about this."

I sank down in a chair at the kitchen table amid the chaos. Locksmiths? In the middle of the day they walk right in? I offered a silent prayer to the *Nina* for keeping us away when they showed up.

One of the cops was at the door, looking at the door bolt. The bolt had been sawed off clean and was still stuck in the doorjamb.

"Hey, Gary, look at this. Saws-all."

The other cop looked and nodded.

"What's that?" I asked him, and went over for a look.

"Saws-all. A sabre power saw. They shove it through and saw through the bolt. There's a bunch using them now."

Only then did I go out into the hall and look at the door frame. There was a jagged slit next to the lock. I hadn't noticed it in my panic, or if I had, it hadn't registered. The super had a look, too.

"They use them to cut out casement windows," he said wisely. "I didn't think anything of it," he told me apologetically. "They said you wanted to change the lock because your car was stolen."

"They just walked in?"

"Yeah. They said they'd be making a racket, you know, changing the lock. They were drilling and pounding."

"Was one of them tall?"

He nodded. "The foreman, I guess he was."

"Did they look like Chinese?"

"Yeah, they did."

My legs turned to rubber. I went back inside, and Kit was sitting on the sofa springs, staring blankly, her face chalk white.

Detective Chen walked in and took it all in at a glance.

"Quishi!" I told him.

Jorge told him what had happened. "There was this big guy, the foreman, and three others. They had drills and workbags and an order slip."

"A what?" I asked. "Let me see it."

He scratched his head, looking sheepish. "They didn't give it to me. They looked okay."

Chen nodded. "The bulldozers."

"What?" I asked.

"That's what I call them. We've seen it a few times lately. They walk right into a place—four, five, ten at a time—and walk out with everything. The owner doesn't know what to do. When we get there, they're gone, and he's trying to identify ten different guys."

Chen looked over the apartment.

"In Chinatown, too. But down there they know the tong is protecting them."

"I woulda stopped them, but they looked okay," Jorge mumbled defensively.

"It's a good thing you didn't try!" Chen remarked. "They had more than drills in those workbags."

Jorge swallowed, and I shuddered. What if we had been there?

Brazen! As nervy as chasing us outside police headquarters. I had written stories about gangs that used such tactics, wide open invasions instead of stealth. A dozen marauders walked into the underground garage of a fancy high-rise near Rockefeller Center in broad daylight, pointed out ten luxury cars—Lincolns, Lexuses, Cadillacs—and told the garage attendant to hand over the keys to them. Then they simply drove them out and away in a caravan. The cops told me they were probably driven right onto a ship ready to sail for South America.

When the bulldozers walked in, you were had if you didn't have a squad of cops right there.

"You'd better not stay here anymore, Fitz," Chen said.

My head imploded! What? Kit can't stay at Ellie's or a

hotel; I can't live in my own place? We're being evicted from wherever we try to hide? Impossible!

"Goddamnit, Jimmy, if they found me here, they'll find us wherever we move! The hell with this! I'm not running anymore!"

Kit was off the sofa springs and at him, too.

"He's right!"

Chen turned his back on her, and there I was. He turned his back on me, too, and stalked out.

Kit paced back and forth, wild and distracted, and declared that she wasn't going home after all.

"But, damnit, honey," I pleaded, "you see what happened here! It's not safe for you in New York!"

She halted and spun, her hands on her hips. "You said it yourself! They'll find us wherever we move! They'll come to Grand Rapids! I can't lead them there."

I caved in. Maybe she was right. Our only chance seemed to be to go after them.

They put a patrolman on foot post out in front after that.

An hour later, when we were still putting things back in place, the phone rang. It was Ironhead.

"Fitz!"

I decided immediately not to mention the break-in. "Hey," I launched in, "I rode the *Nina* today."

"What?" Suddenly, he wasn't interested in tall ships. "I just heard from Dubbs."

"Yeah? Something happened?"

"Something *happened?* He tells me you got yourself burglarized!"

"Oh!" That sounded like a neat trick. "Well, I wasn't going to mention it. There was really a police report on that?"

Of course there was, Ironhead declared. By now there was a red flag on the name Fitzgerald, since reports kept coming in every two hours from all over Manhattan.

"It's okay. They didn't get anything."

"Oh, they didn't?" He wasn't what you'd call concerned.

"They were looking for that Chinese medal."

Ironhead spat and muttered something. "Dubbs checked with Detective Chen, and you've been down there talking to him again! Didn't I tell you to drop that damn story and stick to the ships?"

"Well, yeah, but . . ."

"But what?"

"I'm on the ship story," I protested.

"Then what the hell are you doing down there with Detective Chen?"

"It wasn't my idea. He pulled me in. I wasn't down there on the murder story. I'm on the case."

"You're on what?"

"See, there's a new development, about the return."

Something happened to the phone.

Bang! Errrrrrrrrrrrrrr!

TWENTY-NINE

I WISH I COULD TELL YOU THAT OUR BRAVE AND DESPERate resolution to go after Madame Cheong and Quishi resulted in some idea of how to do it. But the fact is, we were traumatized, besieged, in hiding, prairie dogs in our burrow on the wide open plains of Manhattan with hungry birds of prey circling overhead.

We consoled each other that night, but our closeness didn't bring release. We tossed and turned restlessly, eyes popping open. Kit got out of bed and padded barefoot out into the front room and then came back. A little later, I did the same thing.

I walked to the front window and looked outside. Was the cop on foot post still there? He was, slouched against a streetlight, the red burning coal of a cigarette in his hand. I sat down at the kitchen table and lit a Tiparillo. A moving shadow danced in the dark, and I started. It was Kit, coming out to sit with me.

"Let me have one of those," she said shakily.

There we sat in the darkness at four in the morning, puffing on little cigars, jumping out of our skins.

"Oh, Fitz!"

But there was no way out of our dilemma except to go after Madame Cheong and Quishi, whether we wanted to or not.

"This had to be their last stop," she said.

I had to agree with her. Now we had a cop outside my

place, and Ellie's apartment was a police crime scene. If Quishi and company still didn't have that damnable Dowager Phoenix medal, where else could they go?

"They made Lee Ying tell them," she said gravely.

If they got their hands on us, we would be persuaded, too.

The repeating, clanging fugue played and replayed in my head, Lee Ying to Bobo to Ellie to us.

"The thing is, Fitz," Kit said forlornly, "if that medal is no bigger than a quarter, it could be anywhere."

I had considered that, too. If Bobo and Ellie scrambled around on the floor under the piano grabbing up tips, who knows if they even found it?

"It could have rolled away under a table," she said. "It could have been swept out with the trash. It might just be lost, Fitz."

Is it possible to lose the key to the Denver mint? If such an invaluable item were lost, could they ever stop looking for it? Could the loss of the Chinese medal destroy elaborate plans to return the emperor to the Dragon Throne in the Palace of Cloudless Heaven? The old poem about the fate of a nation riding with the horseman courier flashed through my mind: "For want of a nail the shoe was lost, for want of a shoe the horse was lost, for want of a horse, the rider was lost, for want of a rider the nation was lost . . ."

For want of Tz'u-hsi's ugly face on a medal, their coup was lost?

For want of Madame Cheong's confession, we were lost!

We tried to sleep again, and I guess we did doze off from time to time. But the night was long, our fears like clouds building and reshaping and billowing over us and inside us. We finally gave up at about six-thirty and got up. Kit went into the shower, and I got the coffee going. Then I went in. We were back at the table, back at Go. And frozen. Huddled in our burrow with a cop outside.

Friday morning, I tried to get my mind to concentrate on America Sail. I had to write a curtain-raiser piece for Saturday's paper in advance of the Sunday gala. Not surprisingly, my mind kept wandering to our situation. Madame Cheong and her sly puss. The cops couldn't go after her, but I knew as well as I knew anything that she was behind it and that Quishi was her hatchet man, even though I couldn't prove it.

Kit was on the phone to her mom in Grand Rapids, and from what I could hear from her end of the conversation, she was being urged to come home. Then she wandered around aimlessly for a while, washed the dishes and everything else she could lay her hands on, and started cleaning the apartment.

"I have to do something!" she said when she saw me looking at her.

I let her do it. It apparently was activity to keep her sane.

I gave up trying to write the curtain-raiser and escaped to the bathtub to consult Lao-tzu, seeking enlightenment.

"The more laws and order are made prominent, the more thieves and robbers there will be," declared the Chinese sage.

No democrat was Lao-tzu, and neither was Confucius, who told me, "The relation between superiors and inferiors is like that between the wind and the grass. The grass must bend when the wind blows across it."

Apparently the empress dowager was the wind blowing across her patriotic followers, and they were bending like grass before it.

I turned to my own mentor, Marcus Aurelius, in his *Meditations.*

"Because a thing is difficult for you to do, do not think it is impossible for any man," he suggested. "But whatever is possible for any man to do and right for his nature, think that you can achieve it, too."

I wished I shared Marcus' stoicism and had a couple of his Roman legions to back me up. I tossed him aside and considered what seemed impossible for me: getting a confession out of Anna. The cops' hands were tied, and so were mine as long as I was a witness. That was the source of all my troubles, finding poor Ellie's body sprawled crossways on her bed. A witness to what? The fact that she was dead? Hell, Jack and Missus Hooper and half the people in Ellie's building were witnesses, too. I had just gotten there first.

Of course, that led to the Brooklyn Bridge and Yuan Zhang going into the East River, making Kit and me both witnesses, although it seemed to me we were victims. That's the criminal justice system for you; you get mugged, and you're not supposed to ask the mugger any embarrassing questions because you're a witness. That never seems to stop the mugger from trying to take you out so that you can't even be a witness. How many stories had I covered where witnesses were erased to shut them up?

That's where my bathtub ruminations led me that morning. Kit and I were witnesses, trapped in my apartment with a cop on the door, and we were supposed to shut up, stay out of it, and not bother Madame Cheong, while she and Quishi kept stalking us. What good would it do to be witnesses if we both ended up dead?

I realized I was more afraid of Anna and Quishi than I was of the cops or Gertrude Oppitz and that witness tag. I considered Gertrude Oppitz and her little tape recorder. That's what I needed, Madame Cheong blabbing into a tape recorder. Why couldn't I be like an undercover cop wearing a wire and get her to spill her guts?

Where did that come from? Marcus?

I lit a Tiparillo.

"But whatever is possible for any man to do and right for his nature, think that you can achieve it, too." I hear you, Marcus.

I had a tape recorder, which I used sometimes to record phone conversations with long-winded politicians so I wouldn't misquote them later on. The tape recorder would fit in the side pocket of my jacket, and I had a mike that would fit in my shirt pocket. If Cheong shot her mouth off, I could take the tape to Detective Chen, and maybe that would be enough for him to go after her.

I puffed some more. It wouldn't make Charlie Chan or Trudy Oppitz or Ironhead or Corcoran happy. And maybe I wouldn't be able to get anything out of Cheong. But what was I supposed to do? The tiger was at my own gate.

I tried to imagine what I could say to spook her. "Listen, Anna, I have the Dowager Phoenix."

"What, *waiguoren?* You have it?"

"That's right. I'll trade it to you for Quishi."

Would that work, I wondered? Would she give up Quishi for her patriotic cause? I got out of the tub, dressed, left the bathroom, and got the tape recorder out of my desk. I found the little mike, too.

Kit looked at me from the kitchen, where she was at work with a sponge. "You don't mind if I clean up a little?"

"No, but I'm not sure you'll find any dirt," I laughed.

There are news guys who carry guns, including a TV reporter who used to cover the godfather, the dapper don, John Gotti. There's a *Daily Press* photog who carries a handgun, and there was once a Brooklyn night reporter who had one, too. I always thought it was pretty show-offy, and I don't think any of them ever used their weapons. I'd never had one, but for the first time in my life, I wished I did. No gun, no police shield, no leverage, only desperation.

"Listen," I said, "I have to run to the office and knock out a ship story for tomorrow's paper."

I put on my jacket and slid the tape recorder and mike into the side pocket.

"Oh," Kit said.

"You'll be okay." I stepped to the window and looked out. "The cop's still out there."

"Will you be gone long?"

"No, no. Stay put."

She was looking at me with curiosity and some anxiety. I went out before she could ask me any more. Out front, the cop was still on foot post. He noticed me but didn't say anything or try to stop me. He was watching the building, apparently, and anybody who left was on his or her own. I went to the Daytona and drove off.

All right, maybe it wasn't too smart, but I couldn't think of anything else to do. Sure, I might run into Quishi, but it looked like I'd run into him anyway, sooner or later. Better to run into him on my terms than on his.

I drove down the FDR Drive, parked behind police headquarters, and walked up to Canal Street and to Taylor Lee Trading and Import. The bell over the front door tinkled as I opened it.

I was halfway in through the door, and I glanced up and saw a light from Anna's office at the head of the long, wooden staircase. She was up there planning her coup.

I quickly surveyed the large showroom, looking over the rows of stone Buddhas, bells, fans, and bamboo gimcracks. There was no one on the showroom floor.

I walked toward the foot of the stairs. A shape materialized. Something was stretched out flat on the stairway about halfway up that I hadn't noticed at first. The shape reassembled into a crouch, and then rose up into a World Wrestling Federation–sized, nightmarish hulk, six-foot-five, in blue-denim-and-gunboat-yellow lumberjack boots, with a wide, Buddha brow, squished-in nose, and a protruding chin.

A hoarse snarl came from an enraged water buffalo.

"Waiguoren!"

I gulped five pounds of air, before a thundering avalanche came down on me.

THIRTY

HIS CHARGE DOWN THE STAIRS BOWLED ME OVER BACKward, sending me sprawling against and halfway under a showroom table in a scattered jumble of Buddhas and gimcracks.

"Bastard!" burst from me as I scrambled backward on my knees. He was on his hands and knees facing me, his flat black eyes on me, his silky, black, matted hair tumbling over his wide brow. I scuttled backward on my hands and feet like a crab.

Quishi paused a moment to catch his breath. He glared at me. I noted his thick arms, his tree-trunk body, his great scorpion-claw hands. I cast a fleeting glance to see if he had a dagger.

I didn't see one. Not that this giant needed a stiletto or any other kind of weapon to deal with me. I quickly glanced up the stairway. Madame Cheong would pop out of her office up there, stare down, and direct the destruction and enjoy it.

"Where is it?" growled the water buffalo.

"Go to hell!"

He launched forward, and it was as if Reggie White, the baleful, unstoppable Green Bay Packers lineman, had rushed at me. I stopped scuttling backward and shoved both feet at him. One foot sideswiped his head, and I rolled away. I hoped I had stunned him.

"Stupid *wai low!* We can't wait!"

"You'll wait, you son of a bitch, in Sing Sing on death row!" I yelled at him.

"Where is it? I must go!"

Quishi got to his feet, towering over me, his right hand a wine barrel of a fist. His punch was not like Yuan's, but an unstoppable bowling ball.

Wham! My forearm up in front of me crashed against my face, the bowling ball along with it. Then there were heat and panic and shooting stars and a thud that sent me crashing backward, all but senseless.

I couldn't make him out. A looming form, coming down on me. On his hands and knees bending over me, hands of scrap iron at my throat. I threw a wild punch at his squished-in nose.

He grinned slightly, wagged his head like a dog shaking off water, and yanked me to my feet. His tree-limb arms went around my back in a bear hug, and my feet were lifted off the floor. I was helpless, in the coils of the crushing, breath-killing embrace of a boa constrictor. His Buddha-browed face and black eyes mashed against my nose, his foul breath spraying me. I could not deal with this monster. I felt my spine cracking.

"Now!" came from his volcano mouth.

I was in a half-swoon, passing out, when I managed to grab a stone Buddha off a table and swing it.

Thunk!

Quishi's eyes fluttered and blinked, and his mouth popped open. A deep roar burst out, and his embrace loosened. There was blood on his forehead, soaking his black, silky, matted hair and dripping down onto my face.

He let me go and bent over, holding his head. I collapsed onto the floor at his feet, wasted, the stone Buddha statue in my hand, dripping with blood.

I fought for breath and sat up. My head spun in a red ball of flames.

Quishi had backed off behind a table, but with a roar he turned it over toward me, spilling artifacts helter-skelter onto the floor. He crashed around the table and dug into the rubble for me as I crawled desperately away from him.

I was frantic; I would not survive his embrace.

I staggered away, weak as a kitten, and leaned on a display table. I knew I couldn't fight this behemoth. I grabbed up a stone Buddha statue and staggered backward another step. Impossible.

I needed help. Reinforcements, a backup. Why hadn't I brought Detective Chen and a SWAT team? He had warned me not to come here.

I looked at the stone Buddha in my hand, and instinctively turned and flung it toward the front plate-glass store window, smashing it to pieces and sending glass splintering out across the sidewalk of Canal Street.

Quishi's head jerked around.

I grabbed another stone Buddha and flung it through the window on the other side of the door. A splash of broken glass showered the sidewalk. A passerby skipped away from the flying glass slivers with a yelp and looked in.

Quishi came rushing forward, and I slid around a table. He didn't pause but kept going to the front door, and went out. I saw him shoving his way through a gathering of gawkers out there.

I stumbled forward through the rubble of Madame Cheong's smashed gewgaws and bamboo peacocks, disoriented, crazed with fright and disappointment that he was getting away. Then another thought hit me. Thank Buddha! Let him go! I realized that I was the one who had gotten away.

Chinese faces were peering in, looking in through the shards of glass, and I waved at them.

"Come in! Come in!" I shouted. "Call the police!"

They looked in curiously, but didn't enter. The store looked as though it had been bombed.

I leaned against a table, trying to regain my bearings. I glanced up toward the top of the stairs, toward Madame Cheong's office.

"She can't say she doesn't know Quishi now!" I thought.

"Madame Cheong!" I yelled.

But Anna was still hiding.

Maybe she had beat it out of here during the fight, I considered.

I crept up the long wooden staircase toward Madame Cheong's office at the top. I halted twice, listening and looking upward. I expected the dragon lady to appear, maybe with gun in hand.

But she didn't, and I continued cautiously up the last few steps. I peeked into her office. She was at her desk.

I crouched and peeked into the office. She *was* at her desk, her back arched and rigid against the back of a large leather chair. I halted, and then moved closer. A double strand of white silk was twisted and knotted around her throat, her neck thrust backward at a crooked angle, the red, circular welt under it blooming, spidery blood vessels spreading out. One hand was clutching limply at the silk strand around her throat. Her eyes were open, full of bloodshot veins, and her mouth was agape and gorged with her bloated tongue. If it hadn't been for the ebony, lacquered, beehive hairdo, she would have looked like a roast suckling pig with an apple in her mouth and cherries for eyes.

THIRTY-ONE

I'M NOT GOING TO TRY TO TELL YOU EVERYTHING THAT happened after that because if you want to know I can't remember all of it. There were cops pretty soon—some of the sidewalk gawkers had called in—and before long, Detective Chen got to Taylor Lee Trading and Import, too. And Dubbs Brewer came running up from the headquarters police shack.

I called the city desk and gave Ironhead a quick fill-in.

"Holy Christ," he snapped, "get in here!"

I went out gingerly over the broken glass on the sidewalk and drove back up to the *Daily Press*, leaving Detective Chen sputtering that he needed a statement. When I walked into the city room, Ironhead was all over me.

"What happened!"

"I finally caught up with Madame Cheong and that son of a bitch Quishi," I told him. "He had strangled her. She looked like a roast suckling pig."

"What a pisser!" he said.

"You want me to unload to Tommy?" I asked.

"Unload? Hell, write it!"

"I'm supposed to be a witness," I reminded him.

His face got red, and his voice verged dangerously toward explosion.

"Goddamnit, I am sick and tired of this fucking witness crap!" he yelled. "Nobody gags my reporters! Write the goddamn thing!"

Corcoran was hovering about by then.

"But Arnold . . . !"

"Shut up! This is bullshit! They've had him in a strait-jacket!"

He was in full sail now. Let the district attorney and the cops and forty judges come down on us, goddamnit, this was a newspaper and this was a story and his reporter was right on top of it and nobody was going to tell the New York *Daily Press* what it could or could not print.

"I don't care if they throw you in the fucking Tombs!" he finished. "Corcoran will eat their goddamn subpoenas for lunch!"

I wasn't so sure about having Ironhead on my side, and Corcoran looked a little whey-faced.

But finally I was able to write what I had always thought of as my own story, and the cops and the A.D.A. be damned. I wrote the hell out of it, everything from the beginning, the whole ball of wax. Ironhead ran to his VDT terminal and gobbled the story up as it appeared on his screen.

"Goddamnit, why didn't you tell me all this?" he shouted.

"I tried to!"

"Shut up and write! We'll give it the wood!"

The wood! The largest boxcar type available, so big that the letters did not exist in metal type but were wooden blocks. Of course, in the modern typesetting system used today there were no metal-type letters or wooden ones either. But when we went as big as you can go, we still called it "getting the wood."

And at last there was my byline: *By Edward Fitzgerald.*

Fortunately, Ironhead was so busy handling the copy that he didn't have time to grill me about how this had all come about. When I finished, I jumped up and grabbed my jacket off the chair. I felt the tape recorder in my jacket pocket. Some idea that was.

I beat it out of there, ran to the Daytona, and drove back down to Chinatown and to Taylor Lee Trading and Import. I found Detective Chen with the forensics team, photographing and gathering evidence.

"There you are," he muttered. "Well, you did it this time," he grumbled. Then he sort of sighed, tilted his head, and said, "We can't do any more here right now. I think it's time you had a Chinese beer."

"There's such a thing?"

"Sure. The Germans had a concession in Shanghai, and they taught the Chinese how to make beer."

"I can't accept gratuities from the department," I told him.

"This is on me."

We walked down into Chinatown to Jimmy Wu's, and he ordered me a Chinese beer.

"Ding How," he told the waiter.

Ding How wasn't bad.

"Why do you think Quishi did that to Anna?" I asked him.

"I can tell you why," he said. "She lost the Tz'u-hsi image. She was supposed to deliver it to someone, someone important, I have to think, someone who's part of what's going on over there. And he lost face because of it. Quishi and Yuan came here to get it from her and take it back, and she didn't have it. It cost her her life."

"What about Quishi?" I asked.

"We'll get him now," said Chen. "He's so hot, there'll be no place for him to hide."

My story caused as much trouble as anybody could want, and pitted Corcoran against A.D.A. Oppitz and the cops, and they threatened to indict me. But it all dried up eventually. You might not believe this, but Ironhead cut out of my story any mention of the plot to restore the emperor. When I asked him about it later, he looked at the ceiling and said, "Get the hell out of here."

Kit went back home the next day, after Detective Chen and I took her back to Ellie's apartment to get some of her sister's things. She gathered up some of Ellie's photos and some of her clothes and costume jewelry, and then found her wedding dress in the closet.

"Oh, my God," she wept.

She slumped on the sofa, holding the dress. "She told me she had something old and something new. That would be the dress," Kit sobbed. "She was going to get something borrowed—Mom was going to give her her pearls at the wedding. There must be something blue here, too."

She went through Ellie's bureau then, finding some of Ellie's lingerie, and came up with it.

"Here it is." It was a satin garter with a blue satin rosette on it. "Everything was ready," she said sadly, fingering the blue rosette.

Then she gasped.

"Fitz!"

"What?"

She felt the rosette and then found a slit in the side. From inside she pulled out a gold medal. "There it is! The something old."

Detective Chen took it and examined it. "I'll be damned."

Kit stared at it sadly. Ellie had had the Phoenix medal after all. She had picked it up that night and brought it home with all the tip money. Later, sorting things out, she must have decided it would work as something old.

KIT FLEW BACK HOME TO GRAND RAPIDS THE NEXT DAY, and we've been on the phone ever since.

The story stayed alive for quite a while, and one day Detective Chen summoned me back down to his squad room.

"We found him."

"Quishi?"

He shook his head. "Yuan. His body, what was left of it, finally floated up under the South Street Seaport."

I cringed a little. But it had been an accident, I told myself.

"You can tell Kit we've solved Ellie's murder," he added.

"What?"

"The stiletto was still on him. Forensics was able to lift some of her blood from it."

So it was Yuan, Invisible Fist, who was good with the knife. It figured. Quishi didn't need a knife, not even a fly-swatter.

So I was finally able to call Kit and give her at least a little closure.

I talked to Detective Chen again later, and asked him if he'd had any luck finding Quishi.

"I'll tell you, Fitz. I put out feelers through the grapevine. He's back in Shanghai."

"What?"

"And I'll tell you something else. I think Wei Wang is there too. He's gone from Chinatown; his restaurant, the Golden Goose Pagoda, has been sold. And his Phoenix isn't in the case at the tong office."

"What do you make of it?"

Charlie said he could only guess, but he was a pretty good guesser about Chinese things, unlike *waiguoren*. He thought Wei Wang and Quishi had gone back with the one Phoenix, and who knew what they were up to.

As for Erik Coleman, he walked out of the Criminal Court Building that day, quit his job, and fled back to Grand Rapids, vowing never to return. He's got a job with the Michigan Symphony, Kit told me. There was some legal skirmishing about extraditing him for jumping bail or the forfeiture of his parents' house, but it all dried up when the D.A.'s office finally declined to prosecute. Bobo's ex and Doug the fender banger are still trying to collect on his insurance, I heard.

The Dowager Phoenix, it turned out, *had* been stolen out of the Forbidden City, and the Chinese Ambassador to the United States immediately demanded its return. Chen told me it also alerted Beijing about the followers of T'zu-hsi, which just might torpedo their coup.

That was about the end of it. I watch the wires and TV

about what's going on in China, wondering about the inevitable return of the Lord of Ten Thousand Years.

Second Avenue John finally put my Toyota back together, and the insurance company paid up. But I'm having trouble with that nice lady from Triple A, who arranged for my car rental.

"Mr. Fitzgerald," she called me to say after I'd returned the Dodge Daytona, "you know, there are five fifty-five-dollar parking tickets in the glove compartment."

"It was a temporary *Daily Press* vehicle. Have them call the parking violations bureau and tell them."

"But, gracious, that's up to you or your paper. The car rental place won't pay them."

"I'll tell you what. Tell them to call Charles W. Corcoran, the *Daily Press* lawyer."

"Well, okay."

I don't know how that worked out, because ever since I talked to Corcoran about it once, his phone has been out of order. I can't get through to him.

I know I've been dodging telling you what happened with America Sail, which took place on Sunday, the day after Kit flew home, but I've been trying to forget it.

I took the Lexington Avenue subway down to Bowling Green and walked from there to the Battery, where the press boat took me out to Governor's Island to the *Nina*. New York Harbor, as promised, was a Hollywood production. Small craft, yachts, sloops, cabin cruisers, and little power boats dotted the harbor as far as the eye could see. There were people everywhere, a couple of million of them, lining the shores, hanging out windows, clouds of them on Governor's Island above the old stone ramparts. New York, home of ticker-tape parades and Fourth of July fireworks, knows how to throw a gala, and America Sail was about as big as you could get.

"There you are!" the captain greeted me. "Some turnout!"

I took out the New York Yacht Club flag and the *Daily Press* flag I had brought along.

"How about running these up for us? Would that be okay?"

The captain looked them over and smiled.

"Hey! Sharp!"

And quickly two of his sailors hoisted our gallant banners up the mast of the *Nina*. We were ready to sail.

The gala got under way. Fireboats were whooshing parabolas of spraying water, cannons on Governor's Island boomed out a twenty-one gun salute, a gaggle of VIPs stood on a reviewing stand to watch the Parade of Ships.

And here they came, in a line, majestic and graceful, sails billowing out, crews frantically working them to stay on course, sweeping grandly past us and the reviewing stand behind and above us. Leading the parade came the Coast Guard ship *Eagle* and then, trailing in a proud line, the *Pandora,* the *Christian Radich,* the *Libertad,* the *Sedov*, one after the other, a gallant armada sailing past, tacking to port and up into the Hudson River to head north.

"Shouldn't we get under way?" I asked the captain as the last of the thirty-five biggest tall ships slid by and moved toward the Hudson.

"How's that?"

"Shouldn't you get moving? They're heading up the river."

"Up the river?"

"You don't want to fall too far behind, do you?"

He gave me a puzzled look.

"I don't get you."

"They're moving along pretty fast! Can you catch up?"

"Catch up? Those babies are four or five times our size. We couldn't keep up with them."

"Pardon me?"

"Say, those ships came along a couple hundred years later than the caravels. They're too swift for us."

"I don't understand. Aren't you sailing up the Hudson to the George Washington Bridge?"

"Oh, no! We stay here. Only the big ones are going up and back."

My screen went blank. Perched up there along the Hudson were Pippy McFadden, his yacht club commodore and ritzy sailors, and *Daily Press* photogs. Staying here? The *Nina* with the proud flags of the yacht club and the *Daily Press* hanging limp on her mast, not moving. Somehow in my preoccupation with the murders, I had neglected to note that the little, slow-moving *Nina*, *Pinta*, and *Santa Maria* would be mere decoration, riding at anchor at the reviewing stand and not going up the river with the big ships. No wonder I had the *Nina* all to myself. Why hadn't I ridden the *Pandora!*

The twenty-one cannon salute resounded in my ears. I saw the cannon's mouth, and it was Ironhead's.

Not only could I not get up the river, I could not get off Governor's Island. Nothing could move across to the Battery during the tall ships parade. I was marooned on the *Nina*. Maybe, I thought, I could move to Michigan with Kit. Maybe I could get a job at the Grand Rapids *Press*, as long as they didn't ask for a reference.

When I was finally able to get back to lower Manhattan late that afternoon, I called Ironhead and tried to explain.

But Ironhead uses only one end of the phone, and what he used it for was to say:

"Get your ass in here!"